I0600862

ANNA SPARROWS

Chance's Choice

Littles & Lace Book 5

Cover Design by: Ky at Blue Brolli Graphics

First edition

This book was professionally typeset on Reedsy.
Find out more at reedsy.com

For anyone who has ever beaten themselves up over decisions made when you were young, dumb, and full of...anxiety.
(We've all been there, right? Right??)

Contents

Preface

This is Book 5 of the *Littles & Lace* series, however it can be read as a standalone.

While this is a low-angst (no miscommunication/fights between the MCs during their relationship), sweet & cute romance, this book contains discussion of homophobia, anxiety, symptoms of depression, and panic attacks.

Similarly, this book is an MM Age Play/Age Regression romance between consenting adults, and includes light **pet play/pup play** and some **spanking/impact play**. There are also very brief mentions of other characters indulging in ABDL, but there are no scenes of that type in this novel.

I am still a firm believer in not yucking someone else's yum, so if these kinks aren't for you, don't read them.

Life's too short to read something you don't enjoy.

Acknowledgement

As always, I want to acknowledge and thank my beautiful beta readers for their feedback.

Amur, you always bring a perspective that I hadn't considered, and that is absolutely invaluable to me. I've made adjustments to Chance's initial reaction to seeing Kade, and to his thoughts on Emmett. He's still flawed because he's human, but I hope he's more understandable now. His communication skills still suck, though.

Cindy, you pinpointed one of the biggest issues I was having with the first draft and put it into words, which helped me shape this into something so much more enjoyable to read. You helped me make sure these boys kept the passion going.

And Megan, your feedback helped me smooth out some of the concerns I had with the flow of the first draft. I added a scene between Kade and Don which I think bridges the gap for the tension and drama I was looking for, and it was talking to you which inspired that.

I'd also like to thank and acknowledge you, the reader, for continuing to support me and these characters I've created. I know I'm a nobody, so it means the world that you would pick up my book out of the hundreds of amazing books out there. I genuinely hope you enjoy it.

Chapter One — Chance

"So that's a yes?" My long-time friend Charlie grins at me from across the gleaming countertop of the swanky new bar where we arranged to meet.

Charlie has changed a lot in the last few years. Finding his Forever Boy, ending his career as a cop, and starting a safe haven community center for members of the BDSM/kink community have all played a part in that. He used to be far more serious, less jovial, but now he's quicker to laugh and joke around. Not that he was a stick in the mud before, mind you, but he's more easy going these days. Unless he gets stuck into a new project. A project like the one he has spent months trying to convince me to participate in.

Closing my eyes and giving myself one last opportunity to back out, I sigh. It's a sound of resignation, but I still smile (if somewhat ruefully) at him when I exhale, "Yeah."

Charlie whoops and pumps a fist in the air. "You're the best, man! Thank you!"

"I'm not, like, the only Daddy you've signed up for this thing, right?" *That* thought makes me nervous. This thing I've agreed to? A fundraising auction, where I'm going to be standing up on a stage and (hopefully) having people bid on me. Or, more specifically, on a day of Daddy time. With me.

Now, I'll be the first to admit that I love being a Daddy. Like Charlie and the rest of our social circle, I enjoy the emotional connection between a Daddy and a Little. I like being needed. Nurturing and caring for someone else makes me feel valuable. Even if it's just for the odd scene at The Grove, our local premium BDSM club, I feel *good* after taking care of a Little.

But what Charlie (and, by association, some of my other friends) have been bugging me to agree to seems a bit more daunting.

For one, I'm not going to meet the Little who 'buys' my time until after the fact. Sure, Charlie made sure to ask our lawyer friend, Ted, to write contracts that emphasize the importance of consent for both parties, with a clause that if either me or the winner of the auction are uncomfortable once we meet, a different 'prize' will be arranged by The Center commensurate with the value paid for my time…but it still feels like a lot of pressure on me to make it work, regardless.

Secondly, I might be a Daddy, but I don't consider myself an overly outgoing guy. Standing up on a stage, being *judged* and *bid on* terrifies me. I mean, what if there aren't any Littles in the audience who are into a bearded ginger with a dad bod? I can't imagine I'll feel very good if I don't bring in any money at all. But, on the other hand, what happens if I bring in a ton of cash for The Center? Then we go back to my first concern that there'll be additional pressure on me to make the experience worthwhile.

"No," Charlie answers my question with a shake of his head

and an earnest smile, his blue eyes shining brightly with his excitement, "a few other Grove members have volunteered, too. But the more people that volunteer, the better. And," he leans forward conspiratorially, even though the din of chatter around us makes this a private conversation anyway, "you're my favorite to bring in the big bucks."

I snort at that. I can't help it.

"Me?" I ask, my voice pitching higher with incredulity. "How slim are the pickings at The Grove these days, anyhow?"

Charlie's jovial expression fades into consternation. "Chance, come on. You're a catch."

"Uh huh. That's why all you hot Daddies have boys and I'm still painfully single." I keep my tone light, even if the words themselves are bitter. I can't help it. My social group is kind of aesthetically intimidating to an average Joe like me. Even limiting my assessment to *just* the Daddies in our group, I know I'm the odd man out.

To start with, there's Charlie. He's tall and broad and muscular, not an ounce of fat on him, with biceps that broadcast the fact that he's spent far too long in the gym. He's got one of those generic Hollywood pretty boy faces: an angular jawline topped with neatly trimmed dark stubble, piercing blue eyes and one of those *The Bachelor* style 'more on top' haircuts to his dark brown head of thick hair.

Then there's Ted. Rich, suave, sophisticated Theodore Masters – a silver fox if ever I've seen one. He might be nearing fifty, but his salt and pepper hair only adds to his charm. He's also handsome and lean, and I'd seen many a twink throw themselves at him before his boy, Zephyr, caught his attention.

Next we have young London, a relative newbie to our group and to the world of Daddy/Little dynamics as a whole. He's stocky, but just as broad as Charlie (if a little bit shorter), with lush black hair he keeps coiffed in a rockabilly style, and a square jaw I'd kill for.

Finally, there's Spencer. My closest friend in the group, and probably the next likely to consider himself 'average', though his height and his voice are superior to mine in every way. The latter isn't really a surprise, considering his chosen career is as a voice actor and audiobook narrator. He's tall and lean and charismatic in ways I can only dream of being.

All in all, I've always felt like I've been riding these guys' coattails. They're the cool kids on the playground and they've been kind enough to let me sit with them, but I know I'm out of place.

"Chance," Charlie repeats my name, sounding a little horrified now. He reaches across the narrow counter that separates us, closing his wrist over mine. His blue eyes feel like they are searching my soul, and he frowns as though he's just read my mind. "Do you really feel that way?"

Of all the guys in the group, Charlie's not the one I thought I'd ever share this sort of deep and meaningful conversation with, but here we are.

I shrug and play dumb. "What way?"

"Like you're not one of the hot Daddies, for one." The phrase 'hot Daddies' sounds ridiculously silly coming from him, especially with that serious frown marring his handsome face, but I don't laugh.

"I know who I am, Charlie," I answer reasonably, "and I'm a realist. You put me in a line up with the rest of you and—"

"And you're just as hot as any of us."

I scoff at that.

"I'm serious," he insists.

4

"I'm not looking for sympathy or fishing for compliments," I respond calmly as I take a deep drag from my beer and then smack my lips together once I've swallowed. "I'm just saying, I know I'm...average in comparison. Plain. Boring. Whatever. And that's okay. I don't *want* to work for abs like you and Josh do, or go running like Spence does, or...y'know, anything like that. I'm comfortable with who I am. I just know it's not as...uh...cover model-y as the rest of you. And sometimes I get irrationally jealous of that."

Charlie's still looking at me like I've kicked his puppy or something. "I don't like that, man." He scratches the back of his neck, discomfort etched all over his face. "I never realized you thought of yourself like that, and I don't know what to say to fix it."

"There's nothing to fix," I assure him, feeling stupid for having made the confession to begin with. Sometimes, my brain and my mouth don't connect before the latter engages. This is definitely one of those situations. "Like I said: I'm comfortable with who I am. I am. I just have moments sometimes. But don't we all?"

Something darker and more melancholy flickers in his eyes and he nods, takes a fortifying swallow or three of his beer, then admits, "After I got shot, I questioned whether I'd be a good enough Daddy for Ash. I couldn't physically do things the way I wanted, you know?" He sighs and shakes his head. "And even now, even years later, I have moments where I wonder if I'm still good enough for him now that I'm not a cop." That surprises me, but before I can turn the tables to tell Charlie he shouldn't feel that way about himself, he continues, "So, yeah, I think I get it. I don't like it, but...I get it."

"See," I say instead, understanding that I won't be able to

talk him out of his self-deprecation any more than he can talk me out of mine, "we're all fucked up." I lift my glass to him and he laughs as I add, "Cheers!"

Conversation shifts back to the auction once our strange, emotionally charged moment has passed. I ask him about whether it's just sessions with Daddies and Doms being auctioned, and he explains that The Center and The Grove have both received donations from other kink-friendly places in the city and beyond. Day spas, hotels, photographers, costume designers and even a guy who builds custom adult nursery furniture have all donated their time and services as prizes to be bid on. The Grove has come to the party with discounted memberships for anyone signing up or renewing on the night of the auction, too.

"This whole thing is genius," I tell Charlie as he finishes explaining the deal he's made with The Grove to split the funds and, if the whole thing proves to be a success, the plan to make it an annual event.

"Yeah," he agrees, his smile turning proud, "Josh came up with it."

"No way."

Josh is Charlie's Little brother. And, yes, that's Little with a capital 'L'. He's a cop, like Charlie was, and is generally the joker of our entire group. He's also known to be kind of a brat, though the guy has a heart of gold and we all love him, even if we give him shit.

"Gotta hand it to him, then." I say when Charlie just nods at me. "He's much smarter than he pretends to be. Then again, didn't he just ace his Detective exams or whatever? I've gotta learn to give the kid more credit, huh?"

"He did. Mom threw a party and everything," Charlie

chuckles, but he's still wearing that proud expression. "I'd say we should all start giving him a bit more credit."

"Except when he says something stupid in the chat." Which is almost always. We're all aware that he does it for the attention, but Charlie is almost always guaranteed to take the bait where his younger brother is concerned,

Now it's Charlie's turn to tilt his glass towards me in acknowledgement. "Except for that," he agrees.

After circling back to the original topic of conversation, we start to wrap up our meeting.

"So," Charlie says as he stands and slides on a black, form fitting jacket, "I'll have Cherie send you the contract and we'll go over what else we need from you as we get closer to the date. We'll probably need a bio, some examples of your favorite kinds of Daddy/boy interactions, that kind of thing. A list of your hard limits, too. Pretty much anything you'd bring up during negotiations."

I nod and climb off my own bar stool, draining the last of my glass of beer before placing the empty glass down on the countertop. "Sounds like a plan."

I just hope it's nothing I'll come to regret.

Chapter Two — Kade

My life feels like the lyrics to an old Sinatra song. I've made mistakes but not enough to mention… or something along those lines. I'm paraphrasing. It works for me.

Anyway, I've always sort of flown by the seat of my pants. Mistakes are made and then either forgotten or learned from. I don't dwell or mope: I just keep going.

Hmm. Maybe I'm not like Sinatra. Maybe I'm like a certain forgetful Disney fish, keeping on swimming.

(Okay, this time the paraphrasing is so I don't get sued.)

See, the thing is, I don't like to regret things. I don't like to feel *bad* about things.

But moving back home to the city I grew up in —and left as soon as I fucking could— stirs feelings of guilt I had long ago buried. Guilt and sadness and melancholy and regret so cloying it chokes me.

Did I mention I'm slightly melodramatic?

Now, I know I had a choice. I didn't have to come back to

this landlocked city, hours away from the places I would much rather be. But I've been working for the same company for almost twenty years and the promotion I was offered —with the caveat being I had to come back and work at Head Office to claim it— was too good to turn down.

Of course, my job is tied in to my feelings of regret, but that's not worth going into right now. No. I'm good at what I do, having climbed up the ranks from lowly salesman to the head of the marketing division (with my sights set on Vice President within the next five years) by using my natural charisma and charm.

Still, I can't lie to myself about how I got the job in the first place...

But I can ignore it.

I can ignore feeling used. I can ignore the stab of guilt at having betrayed a friend. (A good friend. A best friend.) I can even ignore the urge to reach out and apologize now that I'm back in town.

I can. I swear I can.

I have to.

I mean, what would I even say? "Hey, I know I fucked up and I totally used your shitty relationship with your dad to my advantage, but could you forgive me so my tummy stops turning over? Oh, yeah, and I came out after I left, too."

Yeah. I can just see that going over well. *Not.*

And that's assuming Chance would even let me get more than three words out before he hung up on me, or slammed a door in my face, or...well, you get the picture.

I did my best friend dirty when we finished high school, and for almost twenty years I've been running from that simple truth.

Chance Baker has every right to hate me. I can still picture the hurt on his face from our last conversation. The betrayal and the heartache.

God, I was such a dick.

Let me make myself very clear: I don't deserve his forgiveness.

But I want it. Fuck, do I want it.

I mightn't have spoken to the man in almost two decades, but that hasn't stopped me from caring about him.

Loving him, even.

And how fucked up is that?

More than I can tell you, considering the way we parted ways.

I've kept track of him over the years. It's unhealthy, I know. But I've stalked his social media, tried to track his career and his relationships as best I could from afar. I told myself I just wanted to make sure that he was happy, but that's a bald-faced lie. I miss him. I've always missed him.

And now I'm back in the city he lives in and the guilt. won't. stop.

"Guess I know what I need tonight," I sigh as I push myself up from the black leather couch in my beautiful, though kind of sterile, lounge room. My entire apartment can be described that way. It's all black and chrome. Sleek, modern and minimalist. Emotionless as fuck.

A bit like me, most people might say. But then, most people don't know the real me. They see 'Professional Kade': a ruthless marketing executive. I don't have close friends. Haven't allowed myself the luxury since I graduated high school.

I don't deserve friends. Not after what I did to Chance.

What I do deserve, though, is a spanking.

And I know just where to get one.

* * *

The Grove comes highly recommended by my former BDSM club. It's exclusive and high-end. They take the safety and privacy of their members very seriously, something I greatly appreciate. It's situated just on the edges of the industrial part of the city, with very little else around. A great big warehouse with a discreet entrance and top of the line soundproofing throughout, you'd never know the wonders that are hidden inside.

When I get to the club, I sign in with the voluptuous maître d and enter through the double doors separating the bright white foyer from the pumping bass and strobe lighting of the nightclub floor. Twin corridors snake around the sides of the building and meet at the back, where the elevators and grand staircase await to lead me to the floors containing the themed playrooms.

I take the corridor to my left, making use of the locker rooms down this way, stripping out of my business attire and pulling on a pair of brightly colored training pants, a rainbow patterned crop top and a pair of bright pink booty shorts. After artfully ruffling my blonde hair, I stash my gym bag in a locker and make my way down the corridor, then climb the grand staircase to the next floor.

Here, it feels like a fancy hotel, with two parallel carpeted hallways lined with doors. I choose the hallway to my right and walk to the end, entering the Littles' Playroom. It's a massive space that runs the width of the warehouse, with high ceilings, couches for the caregivers, and a sunken play space in the center. Down the far end of the 'room', there's even a bouncy castle large enough to hold a couple of adults comfortably.

A bouncy castle.

My former club had a foam pit, the one before that a ball pit and slide. But this one wins hands down, as far as I'm concerned.

As much as I want to go nuts on the bouncy castle, though, I cast my eyes around the room, checking wristbands, looking for an available Daddy. I'm agitated. Restless with simmering guilt. I *need* to be disciplined. It's an itch beneath my skin: a feeling that will only grow until I've been appropriately punished for my poor behavior.

I haven't felt this desperate a need for a spanking in years. I know it's exacerbated by my return to my home city, and I should probably find a therapist to discuss my issues with if I can't get it under control again. But for now, I'm going for the simple solution.

There aren't a lot of people here tonight, which is hardly surprising considering it's a Wednesday and it's not a theme night. But, the benefit is that most people who *are* here are unattached and looking to play.

I'm not searching for a Daddy. Not a permanent one. I just need a scene partner. Someone to take the edge off and make the guilt go away, if only for a little while.

"Well, hi there," a deliciously deep voice says, and I turn to find a middle-aged guy pushing himself to his feet from the couch to my right. He steps in a bit closer with a disarming smile. "Looking for someone —or something— in particular? Or just here to play?"

I give the guy a quick once over. He's substantially taller

than me, which isn't exactly a feat when I tapped out at 5'7" when I was fifteen, with a handsome enough face, chiseled features set in flawless dark skin, and warm brown eyes. He's solidly built, with his dark hair cut in a generic 'short back and sides' style, too. Despite his size, he looks friendly and gentle. I wonder if he's even got it in him to dole out the punishment I need.

"I'm looking for a scene partner," I tell him honestly, shifting on my feet. "I…" I cast my eyes downwards, exhaling as I try to shake out my big headspace and sink into one more appropriate for what I need. My lower lip juts out in a pout. "I've been naughty."

Through lowered lashes, I look up to gauge this guy's reaction. Realization sweeps over him, but he doesn't shy away or recoil. "What do you need, boy?" he asks me calmly, suddenly more Daddy than he was a few seconds ago, too.

I appreciate that he's asking and not just assuming. I could need anything from corner time to a paddling, and some Daddies would just leap in with their suggestions first. But not this guy. That seems to seal the deal in my head, deciding that this one will do. It's just a scene, and we'll have to negotiate limits and safe words before we do anything, but he's already set me at ease and my gut says it's not worth looking any further. Not for what I need tonight.

"A spanking," I answer quietly, biting my lip for effect. I'm the picture of contrition and submission.

Did I mention I'm a *little* manipulative? It's not entirely my fault, but I know my strengths and how to use them to my advantage. Years in sales will do that to a person.

This Daddy smiles softly and extends his hand. "I'm Emmett," he says, and I take his hand and shake it. His palm is warm and dry, his hold firm but not too strong. He's not trying to come off all macho and dominating, even though I'm sure he could if he wanted to.

"Kade," I introduce myself.

"Well, Kade," he says as he releases my hand, "I'd love to be your scene partner if you'll allow me. Can I take care of you tonight?"

That cinches it. There's no other answer than "Yes, Daddy."

* * *

The spanking helps. I'm a sobbing, snotty, sweaty mess by the time we're done. I can feel my ass burning and it helps ground me, making me feel like I've paid penance for my past transgressions. Emmett provides top tier aftercare, too. He rubs aloe vera lotion into my skin and holds me while I come back out of the foggy state a good spanking always puts me in.

"Did you want to talk about it?" he asks once it's clear I'm myself again. He helps me pull up my pants while he waits for my answer.

I play dumb. "About what?"

My Daddy for the scene arches an eyebrow at me. "The reason you needed discipline tonight." Before I can tell him it's none of his damn business, he adds, "You don't have to if you don't want to. But I know talking about it —especially after you've been punished— can help a person process their feelings faster."

I shake my head. "I'd rather not. It's nothing against you. I just…"

"Don't open up to strangers about your personal issues?" He offers, smiling easily. "I get that."

It turns out Emmett is a genuinely nice guy, and the fact that he gave me what I needed and never once turned it into anything sexual only cements my high opinion of him. If I was looking for a Daddy, he'd be a great option.

But I don't want a Daddy. Especially not one as kind as this one. He's going to make some boy incredibly lucky someday. Just not me. I don't deserve a Daddy like him.

And now the guilt is creeping back. Great. That has to be a new record.

"Okay, so, I'm going to give you my card," he says abruptly, pulling me out of my musings. He chuckles when he can see that I'm ready to protest and holds up his hand. "I work down at The Little Community Center as a counselor." He cocks his head. "Have you heard of it?"

"No," I frown. "Is that, like, some sort of social services kind of deal?"

"It's a safe haven, specifically for members of the BDSM and kink community. Set up by a former cop, actually. There's a sweet story behind it, but, essentially, it offers itself up as a safe space and alternative to coming here," Emmett waves his hand around, indicating the club space, "for people who want to explore their kinks without the nightclub or intense sexual overtones. We also provide subsidized, kink-friendly counseling, assistance finding emergency housing, and host Q and A nights and other stuff." He stands from the padded bench in the private room we had booked for our scene, and pulls his wallet from his hip pocket. After rummaging a bit, he hands a little white business card to me. "We're doing a kink-themed fundraising auction and Open House next month if you're interested in checking it out."

Nodding, I look down at the rectangle of embossed cardboard in my hand and tell him, "I'll think about it."

Emmett doesn't push the issue any further than that, and he crosses the room to put the bottle of lotion back into the cabinet it had come from. I thank him again for helping me out, and I'm surprised when he pulls me in for a hug.

Not many people hug me these days. That's a sad realization to have.

"Just think about coming to The Center," he murmurs as he releases me. "I think we'd be good for you, Kade."

There's a softness in his voice that calls to me. Even though I don't feel as all like I deserve it, I long for it. Perhaps that's ultimately why I clutch the business card tight in my fist until I'm back downstairs in the locker room, sliding it into my wallet and making a note to Google the place when I get home.

Chapter Three – Chance

"It's not too late to back out," Spencer teases me as I struggle with doing up my tie.

I roll my eyes and then glare at my own reflection in the mirror. We're in Charlie's office at The Center, getting me all spruced up for the auction. I even trimmed my usually scruffy beard down to something a bit neater, and I'll admit it looks good. Still, this is the first time I've worn a suit in God only knows how long, and this damn tie is causing me grief.

"Dude," Spencer shakes his head and laughs at my increasing frustration, "lose the tie. Pop the first couple of buttons. Leave the jacket open."

"Since when are you a fashionista?" I grizzle, doing as he says and realizing that I actually look pretty damn good like this. Asshole. I hate it when he's right.

"I'm sorry, was that 'thanks, Spence, I don't know what I'd do without you'? Because you're welcome."

Despite rolling my eyes, I turn to him and sigh. "Thanks," I say.

My friend rolls his wrist. "And the rest."

"Thanks is all you're getting from me."

He makes a 'tsk'ing sound. "I hope you're not going to be this surly when you get your ass up on that stage. Nobody wants a grumpy Daddy."

"Lies," Josh interrupts the conversation as he sidles into his brother's office. He grins. "Grumpy Daddies are hella fun."

"You *make* Daddies grumpy, Josh," Spencer argues back. "Not the same thing."

"You say 'tomato', I say 'potato'," the bratty Little of our group sasses back, deliberately turning the phrase into a malaphor to get under Spencer's skin.

Spencer's opening his mouth to take the bait when Josh turns to me and declares, "Anyway, you look great, Chance. Which is good, because it's time to get out there and mingle."

"*Mingle?*" I repeat, horrified.

Josh bobs his head and waves vaguely towards the door. "Yep. They —the events coordinator at The Grove and Cherie, I mean— decided that letting all the patrons get a feel for the merchandise before the show kicks off will help drive up bids…or something like that."

"I don't know how I feel about being called 'the merchandise'," I complain, trying to stall.

Did I mention I have mild social anxieties?

Josh's personality pivots the second he senses my unease. If there's one thing I've noticed about the man, it's that he is ridiculously good at reading people, and has a knack with knowing just what to say or do to ease a person's discomfort. He's immediately serious when he says, "All joking aside, Chance, if you don't want to do this, you don't have to. Charlie will understand."

I shake my head. "I can't do that to him. Or to The Center. I'm doing this thing."

It's just one night. I can handle a little bit of mingling and a few minutes on a stage. It's for a good cause.

"In that case, we'll keep close," Josh tells me, definitively. "It can look like you're chatting, but you'll have the safety buffer of your friends."

It's times like this that I question why he's earned himself a reputation as a brat. He's obviously a sweetheart, so it surprises me that he enjoys being bratty. Still, different strokes for different folks and all that jazz.

I shoot him a grateful smile. "Thanks, man. I'd like that."

The three of us traipse out of Charlie's office and Josh locks the door behind us. The auction itself is being held in the community hall, which is a large open room on the far end of this building from the offices. In between the offices and the hall, there's a big open rec room which is usually full of beanbag chairs, couches, and coffee tables. But today the space has been cleared and is being utilized as a reception venue of sorts.

People are milling about in an eclectic mix of cocktail attire and kink-related clothing. The invitations had listed the dress code as 'whatever you're comfortable in' with a reminder that this event is kink-friendly. So there are people in leather, in harnesses and pet hoods, some in onesies and others in a mixture of both cocktail and kink, like the lady in the beautiful body contouring black dress and the whip holstered to her hip.

Servers with gleaming silver platters topped with appetizers and flutes of bubbling wine weave between the clusters of people, and there's a dull rumble of conversation in the air.

On long tables down the sides of the room, pictures of all the items on auction are displayed for the attendees to check out and read about where bios and blurbs have been included. I know my photo is on one of those tables, along with a bio I asked Tony, Spencer's boyfriend, to write for me. I'm not going to go look to confirm this, though.

Spence and Josh usher me towards the groups of people, and I find that I recognize a lot of them from The Grove. This sets me at ease, and, after snagging a glass of bubbly white wine from a passing server, I settle in to make conversation.

It's not so bad after all. Maybe this auction's going to work out well for me, despite my misgivings and my fears.

I manage to hold onto that positivity for the entire time before the auction begins. When I'm on the little stage as the third Daddy to go up for bidding, I'm relieved to find that the spotlight on me makes it impossible to see into the crowd of people in the audience.

The auctioneer —a master Dom I've seen around The Grove over the years— reads my bio before the bidding commences. I have to admit that Tony did a pretty fantastic job hyping me up. He wrote about how much I enjoy taking on a nurturing role, but that I like to get involved in play time, too. He also discussed my goofy sense of humor and how close I am with my friends.

Listening to Tony's description, even *I* want to bid on some time with me. I make a note to buy him a new stuffy or something to show my appreciation. He's a sweet kid, and he makes my best friend stupidly happy to boot.

I try not to pay attention when the bidding starts. I'm still afraid that nobody will bid. After all, I visit The Grove regularly, and I'm almost always open to play. Why would anyone pay for a day with me, when they can find me at the club for free?

But then I hear the price escalating, and it almost sounds like there's a bidding war happening, and it's not that much longer before the gavel goes down with an echoing *crack* and I've been sold for a day to the highest bidder.

I walk off the stage with wobbling legs, and Charlie's there to pat my back and grin. "Did you hear that?!" He asks me, his blue eyes twinkling with the reflection of the stage lights at my back. "You outsold Bryce."

I had assumed Bryce would bring in the most money, and I'd told Charlie as much. Bryce is hot as fuck and pansexual, so open to play with Littles of all genders, and a day of Daddy time with him had sold for almost two thousand dollars. I can't imagine being worth anywhere near that sort of cash.

My fears of living up to the value start to simmer away at the back of my brain. Talk about pressure!

I blink at Charlie, genuinely surprised. "I did not."

"You did, man, I swear."

"Who the hell would be insane enough to pay that kind of money for time with me?" I ask, feeling bewildered. I turn around, trying to peer back over the stage and towards the audience. "Do we know him?"

Charlie shrugs and shakes his head. "Emmett does. Says he's new to town. Has seen him at The Grove a couple of times. About our age. Short. Slim. He's private, but a nice guy...according to Em, anyway."

Charlie's answer only leaves me with more questions. Why would a random Little who has never met me want to pay that kind of cash for a day of my time? Especially if he's been hanging out with the attractive counselor Charlie just mentioned?

Emmett also volunteered a day of Daddy time for the auction and he's up next, so it's not like I was a second choice or anything.

Charlie claps a hand on my shoulder and leads me through the door that lets us back out into the main room. "Come on: you can meet the guy and ask him all your questions yourself. He should be paying Cherie about now."

We walk down the narrow aisle of space between the wall and the chairs that have been set up for the bidding audience, and I'm dimly aware of Emmett's bio being read to the crowd. I don't turn back to watch the proceedings, though. I'm too curious to meet the man who bought a day with me.

Charlie opens the door at the back of the room, guiding me through the rec room and towards the back offices. Cherie usually mans the reception desk, and as we turn the corner from the rec room, her little office is brightly lit up and she's sitting in her usual spot at the desk in front of the wall, chatting with a short, blonde man whose back is currently to me.

There's something vaguely familiar about the set of his shoulders, but it's not until Cherie brightly declares, "And here they are now," that the guy tenses and then turns slowly to face me.

I feel the air leave my lungs at the same time as Charlie walks into my back because I've frozen unexpectedly in place.

"Hey, Chance," Kade says, as if the past twenty years haven't happened. As if our final conversation didn't leave me hurting and alone.

He's aged well, I realize dimly. He still looks like himself, though his face has filled out and his shoulders and chest seem more solid beneath the figure-hugging Henley he wears. He's still as short as he always was, still as slim and still as pretty, but very much a man opposed to the angry eighteen-year-old from my memories.

When I fail to speak, he steps a bit closer, his smile a little bit rueful. "Surprise?"

I exhale, reminding myself that I let go of the hurt between us a long time ago. I even forgave him. But there's an echo of pain and embarrassment as I look at him which makes me uncomfortable.

The conversation ahead is inevitable and I know it. Honestly, we should have had it twenty years ago.

Turning to Charlie, I softly murmur, "Refund him," before I turn on my heel and walk away.

I know that Kade will follow me.

Chapter Four – Kade

"Don't refund me," I tell the tall, dark-haired man with the impressive biceps. Usually, I'd pause to admire such a handsome specimen, but I'm too concerned with catching up to Chance and begging him to listen to me.

Honestly, I know I don't really deserve it. But when I arrived tonight and saw his picture in among the Daddy Day auction 'prizes', it was like a sucker punch to the gut before instinct took over.

I mean, how unlikely is it, really, that my best friend from high school is a *Daddy* when I'm a Little? It's either a cruel joke from fate, or a sign that we've always just been that compatible.

When I stared at his photo, a little voice in my head had snidely reminded me that if I hadn't fucked up twenty years ago, we might have been able to explore that compatibility together, but I'd managed to swallow it back and settle in for the auction, waiting patiently for my chance. (Ha, see what I did there?)

Originally, I only turned up because Emmett gently reminded me the last two times we bumped into each other at The Grove. If I were to let myself have friends, I imagine Emmett would make a good one, so I said I'd come and check the place out tonight. I said it partially to shut him up, and partially because the loneliness of my life really is starting to wear on me.

It's my own fault. I know this. And being back in my home city is exacerbating it. But I think I've hit a wall and I need to finally deal with the mess I made.

Which then leads me right back to why I bid on Chance. I expected that he'd take one look at me and tell me to fuck off, but I just couldn't help myself. I need closure, if nothing else. Besides, dropping a couple of grand on a worthy cause isn't something I mind doing anyway. It's not like I've got anyone other than myself to spend my money on, and this kink-centric community center is doing amazing things. Honestly, they need to spread the word more, because the services, inclusion, and help they are offering is phenomenal.

Maybe once I've been able to talk to Chance, I'll volunteer to help their marketing and social media team, or something.

But Chance is my priority right now.

I race after him, following him through the bright, welcoming rec room and then through the double doors that lead out into the beautifully manicured entrance and front lawn. From the street, this place looks almost like a large day care center. It's got a friendly vibe, from the colorful fencing, to the rainbow pattern of the building's front façade, and also the neat lawn and garden beds. I'd stood outside admiring it for a few minutes earlier tonight.

"Chance, c'mon, please wait," I call after my former friend, trotting to try and catch up to him.

He's reached the sidewalk and I watch as he stops and his shoulders slump before he turns to face me, his mouth set in a grim line. "What the hell, Kade?"

Even though I wasn't exactly expecting sunshine and roses, the fire in Chance's hazel-brown eyes makes me stop in my tracks. Maybe it's my guilt, maybe it's our past, maybe it's the fact that he's a Daddy and I'm a boy, but I can feel my lower lip quiver in the face of his frustration.

He steps closer, still frowning, the look far more intimidating now that he's a grown ass man than it ever was when we were teens. The hair on his cheeks —also a new addition— intensifies the expression on his face.

"Seriously, what…" Chance trails off and shakes his head. "How'd you even know I was gonna be here?"

"I didn't."

Chance blinks at me, then scoffs, "So you just *happened* to turn up to a kinky auction? You expect me to believe…" He does the trailing off thing again, then frowns. "Charlie said Emmett knew you from The Grove." Now he's starting to sound genuinely confused, his ire deflating.

It's so very much like the boy I used to know that I can't help smiling. "Yeah. I…I'm a Little, actually. I've only been back in town a short while, and word on the grapevine is that The Grove's the best club around, so…" I shrug. When he doesn't say anything, I press on. "I had no idea you'd be here. Hell, I had no idea you were a Daddy. And then when I saw you, I just…"

"Acted on impulse." Chance finishes for me in a tone I can't really read. He sounds flat and resigned, sure, but am I just being hopeful, or is he also a little amused?

"Yeah," I answer, another smile tugging at my lips as I shrug, "you know me."

That proves to be the wrong thing to say.

"Funnily enough, no, I don't." Chance folds his arms, the suit jacket he's wearing pulling tight across broader shoulders than I recall him having. "And that's your fault, Kade. Hell, I came out to you and…" He stops himself, sighing. "It doesn't fucking matter. It's been twenty years and I don't know what you hoped to achieve by buying a day with me, but you're not getting that day. I hope you realize that."

"I know," my reply is soft and resigned. I want to reach for him, want to offer him physical comfort because I know he's a tactile man, but I keep my hands to myself. "I just…I wanted to…to see you. To apologize to you."

His eyes snap to mine at that. *"What?"*

I swallow, feeling my palms sweating and my heart racing.

I've thought about what I'd say to him so often for the last twenty years, and certainly more frequently since I've been back in town, that it's almost seared into my brain. An elaborate, heartfelt apology, listing my crimes and expressing my understanding that I don't expect his forgiveness, but that I know he deserves to hear me say the words.

But now, knowing that this is my only opportunity, my mind blanks.

Twenty fucking years of remorse, and all I manage to offer him is, "I fucked up, Chance. I fucked up, and I'm so sorry."

I want to say more. I do. But the words won't come. I try to implore him with my eyes, begging him silently to hear them even though I can't put them out there.

"Kade…"

"I'm so sorry." I repeat.

Then I burst into tears.

Chapter Five – Chance

What the fuck is happening right now?

This is the question I ask myself as my best friend from high school breaks down in front of me. Weak resentment wars with my instinct to comfort him. It's not even an instinct borne entirely of our former friendship, either. No: he's a Little. He's an upset Little and I'm a Daddy. He's also someone I cared terribly deeply for before we parted ways, and I've never liked seeing him upset.

It is pure instinct driving me to step forward and pull him into my arms.

Kade becomes a limpet, clinging to me as he sobs. He babbles while I hold him, and I catch bits and pieces of the apology I'm assuming he wanted to make. Snippets like 'I was a coward' and 'I know I hurt you' and 'you should hate me' ring in my ears.

It's all the closure I ever wanted from him, but it feels hollow now.

Yeah, twenty years ago I was so hurt that I had come out to

my best friend, hoping that he'd do the same with me (because, *hello*, the fact that he's gay was never going to be a surprise, even if it does make me a bit of an asshole for stereotyping), only to have him brush off my world-changing revelation to tell me that he was taking the job with my father that I had turned down only hours earlier.

I'd felt betrayed.

Not that he hadn't felt ready to come out to me in return, because I understood *that*.

No, I felt betrayed because he knew how rocky my relationship with my dad was, and he was playing into my father's manipulative tactics by accepting that job.

When I'd told him as much, he'd gotten defensive. We'd exchanged bitter words. He'd told me I was stupid to turn down my father's connections. I'd told him *he* was stupid if he thought Dad wasn't just hiring him to get back at me. In hindsight, it's stuff we could have talked through, but we didn't have the maturity to do so. But back then I'd been left a child on the cusp of adulthood, without my parents' support *and* without my best friend. I'd seen his actions as him taking their side, and that had been that.

It had taken me a while to work through that, and at least a few years to let go completely. I thought that I'd forgiven when I'd tried to forget, but a few minutes ago, I still felt the pang of hurt that he'd turned a pivotal moment in my life —my coming out to my best friend, someone I trusted and loved— into a painful memory.

When I laid eyes on him, I felt like that eighteen-year-old version of myself again: lost, hurt, and unsure about where to go from there.

But I've never once hated Kaden McDonnell.

As I've aged, I've been able to look back on those memories through an adult's eyes. Kade wasn't like me. He didn't have wealthy parents or a guaranteed career waiting for him. He'd grown up with just his mom, and she'd been vocal about him needing to move out and support himself once he was 'an adult'. Growing up, he'd spent more time at my house than at his own, and the amount of pressure he'd put on himself to succeed in life, even at such a young age, is soul crushing in hindsight.

Yes, he'd hurt me. Yes, I'd been angry with him for a long time. And, yeah, I thought I'd never wanted to see him again for those reasons. But I can admit to myself that they were flimsy reasons, and hearing how much he's been beating himself up over what happened between us puts a sour taste in my mouth. It's been twenty years, and he's been agonizing over it this whole time?

I moved on. I've lived a happy life for the last two decades. It sounds awful, but in the last ten years or so, I really haven't even given that much thought to Kade and what happened when we graduated high school. It only ever comes up when my mom calls to beg me to try reconciling with my father – on my birthday, and at Christmas.

Seeing him in person was a shock, and my reaction to turn my back was a knee-jerk one, but as quickly as I was reminded of the hurt and embarrassment from our teenaged falling out, it's becoming clear to me that he's spent a lot more time punishing himself for what happened than I have done dwelling on it.

I'm rubbing Kade's back and murmuring words of comfort before I even realize it's happening. He fits in my arms as easily as he did when we were teenagers, though I don't think he ever understood the way I'd felt about him back then. He was my best friend, and I was pretty sure I was in love with him.

You know, until shit went down and I never spoke to him again.

I guess that played a big part in how hurt I was by what happened, too. I mean, I came out to him and, not only did I feel betrayed, but I was also heartbroken that he didn't seem to reciprocate my feelings.

The sound of footsteps approaching has me looking up and over the top of Kade's blonde head, and I'm not surprised to see Charlie and Ted making their way over to us.

"Everything okay here?" Charlie asks, furrowing his brow as he looks from my face to Kade burrowed against my chest and then back up to my face again. Considering the way I reacted when I saw him, I understand his confusion.

Kade stiffens when he realizes that we have an audience, but I shush him and hold him in place.

"It's fine," I answer my friend, unsure of what else I could, or even should, say.

"Did you guys want to use one of the offices to talk?" Ted suggests gently. "It's getting a bit chilly out here."

And we're making a scene in public. That's not a great look for The Center, but they're kind enough not to mention that.

"Yeah," I agree, still a bit lost as to what the actual fuck is happening, "that'd be great."

"You can use the office I share with Gabe," Ted says. He's recently volunteered pro bono hours to The Center and works here every other Wednesday. Gabe, a social worker, was kind enough to share his space with our lawyer friend. "The couch in there is pretty cozy. Much better than hanging around out here."

Giving Kade a squeeze, I tell Ted, "That sounds great. Lead the way." Then I gently push my former best friend away and, with my hand on the small of his back, guide him to follow behind my friends.

He mutters a croaky "Thank you" to Ted and Charlie as they get us settled in the office. It is decorated in neutral tones, with a worn, solid timber desk and chair along one wall, and a squishy brown couch along another. Next to the couch, there's a large potted plant of some kind. A ficus maybe? I have no idea, but London would know. I doubt I'll remember or care enough to ask him, but the greenery adds a brightness to the space.

Both my friends level me with pointed looks before they leave Kade and I to our own devices, quietly pulling the door shut in their wake. I'm not going to get away with brushing them off over this.

"Well, this is embarrassing," Kade eventually sighs, scrubbing a hand over his face. He leans his head back over the soft, suede couch and stares at the ceiling, his cheeks pink. "Sorry. I mean, for—" he gestures vaguely in the air "—all this. I wasn't expecting to melt down like that. That's never happened before."

I frown, because who hasn't lost control of their emotions before? Let alone a Little. "Never?"

Kade shakes his head, still resolutely staring upwards. "Nope. Well, I mean, except for after a proper spanking. But I expect to let go then. That's why I…" He stops abruptly.

The Daddy in me is alert and determined to know more. "Why you what, Kaden?"

He doesn't wrinkle his nose or scold me for using his actual name like he used to when we were kids. If anything, a tiny half-smile tugs at the corner of his lips.

It takes a few more moments of silence before he exhales and admits, "I go to the clubs specifically for that. For the domestic discipline. To get control of my emotions. To take my punishment and cry it out and make everything better for a little while."

Something in my chest squeezes tightly at the murmured confession. A couple of tears leak down the sides of his face. With his head tilted back the way it is, they track down into his hairline and ear. He doesn't move to wipe them off.

I surprise us both when my hand reaches out for the side of his face that I have access to, and my thumb carefully brushes away the remnants.

Kade's lower lip quivers again, much like it did during our initial confrontation (if you can even call it that), and then he launches across the space between us, burrowing his face in my chest again. He's not sobbing like he was earlier, though. He's trembling, and sniffling, but he's still coherent when he says, "I missed you."

And just like that, any lingering frustration at our history seems to completely dissolve. I've never liked seeing him upset. I bring my arms back around him and answering the only way I can: honestly. "I missed you, too."

We sit like this for I don't know how long, until Kade takes a deep breath and rights himself. He looks a mess, with his hair in disarray and his eyes rimmed with red, but he's lost the tense set of his shoulders and the tremulous smile he offers me is genuine. It's a glimpse of the boy I'd once loved.

"I really am sorry, Chance," he says. "I spent the first year or so telling myself I should just man up and call you, but I chickened out every time I got close. And then time went on, and it seemed more and more awkward, and then I just… decided you were better off without hearing from me."

I don't like the defeat that enters his voice, or the way he looks down at his lap, where he's fidgeting with his fingers. He was always the outlandish, confident one of the two of us. Seeing him subdued and broken just feels wrong.

Before I can say anything, though, he's speaking again, "But then I saw your picture tonight and I couldn't not bid. It was like a sign, or something, you know?" He looks up at me, his blue eyes startlingly bright and wide. "I mean, what's the actual likelihood of that happening? I had no idea you were an age play Daddy, or that you had affiliations to The Grove. It's not like it's that common a kink."

"True," I acknowledge, a bit weirded out by how easy it is to talk to this man, like the past twenty years of radio silence never existed. However, I stopped being angry with Kade years ago, and, yeah, I really have missed him. I didn't realize how much until I saw him again. Getting comfortable, I ask, "How did you come by age regression?"

Kade chuckles mirthlessly. "You don't have to do this. Make small talk, I mean." He shrugs, and offers me another rueful smile, those perfectly pouty lips of his twisting bitterly. I practically can feel the self-deprecation radiating from him. "I appreciate you giving me a chance to apologize. And for…" he waves his hand over his face, "dealing with that whole mess. You're a good guy, Chance. You always have been, and I'm—"

I've had enough. Cutting him off, I bring out *Daddy voice*. "Kaden, if you apologize one more time, you're going in the corner."

His jaw drops. "What?"

"You heard me. You've apologized. I've accepted your apology. We were kids, Kade. We said stupid shit to each other and didn't have the emotional or mental maturity to fix it."

"But—"

"But nothing. Yeah, I was hurt. Yeah, seeing you tonight brought that feeling rushing back in those first few minutes. But I've thought about it a little—"

"What?" Kade snorts with disbelief and amusement, a hint of the feistiness I knew so well peeking through, "In the last half hour while I was sobbing all over you?"

I roll my eyes. "Well, yeah?" At his arched eyebrow, I chuckle and continue, "Honestly, I overreacted tonight. And probably when we were kids, too. You taking the job didn't ruin my life. I'd already broken ties with my dad. I just…" Am I really doing this? Am I really about to make this confession? Twenty fucking years too late? "I loved you, Kade. As my best friend, yeah, but…I was *in* love with you. And when I came out to you, I'd hoped…" I let him fill in the blanks, feeling my cheeks heat up as his jaw goes slack.

Clearing my throat, I steamroll over his whispered, "*What?!*"

"So, yeah. That's why I was hurt. But…it's been twenty years. It's time to put that shit behind us."

Chapter Six – Kade

Did my former best friend just tell me he was in love with me? *Was* —past tense— but still…*Holy shit*. I know his words should make me feel better, but guilt roils my belly all over again. He was in love with me, and I threw it in his face. Worse still, I struggle against the knowledge that I'd had feelings for him in return. Not for the first time, I wish I'd handled things differently.

Sure, I didn't know that he had feelings for me at the time, but he'd still come out to me and, instead of supporting him like a best friend should have, I'd panicked and blurted out the deal I'd made with his father only hours earlier.

If I could turn back time…

No. No, thinking like that isn't going to help me. Not even if I let the voice in my head sound like Cher. Of course, now that I come to think of it, the lyrics to that particular song are more relatable than ever. *Hmm…*

No. Getting lost in 'what if's and regrets will only make it hurt more.

"I was too scared to come out," the words tumble from my mouth without even connecting in my brain first. This is clearly a behavioral pattern around Chance. "I know I didn't exactly scream *straight boy*, but…"

"Your mom." Chance finishes for me, his voice soft with understanding.

"My mom," I agree on a sigh. While I was living under her roof, there was no way I was rocking that boat.

"I get it," Chance tells me, and he startles me when he reaches for my hand and squeezes it. "I *never* begrudged you for waiting to come out. Nobody should be forced to do that."

Slivers of relief pierce through the churning guilt. "I came out the day I moved out," I explain anyway, and Chance squeezes my hand again. My heart thumps wildly at the realization that he's not letting go. "Mom took it about as well as I'd expected. But…we're okay now. It took a few years, but…yeah. We're okay."

We've never really been that close, Mom and me. My Dad was a Navy man and he died when I was little. Too little to really remember him. Mom did her best raising me, but she never really recovered from the loss. And our ideologies and values never really aligned either.

The fact that I've been out and proud for two decades and she's never once asked me about my love life or whether I'm going to bring someone home to meet her is equal parts a relief and depressing. I'm living my own version of 'Don't Ask Don't Tell' with her, but for the two or three conversations we have a year, it works well enough.

I look up to find Chance's eyes on me. They're narrowed, like he's gauging the truth of my assessment of my relationship with my mother.

My heart beats even faster.

"I'm sorry I wasn't there," he says.

I shake my head. "If I can't apologize anymore, neither can you."

That earns me a wry laugh, and the sound sets about a thousand butterflies loose in my belly. I haven't made Chance laugh in twenty years, but the sound is as pleasant as it always was, if a bit deeper and containing more gravel now. His whole Daddy vibe is on point.

"All right, that's fair," he agrees, then pulls his hand from mine to offer it towards me for a handshake. "Clean slate?"

Hope blooms inside me for the first time in what feels like forever.

Admittedly, I feel like I'm getting off light here. That his forgiveness has come too fast, too easily. But that has always been Chance. He always was too quick to forgive me when we were kids, as well, not that I ever fucked up as monumentally as that last time. Still, I would be stupid to look a gift horse in the mouth, and I have to trust that he knows what he's doing.

The guilt starts to fade away as I clasp his larger, meatier palm with mine. His skin is smooth and warm to touch. I grin and nod, "Clean slate."

* * *

"You didn't have to drive me home," I tell Chance later as he pulls up outside my apartment building. I hadn't driven to the auction as I'd planned on drinking at the event. Now I'm glad I didn't do either of those things because I have a clear mind and more time with Chance.

If someone had told me that I'd be ending tonight on

speaking terms with my former best friend —and my biggest regret— I would have laughed my pert little ass off. But here I am, and so is Chance.

He's in the driver's seat of his shiny red truck, and I'm beside him in the passenger seat. This is his baby, he'd told me, and it's obvious he takes great care of it. It's not a super new model, but the dash and steering wheel are practically gleaming from polish, and there's not a speck of dust to be seen. The leather seats are also well conditioned, with no scuff marks, tears, or cracking.

Chance's suit jacket is discarded on the bench seat between us, and he's already unbuttoned his cuffs and rolled his sleeves to his elbows. I feel like a Jane Austen character, getting giddy at the sight of exposed, masculine forearms – thick, strong, and covered in cinnamon colored hair.

Flash me some ankle, Daddy...

I smother a chuckle at my absurd thought, then swallow the panic over my brain's choice of title. Chance is a Daddy, yes. But he's not my Daddy and I, more than anyone else, have no right to think of him that way, forgiven or not.

But I can't help acknowledging just how attractive he is.

When we were kids, I'd tried to ignore my attraction to him. I'd tried not notice the flecks of gold in his eyes, or the *almost* dimple in his left cheek, now hidden by a thick, rusty brown beard which glints with copper when the light catches it right.

God, that beard. Chance was a handsome eighteen-year-old, as far as any gangly teenager can be considered handsome when you are also a weedy young adult. But his aging has been beyond good to him. He's filled out, the lean abdomen of his teens now a soft paunch, his face rounder, and his thighs and arms bigger. He's the perfect build for a Daddy in my estimation: an alluring mixture of masculinity and comfort.

"I wanted to, Kade," he says, and I frown.

"What?" I let myself get distracted, so it takes me a second to realize that he's responding to what I said a few seconds ago. "Oh. Right. Yeah. Thank you."

His eyebrow quirks upwards, and there's amusement dancing in his gaze. "Lost in thought?"

"Something like that."

Awkward silence descends.

"Did you wanna—" I start.

He simultaneously says, "Well I—"

We fumble over each other's words next, both of us doing the "you go" "no you first" dance, and it ends with us both laughing off the strained moment.

"Did you want to come up for a coffee?" I ask into the comfortable silence that follows.

I'm expecting a rejection, but he surprises me by smiling and agreeing.

Great. Now I don't know what to say to him.

He kills the ignition and we climb out of our respective sides of his truck, the park lights flashing when he presses the button to lock it behind us. Then we walk in what I hope is companionable silence together, through my building's gleaming white lobby, to the bank of elevators and up to the sixth floor.

Chance whistles when I unlock the door to my apartment, taking it in for the first time while I drop my keys into the bowl on the side table in the little entryway. Toeing off my shoes and barely noticing him doing the same, I follow his gaze, trying to see my new home from his perspective.

It's cold. Clinical. All white tiles, white paint, white

cabinetry, and chrome accents. It's like something out of a magazine, with very little personality. The only splash of color comes from the living area, where a bright rainbow patterned rug takes up most of the floor space between the black couch and matching entertainment unit where the TV sits. To the right of that space, there's a floor to ceiling window stretching the length of the room, showing off my view of the city. As it is nighttime now, colorful lights in reds, yellows and oranges twinkle in the inky blackness.

Feeling self-conscious, I begin, "I only just moved in a couple of months ago, so..."

"It's great," Chance cuts me off, heading towards the living room. If we had turned left, we would have gone past the combined kitchen and dining area and into the hallway which leads to the two bedrooms and two bathrooms.

Standing just at the corner of the rug, Chance's lip quirks upwards. "I like this," he toes at the soft floor covering, "it's very you." Then he frowns and looks around the space again. I wish I knew what he was thinking.

Before I can second guess myself, I ask, "What's wrong?"

"You said you're a Little," he begins, then casts his gaze around my very minimalist home, "so...where are your toys? Your comfort items? Hell, your Disney DVDs?"

Laughter bubbles up out of my chest and escapes through my lips before I can rein it in. "DVDs? I have a Disney plus subscription. What year are you living in?"

"Shut up," he huffs back at me, but there's no heat to it.

Some more of the awkward tension I was feeling melts away. It's starting to feel like our old interactions again. Like we've always been this way. Like the last twenty years never happened, and I never screwed up and—

"Kaden, stop spiraling."

I blink, surprised to find that Chance has closed the space between us and is frowning down at me. He always could read me well.

My cheeks burn and I take a step backwards. "Sorry," I mutter. "I just—"

"I know," he assures me. "But we agreed. We can't change the past, and I'm done being angry about it. To be honest, I was done being angry a long time ago. You need to stop feeling guilty." And, to emphasize the fact that he doesn't want to revisit the topic, he goes back to his original line of questioning. "So, where are your toys and comfort items?"

He really is such a Daddy, isn't he?

"In the spare room," I answer, jerking my head in the direction of the rest of the apartment. "I'm not a lifestyle Little. A scene here and there is enough." It's not the whole truth, but it's how I've lived my life to this point. I haven't allowed myself relationships, and indulging in age play on my own just felt sad and empty.

Chance's eyebrows wing upwards, but he doesn't question me. He just says, "Huh," and shrugs.

I want to find it amusing that he still knows me so well, but it just stirs that guilt and melancholy back up again.

"*Kade*," he sighs, and this time I do laugh.

"Stop reading me like a fucking book."

He rolls his eyes, but he's grinning. "Stop being so easy to read."

God, I've missed this. Missed him. Missed our friendship and our stupid-ass banter and just feeling *seen*.

"Come on," I shake myself from that train of thought, knowing it'll only send me back into a remorseful spiral again,

"I'll give you the tour."

It's not a huge apartment, but it's more than enough for just me. I don't entertain people here, so the second bedroom is unnecessary, aside from being the place I store my few items of Little paraphernalia.

The bedrooms are just like the rest of the apartment. Modern and sparsely decorated. In the spare room, there's a single teddy bear sitting on the bed, propped up against the fluffy white pillows. In the closet, I have a few Little outfits neatly folded away in the drawers. I've never worn diapers (it loses its appeal when I know I'll be on my own) so I really only have a few pairs of training pants to accompany my outfits. I have a selection of pacifiers in a veritable rainbow of colors, though. Sucking on one of those is calming.

Chance steps towards the bed and picks the bear up, turning to face me with an almost sad set to his expression. "Have you ever tried…" he starts, then stops himself and shakes his head. The bear is set back down in front of the pillows gently. "Never mind. That's none of my business."

"No," I lean against the doorframe, doing my best to keep my body relaxed. I leave my hands at my sides, despite the urge to fold my arms across my chest. "Have I ever tried what?"

"It's just…I know you, Kade. Well, I knew you. And you never did anything by halves, especially when you enjoyed it. So it surprises me that you haven't brought age play into your home or made it a bigger part of your life."

"Yeah, well, it's not as fun when you're alone, is it?"

As soon as they've left my lips, I want to take those bitter words back.

Chance's frown deepens. "You're not perpetually single, though?" He cringes. "Shit. That's insensitive and also none of my fucking business." The realization is followed up by a muttered, "Where's Spence when you need him?"

I shuffle my stance and let my head fall back against the doorframe. "You're right: it's not really any of your business, but…"

Am I really doing this? Am I really about to tell him just how lonely my life has been? He was my best friend, and there's a part of me straining to reclaim that relationship, if nothing else. To lose myself in the familiarity of his comforting presence. It's been my own doing, this self-imposed isolation, but it doesn't make it any less painful. I want to talk to someone about it.

I want to talk to Chance about it.

Steeling myself with a deep breath, I confess, "I've never had a relationship last more than a couple of nights, and that's being generous on relabeling an extended hookup. I told myself I didn't deserve anything more and—"

"Jesus, Kade," Chance closes the space between us and pulls me in for an unexpected hug, holding me tight against his warmth. "You're an idiot."

I snort. "That's comforting."

"Shut up." His voice vibrates through his chest. He squeezes me a bit more tightly, as though I might push away at any second.

That's not likely. I haven't been held like this in…well, longer than I care to think about, not counting the aftercare I've received from Emmett.

I've missed Chance's hugs the most.

"This might sound kinda' self-involved," he says after another beat or two have passed, "but have you honestly spent the last twenty fucking years punishing yourself for a melodramatic moment between us when we were kids?"

"I…" Clearing my throat, I tuck my face into the crook of his neck. "It was mostly that, yeah."

Chance's frustrated groan is his only response, but he doesn't let me go.

Hating the silence, I try to explain, "I mean, I'm probably also fucked up from my issues with Mom, too, so it's not *just* what happened between us, but…you meant everything to me, you know? And I hurt you and destroyed our friendship and I figured if I could do that to you, I could do it to anyone and I didn't trust myself anymore. Plus, I didn't deserve to find love or whatever."

Chance is silent again, whether because I've shocked him speechless or because he's mulling over my admission, I don't know. Not for the first time, I wish I could read his mind.

He startles me when his lips find my temple, bestowing me with a gentle kiss before he sighs. "What am I going to do with you?"

I can't help that the only suggestions on the tip of my tongue are inappropriate.

Chapter Seven — Chance

This is so far out of my realm of experience, it's not even funny. It hurts me that Kade's been denying himself happiness out of some deeply ingrained sense of guilt. And for what? A heated moment when we were teenagers? Fuck it all, I'd thought myself heartbroken and I still managed to move on and date people. But he just…what, exactly? Lived half a life? If I hadn't already moved past my anger years ago, this would be the moment that I truly forgave him. He's been punishing himself enough.

"I'm going to be honest here," I tell him when hugging in the doorway of his guest room starts to feel a bit weird, "I'm not good with words. With emotions. I don't know what to say or do." Which is stupid because I'm a Daddy. I'm supposed to know how to comfort someone. But Kade's *different*. I know him so well and I simultaneously feel like I don't know him at all. "But I *do* know that you need to stop living in the past. You need to let people in. You need—*mmmph*."

I stumble backwards at the unexpected press of his lips to

mine. The almost feverish way he's clinging to me and kissing me. With my knees hitting the edge of the bed, I drop my ass down to the mattress, pulling him with me until he's straddling my lap and my hands are gripping his undulating hips.

We make out like horny teenagers for longer than I care to admit, before I tear my mouth from his with reluctance. Breathing heavily, I chuckle, "Well, that escalated quickly."

Kade's cheeks are flushed pink and his lips are swollen from our efforts. There's a hint of beard rash around his mouth which I refuse to feel guilty for. He's disheveled, his blue eyes blown wide with lust and surprise, likely at his own actions. He's hot as fuck, and it takes every bit of willpower I possess to not dive in for another kiss.

"I..." he begins and then stops, casting his gaze away. "Sorry."

"Hey, no," gently holding his chin between my thumb and index finger, I turn him back to face me. "That was unexpected, yeah, but welcome." Didn't I tell him earlier that I thought I was in love with him way back when? And he knows I've promised to forgive and forget. Plus, we're both single, consenting adults now, with compatible kinks, even if he hasn't yet explored his interests outside of a club setting. Why should this new development be a problem? "That was eighteen-year-old me's fantasy brought to life." I clear my throat and shift uncomfortably, ignoring my throbbing cock. "And, not gonna lie, thirty-eight-year-old me enjoyed it, too."

The corner of his lip twitches, but he turns adorably shy. I find that more amusing than anything, considering just how fiery and flamboyant he used to be.

Perhaps the shyness is indicative of his Little side? Or a new development of twenty years spent in self-enforced solitude. Either way, it's adorable.

"Why'd you kiss me, Kade?" I ask him softly, smoothing my hands up his sides in what I hope is a comforting gesture.

He nibbles his bottom lip and shrugs.

"*Kaden*," Daddy voice proves effective, if the way he straightens up is anything to go by, and I fight the urge to smile. "An actual answer, please."

"I…" he works his jaw, then seems to give himself some sort of internal talking to, because the next thing I know, Kade is lifting his chin defiantly and his blue eyes are blazing with the confidence I recall from our youth. It makes my stomach flip, even if I have enjoyed seeing him softer and more vulnerable. "I wanted to. You were telling me to let people in and put myself first, or whatever, and so I did. Put myself first."

I don't correct him or tell him that I hadn't actually told him to put himself first, because I was about to do just that before his kiss distracted me. Instead, I grin back at him. "Kissing me is putting yourself first?" He's still straddling my lap and if he doesn't have a problem with it, neither do I.

Kade rolls his eyes and shoves at my shoulders lightly. "As if you didn't know I've wanted to do that since we were fifteen. Maybe even before that."

I didn't know that.

I try not to let my face fall. Try not to tell him that if he'd just said something when I came out to him, the last twenty years might have been different. I've promised us both that the past is behind us. But damn if those words don't bring up a little pang of regret again.

Determined not to let the jovial mood between us slip away, I muster a laugh. "We would have disappointed each other back then. Two virginal, closeted boys with no idea what we were doing. Could you imagine?"

He makes a face. "Yeah. Okay. Fair point. My first time was…memorable for all the wrong reasons." He shudders. "It's how I found age play, actually."

My hands tighten on his hips again. "Yeah?"

"Yeah. After the disaster that was my first time with some guy my age with about as much knowledge and experience as me, I decided I needed to find older men. More experienced men. Men who could look after me and make it good for me, you know?"

I nod, trying not to feel jealous. It's not like I've spent the last two decades a monk, either.

"So I started Googling how to meet men like that," Kade's cheeks redden again. "The word 'Daddy' kept popping up. At first I was just curious about finding a Daddy without the age play. But the more I read about regressing, the more interested I was in trying it. So," he pauses, "then I found a munch and, after talking about it with some Daddies and Littles, I figured what the hell. I arranged my first scenes and never looked back." He stares past me, his expression wistful. "It was great stress relief. The spankings in particular helped me to deal with…everything. So, any time I got too overwhelmed, I'd head to my local BDSM club and find a Daddy to spank me and, if the mood struck, get off with."

It's a lot to take in, and I resolutely try not think about him meeting Emmett at The Grove for either of those purposes. I like Emmett. But damn if a simmering, albeit irrational jealousy doesn't tingle in my veins for a brief moment.

I am not that person, I tell myself, shaking the momentary feeling off. *Jealousy is not an attractive trait. Besides, it's not like I've been a monk over the last twenty years, either.*

My irrational thoughts now settled, I think about what Kade

hasn't said. "So you've never really *played*, then? Never given in to the little boy inside you and just…" I roll my wrist, searching for the right words, "been silly?"

"I didn't deserve those kinds of scenes," his answer is swift and heartbreaking.

"Oh, Kade, of course you did. You *do*." We're going around in circles now, but I can't help trying to convince him that he's worthy of so much more than just punishment scenes. Because that's what I've inferred from his vague story: he's using punishment scenes to deal with his guilt. He's not enjoying himself. Not really. I nuzzle his nose with mine. "If you could try anything —any kind of scene at all— just for fun, what would it be?"

"Anything?"

I nod. "Anything."

He's silent for a bit, then his answer throws me for yet another loop.

"I'm curious about puppy play."

I don't know what I was expecting, but it wasn't that. Kade said he was a Little, so I thought maybe suckling, or diapers, or stuffies. But…puppy play?

"I've never had a pup before," I blurt, then cringe because *he's not mine*.

Yeah, we're making out and cuddling, but until a couple of hours ago, we hadn't spoken in decades. So we need to talk about what this kissing and cuddling actually means, and I need to stop letting my past feelings for him dictate my hopes for the future.

But I'm still holding him in my lap, and I *really* don't want him to explore these new things with someone else.

I want him to be mine. My boy. My boyfriend.

My…pup.

Huh.

Do I actually want that? Or is this just a knee jerk reaction? Am I only feeling these things because I'm fulfilling my eighteen-year-old self's fantasies just by holding this man in my arms right now?

Possibly.

What does puppy play even entail? Is it something I would even enjoy? I've never looked into it because being an age play Daddy was my thing. It's *still* my thing. I certainly haven't changed in the last couple of hours. Would I still be a Daddy or would I be a Master?

I don't think I want to be a Master. That word alone sounds cold. Dominating. Distanced. Too much like my father and the man he wanted me to be.

"You're freaking out," Kade says, his long, elegant fingers gently caressing my cheek. "It's just a curiosity. You asked, I answered." He shrugs. "Besides, just because we're doing this," he gestures between us, "doesn't mean you're obligated to stick around."

The way he says that is telling, though. He's putting the ball in my court. I know him well enough, despite not having seen him for years, to know that he only does that when he really wants something but is too afraid of being embarrassed to admit it.

This thing between us, whatever it is, means something to him, too.

That realization is a relief. Even if I'm getting attached too quickly, potentially because I loved him all those years ago, it's good to know that he's not unaffected by this new development between us.

Smoothing my hands up his sides again, I ask, "You think you can walk back into my life, kiss me senseless, and then expect me to walk away? Really, Kade?"

"I'd deserve it."

"For fuck's sake," I groan. "We're not going around and around in circles about the past anymore. I can't take it. Forget that last conversation. Forget the wasted years. It's over, it's gone, it's not coming back. I said we're starting fresh again and I meant it. So, because it's a clean slate, you don't deserve to be punished or ignored or…or anything like that. And I swear to God, if you bring it up one more time, I'm putting you over my lap and giving you a proper spanking, understood?"

Chapter Eight — Kade

Was that supposed to be a threat? Because, honestly, the thought of Chance spanking me isn't making me want to change my ways. If anything, I want that spanking. Badly.

"You should," I tell him, smirking when he arches a bushy cinnamon colored eyebrow at me.

"I should what?"

"Spank me."

He blinks. "I didn't mean for pleasure, Kaden."

God, his Daddy voice is everything.

Focus, Kade.

"I know. And that's what I want. I want *you* to punish me for what I did." As the words tumble from my lips, I'm filled with certainty. "Bring the whole thing round circle, you know? Punishment and absolution from you directly are *exactly* what I need."

I don't know why I didn't think of it earlier. Not even when I bid on him at the auction. Not that I ever imagined he'd talk to me, let alone give me the Daddy time I'd bought. And I certainly never imagined that he would forgive me so easily, if at all. No, I knew that it felt *too* easy, and now I know that I *need* him to punish me.

Chance is quiet for a while, and I wish I could read his thoughts. Eventually, he sighs with reluctance and butterflies fill my belly. He's going to agree. Holy shit, he's actually going to spank me.

"One and done, Kade," he says firmly. "After I spank you, that's it. That's the only punishment you're getting for... God, you don't even deserve a spanking for something that happened so long ago, you know that, right? Not when you've been getting them regularly for the same damn thing."

"Chance, please...I do need this. I need this from you."

Even though I don't have the right to ask for it, I can't let the idea go now.

"Then what?" He prompts, looking me in the eye. "What happens after? Do you want us to go our separate ways?" My stomach clenches at the thought and I'm shaking my head vehemently. His expression softens. "Good," he says, "me neither. So, aside from absolution —which you've already earned verbally, I'll remind you— what do you want from me? Casual hookups? A relationship? Friendship? Though, I gotta say, I don't let any of my other friends snuggle in my lap like this."

I snort. "I'm glad to hear that. I wouldn't wanna get jealous."

I squeal when he pinches my ass. "Stop deflecting."

"I've never had a relationship," I remind him softly, looking away. "But, if I was going to try that with anyone, I'd want that to be you." If I'm being honest with myself, I've always wanted it to be him. I was too cowardly to say anything as a teenager, and then I fucked things up. Then I didn't want to be in a relationship at all, because if I couldn't have Chance, I didn't want anyone.

That's probably a sad realization to have after twenty years, right? Pining after someone for that long isn't healthy, and I know it. Maybe if we'd drifted apart under more normal circumstances, things might have been different. Who knows? All I know is that I'm starting to feel alive and more like my actual self for the first time in a very long time, and that's from being in his proximity again. From talking to him again.

He said he thought that he loved me when we were kids. Well, I'm pretty sure I reciprocated those feelings.

God, I was an idiot.

"That's not a direct answer," Chance tells me softly, and I rein my thoughts back in again. He's once again turning my face towards his, looking me in the eye, refusing to let me hide from him. "Do you want a relationship with me? Do you want me to be your Daddy? Because, I'll be honest here, Kade, I *do* want to be a Daddy with a Little as part of my relationship. It's something I look for in a partner. It doesn't have to be a 24/7 thing, but…yeah."

This entire night has been a whirlwind, full of unexpected events that I just can't wrap my head around. If I'd never gone to that auction, if I'd never perused the photos of Daddies volunteering their time, if I'd never given in to my gut instinct to bid on him and apologize, I'd be sitting here alone in my apartment, miserable and still punishing myself. Instead, tonight's happenings have led me to this moment, straddling Chance's lap while he asks me a question I wish he'd asked me twenty years ago, not that either of us even *knew* about age play back then.

My throat is tight when I answer, "Yes. Yes, I want all of that. With you."

"Me too, baby," he says, then brings our lips together again for a sweet kiss.

Our mouths move together slowly, almost carefully. I melt into Chance's embrace and let him set the pace. The fire and urgency from our previous kiss is nowhere to be seen. Instead, this kiss feels intense in a different way. It's laden with emotions I'm too scared to name, with lament of time lost, and also joy for a potential future together. It's the reclamation of an old friendship, but a promise to take that original foundation and turn it into something even more special. It's perfect and sweet, but still kind of poignant and overwhelming.

It's not until Chance pulls back and brushes his thumbs over my cheekbones that I realize I've been crying.

"Too much? Too fast?" Chance asks, his voice low and calming.

I shake my head. "No. I just can't believe this is happening. That you're here with me. That you're kissing me."

"Mmm," he agrees, his lips quirking beneath his scruff, "I know the feeling. Eighteen-year-old me would be doing a happy dance right about now."

I'm reminded again of my past mistakes and I swallow roughly. His earlier promise bounces around my head and I know that I need his punishment before I can truly move forward with him. "I need you to spank me, Daddy," I tell him with all the earnestness I can muster. "Please? Tonight. Now."

His whiskey-colored eyes soften and he presses his forehead to mine. "I'm not going to do it again for the past stuff, Kade. Once it's done, it's *done*. Understood?"

I nod, not trusting my voice. I can almost taste the closure. For real this time. That thought alone is making me more emotional than I've ever been. I've held on to the hurt and guilt from the past for so long that it's become a part of me. But I'm finally ready to let go of that if it means a future with Chance might be on the cards after all, however hard that is to believe.

"Where do you want to do it?" he asks me when I don't say anything further. "In here? In the living room?"

"My room," I manage to croak out. "I've never done this at home before, but…I like to be held afterwards. And," I swallow, "it's late. I…I mean…could you stay with me? Just to hold me? We don't have to rush into anything else. I just…I just don't want to let you go tonight." Especially not once he's spanked me.

Chance doesn't have a change of clothes, but tomorrow is a Saturday and we can deal with everything else then.

His lips brush my forehead, the hair of his beard tickling my skin in the most comforting way. "Of course, baby." After another kiss, he says, "Lead the way."

With reluctance, I climb off his lap and he takes my hand in his. I smile a bit at that, then guide him back out the door of the guest room and down the short hallway in the other direction, into the master suite of the apartment.

This room is larger, with a black leather armchair in the corner by the window which looks out over the rest of the city. It's one of the benefits to my corner apartment. The window here is tinted, so I can see out but nobody can see in. I still draw the curtains at night, though, because I hate the sun waking me up.

My bed is king sized and pressed against the middle of the

wall on the left side of the room, the headboard padded white leather and the comforter also crisp and white. A few black throw pillows and a black throw blanket tie the space together, but it's just as sterile and lifeless as the rest of my apartment.

Chance doesn't say anything about my minimalist decorating, though. Instead he walks over to the bed with me and lets go of my hand as he sits himself on the edge of the mattress. He makes quite the picture like this, in his suit pants and rumbled dress shirt, the collar unbuttoned and the sleeves rolled to his elbows.

"Pants off, Kade," he instructs when I fail to move, and I fumble with my belt with trembling hands. After taking a couple of calming breaths to get myself under control, I manage to slip the leather from my pant loops, and it's not long before I'm stepping out of my pants entirely, pulling off my socks next. I'm left in my shirt and briefs, and, at Chance's raised eyebrow, I tug my underwear down my legs, too.

He pats his thigh, and I drape myself over his lap as though it's second nature to me.

I guess it kind of is. I've done this countless times over the last twenty years, and I've never been ashamed of that, but it's never felt as right as this does.

Chance is about to spank me.

Chance. My former best friend. My former teenage crush. The man whose heart I accidentally broke and never forgave myself. I hadn't even realized how badly I'd hurt him, either. Even if he moved on and I didn't, I still did a number on him. I need this punishment more than I can properly express.

I'm over his lap only minutes after telling him that I want him as my boyfriend and my Daddy, and it's everything I've ever wanted and still so surreal.

Is this a dream? If it is, clichéd as it sounds, I don't want to wake up.

Chance shifts his weight under me, making sure I'm settled comfortable across his thick thighs, his legs spread wide with feet planted firmly on my lush gray carpet for stability. As Chance's hand rubs my ass cheeks, my naked cock twitches where it is pressed against the fabric of his suit pants. But this isn't about sex. Not tonight, anyway.

I brace myself for the first slap, but Chance —*Daddy,* I remind myself, feeling my throat tighten with unexpected emotion— smooths a hand down my spine. "Relax, baby," he says gently. "I've got you. And when I say we're done with this, that's it. You're gonna stop beating yourself up for what happened between two dumb, hurting kids. Okay?"

I nod.

"I need your verbal acknowledgment, Kaden."

"Yes."

That earns me a light swat to my backside. "Yes *what*, Kade?"

It takes me a moment longer than it should to understand. The tightness in my throat returns, but I manage it. "Yes, Daddy."

"Good boy," he says, and I don't think I'm imagining the sudden gruffness in his voice. Then, almost like an afterthought, Chance clears his throat and confirms, "Traffic light system for safe wording?"

"Yes, Daddy."

His hand strokes down my spine again, then rubs at my left butt cheek and then my right.

Then the first smack finally lands and I jolt in his lap, simultaneously relishing and lamenting the sting. My hands clutch at his thigh, and I tuck my chin towards my chest as the next slap sounds out in the quiet of my bedroom, accompanied by another sharp throb.

The next few smacks pack the same sort of wallop, and I can feel my ass burning as Chance starts to rain them down on my bare skin, never quite landing his palm in the same spot, but managing to catch skin that was already stinging painfully.

Neither one of us are counting, and the pain is starting to make me feel exposed and raw, but I'm holding on to my tears, not yet ready to let go.

"You're taking this so well, baby," Chance says after delivering another firm swat to my throbbing rear. "But it's time to start forgiving yourself. I," he says, punctuating the word with another slap, "forgive," another, "you."

On the final smack, I break.

Already feeling vulnerable, I don't know if it's the additional pain or the perfectly timed words that do me in, but I start to cry. At first, it's quiet whimpers and tears trickling down my cheeks, until Chance starts murmuring again.

"That's it, Kade. Let it out." He spanks me some more, lighter this time, but my cheeks feel so tender that even light touches hurt now. "You're being such a good boy for Daddy."

My whimpers morph into sobs now: deep, heaving, ugly sounds that seem to be pulled straight from my belly. The tears are no longer trickles but streams, and I can feel snot dripping from my nose.

Chance is still talking. "Just a few more, then I need you to let go of your guilt once and for all."

"I'm sorry," I howl and clutch even harder at his leg. I press my face into his pants, making a mess of the black fabric, "I'm sorry, Daddy."

"I know, baby," he soothes, lands three more smacks, then

strokes my shaking back. "Good boy. It's over. All is forgiven."

I'm still bawling as he maneuvers me up and cuddles me close. I'm still apologizing and shaking and letting out years of pent-up guilt and grief. I lose track of what I'm saying, letting my mouth run until I've lost steam.

Chance holds me through it all, rocking me in his lap, uncaring of the tears and snot seeping into the shoulder of his shirt. His hands never stop moving over my back and my hair, and it's only once I'm heaving in shaky breaths to properly calm myself that I realize he's nuzzling his cheek against the top of my head.

I feel woozy once the emotion fades away. Exhausted and drained. But...*light*. Liberated.

Absolved.

It's different to any of the other times with the other Daddies I've had spank me over the years. With them, the release had never been as intense, and I'd always held on to just enough of my guilt that it would fester away again. But this time I did as Chance told me to: I let it all out. He forgave me and I accepted my official punishment from the only person whose perspective ever mattered.

With the absolution, though, comes uncertainty. I've spent so long fixating and hating myself that I honestly don't know how to act now that I've promised to let it go.

My head is hazy with the release, with the high of feeling free and new. Chance kisses my sweaty temple and, still rubbing my back, eventually asks, "Feel better now?"

I nod, and my voice is raw and scratchy when I answer, "So much better. Thank you." My breathing hitches on the last two words, but I manage to swallow back a new round of tears.

I swear, I've cried more tonight than I have over the last

two decades. There's something about Chance that sends my carefully constructed walls tumbling down effortlessly. Though I usually hate feeling weak and vulnerable, I don't mind being this way with him. I never want to hide from him again.

I hiss and flinch when his calming hands coast over my ass. I'm not going to be able to sit properly for days. But that thought brings a smile to my lips because Chance did that for me. Chance said he'd be my Daddy, and he gave me exactly what I needed. The lingering pain will be a reminder of that.

Chance makes a sound of commiseration and kisses my temple again. "Okay," he coos (*he fucking coos!*), "I think someone needs a cool bath and a slathering of lotion before bed, hmm?"

Unconsciously snuggling further into his embrace, I nod. "Mmm."

His chuckle rumbles through his chest. "C'mon, baby. Let's get you sorted out before we both crash here."

I whine as he shifts me out of his lap, already missing the warmth and safety of his arms.

He's unmoved by my complaints, though. "Is the tub in your master bath, or in the other bathroom?"

"Master," I tell him, trying not to sound too sullen. He takes my hand and squeezes it.

"Show me."

With a final dejected sigh, I pad across the carpet and to the door on the wall on the left side of my bed. My walk-in wardrobe is actually behind the wall my bed sits on, something Chance notes as we pass the space where the wall ends, leaving a doorway-sized gap. There's a matching one on the other side of the room, too. I think it adds to the modern, minimalist vibe of the whole place.

Opening the door to the master bathroom, I show Chance through to the generous space. It's all white subway tiles and chrome accessories. The tub is a thing of beauty – a large, deep, freestanding bath in the middle of the wall between the shower which runs lengthways down the left side of the room and the double vanity running lengthways to our right. The toilet is segregated in its own little room next to the double vanity.

Chance steps up to the tub and fiddles with the faucet until the water pouring through it is to his liking, then he turns to me and gestures me over with a crook of his fingers. I go willingly.

His fingers pluck deftly at the buttons of my dress shirt, first the cuffs and then the row down my chest and belly. Like him, I wasn't wearing a tie, and I ditched my jacket when we came into the apartment, so the shirt is the only thing he needs to help me out of, but he takes his time with it as if he's savoring the experience.

It makes me feel special. Even more special than being laid over his lap and spanked just the way I'd needed.

The silence between us is comfortable as he finally slips the material over my shoulders, then tosses it towards the hamper concealed next to the vanity on the end near the bath. His eyes are dark and hungry as they take my naked form in.

"You're beautiful, Kade. Always have been."

I catch sight of my reflection in the mirror above the vanity and cringe. My eyes and nose are puffy and red. There are tear tracks streaming my face, and a shiny trail of drying snot along my left cheek.

"Shit," I exhale, turning away from the mirror.

"Kaden," Chance reprimands me. I look back up at him with wide eyes. He frowns. "The only reason I'm not swatting your butt for that is that it's red raw. And we haven't gone over the rules yet, but I'm telling you right now, rule number one is that I won't have you disparaging yourself. Rule number two is no swearing. Big or Little, I'm pulling rank as Daddy on that. Understood?"

Dear God, but he's hot when he's in Daddy mode. Have I mentioned that already?

Swallowing, I nod my agreement with perhaps a hint too much of eagerness. "Yes, Daddy."

His expression softens again, and he cups my cheek with a broad, warm palm. He strokes my cheekbone with his thumb and I lean into the affection like a cat. "Good boy," he murmurs and my heart flutters.

I'll do anything to keep hearing him say that phrase to me.

When the bath is full enough to Chance's standards, he holds my hand and helps lower me into the tepid water. I try not to wince as my sore ass protests both the temperature (despite it being relatively cool) and the pressure of the porcelain once I'm seated.

Chance locates a washcloth and shower gel, urging me to relax as he cleans me up. His movements are gentle but confident, and I try not to think too hard about the boys that have had this honor before me. Instead, I close my eyes and think about how lucky I am that this is happening.

Never in my wildest dreams would I have thought that Chance would ever want me in any capacity. But he said that he does. He said that he wants me as his boyfriend and his boy, and he's proving to be a better Daddy than I've ever allowed myself to fantasize about having.

Whatever crush I had for him as a teenager is swamped by the feelings building in me. I've never not had feelings for Chance, so I'm not surprised to feel them coming on so quickly now. But I keep them to myself, knowing that what we have is still so tentative and fragile. Even though he's forgiven me, I can't help but think that Chance will need time to process all these new developments between us and I resolve to be patient with him.

As such, I know that I can't push him too hard or too fast. I need to reel back and give him time and space to really think about being with me. I need to know that he's properly considered it before I get too attached.

After all, I've waited twenty years, what's a few more weeks or months?

Chapter Nine – Chance

"I'll be sure to get you some bath toys for the next time we do this," I hear myself promising as I slowly wash Kade's body.

He startles and blinks at me. "There really will be a next time?" He brings a hand up out of the water, an elegant index finger held up to stall the protest he knows I'm about to make. "I believe you've forgiven me, Ch—*Daddy*," he tells me quietly, and my stomach clenches pleasantly at the honorific, "but... I just...you don't *have* to..." Kade pauses. Exhales. Visibly fortifies himself. "Tonight has been a lot for me, and I'm sure it's been a lot for you, too. So, if you want to leave it as is, you can. I won't hold it against you if you want to pull back and think about it before we commit to a relationship."

There's a part of me that wants to rail against his assumption that I need time to think things over, but I understand where he's coming from. When I first saw him tonight, my initial reaction was fueled by hurt and frustration. If the tables had been reversed, I'd be questioning the swift turnaround of attitude, too, even though we have talked it to death by now.

"I don't need time to think about it, baby," I answer him softly. "Hearing you call me Daddy —whether you're a Little or it's just a kinky title— is like having all my fantasies come to life. Only, okay, I never considered Daddy kink of any kind when we were eighteen." I shrug, then return to smoothing the washcloth over his skin. "If you want to slow things down because this is too fast for you, we can, but I'm not worried that we're jumping ahead."

It's so hard to describe, but he doesn't feel like a stranger. He feels like the close friend he was before our emotionally fueled falling out. He feels safe and comfortable. He feels like home in a way none of my previous relationships ever have, and I've only spent a couple of hours with him. I can only imagine that it's a sign that we're good for each other. It wouldn't feel so easy —so right— if we weren't, I'm convinced of that.

Kade practically melts at my declaration. "Thank God," he says on a sigh. "It was killing me being all responsible and mature and shit."

"*Kaden,*" I shut my eyes and shake my head, fighting my amusement. "Rule number two, remember?"

When I reopen my eyes, his cheeks are flushing pink and he smiles sheepishly. "Sorry, Daddy. That's gonna take some getting used to." Then his blush deepens, and he asks, "Does it, um, does it count during sex? The no swearing thing?"

This time I lose the battle with my amusement, snorting inelegantly. I bring a wet hand up to cup his jaw. "I think we can negotiate, don't you?"

"Yes please," Kade nuzzles into my hand, and I'm reminded by his earlier statement about puppy play.

Guess I've got some research to do.

But, for tonight, I'm going to finish bathing him, I'll lotion that pink ass, and I'll cuddle him to sleep.

And that's exactly what we do.

* * *

Katie startles me when she drops into a chair across from me at the café where I tend to take my lunch breaks.

"Okay," she demands with a Cheshire cat grin, crossing her arms over the marble-patterned Formica table top and leaning forward with blatant eagerness, "spill. Mommy and Charlie said some Little you knew bought you at the auction and then you disappeared with him for the entire weekend." She waggles her eyebrows. "So…*spill.* Who was he? Musta' been something special for you to go *incommunicado* and all."

I groan, despite knowing that the inquisition was inevitable. The group chat has been pinging with notifications with tags on my name since Sunday morning. I'm honestly surprised that my friends waited that long, considering the auction was Friday night. We hadn't been anywhere near as kind to Spencer when he started dating Tony.

At my mixed sound of protest and resignation, Katie wiggles with excitement in her seat. She's become a close friend since London introduced her and her Mommy, Cherie, to the group, and we often meet for lunch because —out of sheer coincidence— our offices happen to be in the same building, but we work for different companies.

"So there *is* something to tell!" my curvaceous companion all but squeals, clapping her hands. Then she straightens and levels me with a look she's borrowed directly from Cherie, pointing a bright pink polished nail my way. "Start talking, mister."

Despite a tiny desire to keep this new development just to myself for a little while longer, I do. I start telling Katie about Kade (and she giggles when she notices how similar their names sound), starting at the beginning. How we met in grade school when his mom moved the two of them into the area. How the other kids picked on him, and I —not giving a shit— went and sat with him in the cafeteria, trading him my (gross) healthy salad sandwich for his bologna one. How we'd bonded over shared interests (we both thought Scooby Doo was the shit back then) and how we'd become inseparable as only a pair of eight-year-olds possibly could.

Katie listens patiently as I continue to summarize our friendship into our teenage years, my thoughts on his relationship with his mom and my own distant one with my parents, my father in particular. My realization at fifteen that my spontaneous boners had somewhere along the lines become boners for Kade without ever knowing it. Keeping my crush (and the knowledge that I was definitely not straight) hidden for the next three years.

Then I tell Katie about our falling out.

About never speaking to Kade again.

About my surprise at him appearing twenty years after our fight. A fight we should have been able to talk through if we'd been more mature.

Somewhere along the lines, Katie lost the mirthful glint in her eyes and reached out to squeeze my forearm in support. She does it again when I tell her that we talked everything out and that he begged me to spank him properly as penance, even though I'd already forgiven him.

"He needed it," she asserts with the weight of her own

experience as a Little backing her conviction. "You did a good thing, Chance." After another moment, she smirks, "But that was just Friday night. You vanished for the whole weekend."

I can't help laughing. She's like a dog with a bone. Nodding, I admit, "We acknowledged that we both have lingering feelings for each other which we never quite managed to get rid of, and that we'd like to give a relationship a go." Before she can squeal, I hurry to get the rest out, "We actually spent most of Saturday apart, to clear our heads and make sure that the night before hadn't just been a fluke, or because it was so highly emotionally charged or whatever…" Fondness and frustration still war within me over that, and it carries into my tone.

Katie snorts. "Not your idea, I take it?"

"Nope. That was all Kade. I think there's a part of him that still thinks I'll regret being with him, or that I forgave him too quickly, or that he doesn't deserve me, or…whatever."

Her thick dark hair, pulled into a high ponytail, sways as she shakes her head. "The only thing that'll help him move past those fears is time. Well," she shrugs, "and, obviously, you demonstrating that they're just that: fears and nothing else." Then she cocks her head again and asks seriously, "Don't you have your own concerns about it all?"

Immediately the words 'puppy play' spring to mind, but I don't think that's what she's asking.

"I mean, yeah, of course I do. We're coming at this thing with a history behind us, but twenty years of distance, too. So, while we know each other, we don't really know each other…if that makes sense?"

"It does. But the not knowing part isn't all that different to meeting someone new, is it? You're getting the best of both worlds here. You already know the basics, and a lot of the hard stuff. But you also get the exciting 'getting to know you' stuff for the changes over the time you've been apart."

I sit back in my chair, impressed by that logic. "I…hadn't thought of it that way."

Katie winks. "I know. That's what I'm here for." Then she snags a fry from my forgotten lunch plate and pops it into her mouth.

"Oh," I tease, "so you're not just here to mooch my meals, then?"

"That's just a bonus," she responds with cheek.

I check my watch and sigh. "Well, on that note, I've gotta get back to the office." I'm on the project management team for a large retail chain. It's not the most thrilling job, but it pays the bills. I push myself up out of my seat and then bend to kiss Katie's appled cheek. "Thank you for listening."

Before I can walk away, she grabs my hand and squeezes it. "Always, Chance. You know that, right?"

"I do." I nod. As much as I love the guys and still consider Spence my closest friend, I'm beyond grateful to have found this extra support in the form of Kate and Cherie's friendship. They just offer a different perspective and brand of comfort to the rest of the gang, and I appreciate it more than I can put into words.

And, as I'm making my way back to my office, I can't help but think that they'd be really good for Kade, too.

Chapter Ten – Kade

After spending Friday night, Saturday night and all of Sunday getting properly reacquainted with Chance, returning to the daily grind of my day job is a shock to the system. Especially when my first meeting on Monday morning happens to be with Donald Baker – the CEO of the company, and also Chance's father.

Donald has always been an ass. I knew it as a teenager, and I've known it for the twenty years I've been his corporate slave. But I've proven myself to be an asset to the company, which is why the guy has begrudgingly kept me around. I'm not an idiot: I know that Chance was right all those years ago. Don hired me to upset Chance. The fact that he lucked out and got an awesome salesman out of his scheme was unintentional.

Despite my spanking having rid me of the guilt of everything that happened, I can't help but feel a bit dirty for having stuck with Don's company this whole time. Even though I was climbing the corporate ladder for my own gain, I was also increasing his profits as I went.

This was something else Chance and I discussed over the weekend: the fact that I'm still employed by his father. Instead of being annoyed, or revolted, or even hurt, though, Chance said he understood. Apparently, he hasn't spoken to his dad since we were eighteen, either, but it's not eating him up inside. That knowledge is the only thing keeping me from screaming when I'm greeted by Don's smug smirk when I enter his office for our scheduled meeting.

Thankfully, he looks nothing like Chance. Or, rather, Chance looks nothing like him. This man is short and stout, with ruddy cheeks and a hairline that receded before I ever met him when I was a child. His brow is marred with deep set frown lines, the wrinkles around his mouth set the same way. It's as though he's constantly scowling, even when those thin, cracked lips curl upwards into a sneer or smirk much as they are now.

"Kaden," he greets me from his cushy office chair behind his desk, not bothering to get up or even offer his hand in greeting. He just nods curtly at the pair of less than comfortable chairs facing his desk and barks, "Sit."

I comply and we launch into my weekly reporting. I give him information about our sales figures across the board, our intentions for the week ahead, whether we're on track to meet our monthly sales and advertising targets, and my expectations for the end of the financial year. He asks probing questions, demands more of me —of my team, of the sales guys, and of the company in general— and I know that there's no point in telling him that we are working to capacity. I make non-committal sounds which he interprets as agreement, and then he calls the meeting to an end. All in all, it's relatively painless.

At least, it is until I reach the door. Just as I'm turning the knob, his grainy, aging voice says, "Oh, and Kaden?"

"Yeah, Don?" I turn my head, hoping my expression is blank. Giving away the frustration I feel would be detrimental to my career.

"I can't tell you what to do with your *private life*," he spits those words with the same disdain my mother does, "but I can tell you that seeing my son again is a bad idea."

I don't know if he saw me with Chance on Sunday, or if he's just giving me a general warning, but it has my hackles up. Playing it cool, I keep my reply vague. "It's been twenty years, Don."

His stare is a knowing one, even though he raises both palms in mock surrender. "I'm just saying you should think about your priorities. He's bad news, and I won't have him and his type implicated with my brand. Understood?"

His type. Those words bound around in my brain for the rest of the day. 'His type.' I'm guessing Don's alluding to the kinky community Chance is a part of. The same one I am also a part of, though Don seems oblivious to my own involvement.

Obviously, he's had someone keeping tabs on his son. I know I should tell Chance, but our current relationship is so new and tenuous, I can't bring myself to do it. I mean, what would I say? "Hey, so your Dad said I shouldn't be hanging around with you and your type, so I guess he's spying on you?" Yeah…that's a no from me. It would only cause more drama than is healthy for us right now. Besides, he knows his father better than anyone: he's probably already aware that the guy's keeping track of him, even if they are estranged.

Thankfully, nothing else out of the ordinary happens during the rest of my week. My days are filled with campaign proposals, overseeing the results of our latest catalogue release, negotiating rebate deals with our suppliers and trying to get the sales guys excited about our increased targets. I would have liked to have gone out on a date with my new boyfriend (and thinking those words still gives me such a thrill) but he's also been swamped at work, so we've had to make do with phone calls and texts.

By the time Friday night rolls around, I am a jittery bundle of energy. I'm excited to see Chance again, to spend the weekend with him, but I'm also feeling...*odd*. It's like a thrumming under my skin. A need I can't quite express. Excitement and anxiety and yearning all bundled up together in a strange mishmash of emotion.

Chance takes one look at me when he opens his front door —because his place is bigger and more private, given that he lives on a property twenty minutes' drive outside the city proper— and his eyes soften as he reaches for me.

"Oh, baby," he croons, pulling me in for a hug, I melt against his larger frame, soaking in the affection like a sponge. "Long week?"

"The longest," I complain with a whine that sounds so unlike the man I've tried to be. Chance's presence does this to me. He brings down my walls, sending me hurtling back to a much younger headspace just by reminding me of my youth.

"Come on, let's get comfy on the couch and see if we can't get you relaxed." He gently tugs me forward, taking my overnight bag from my hands and placing it on the worn timber floor inside the foyer, shutting his front door behind us.

His place is the antithesis of mine. Where mine is modern, his is dated. Mine is a high-rise apartment, his is a single-story cottage. Where I have gleaming tiles and chrome, he has scuffed timber and gingham. His is colorful, warm, and cosy.

Mine is stark, cold, and impersonal.

"It's not much," he says self-consciously, leading the way from the front door into a little living room with a big, plush beige couch and a crackling fireplace, "but it's home. And I got it for a great price about ten years back."

I can tell Chance is trying to sound casual and nonchalant, but the tense set of his shoulders and the rosy tint to his cheeks tells me that he is actually worried about my impression of his home. I let my eyes sweep over the room we're currently standing in, taking in the reds and golds of the decorations, the knickknacks on the side table and the photos on the walls, and I grin.

"I love it," I tell him honestly. It's very *him*. Comforting. Inviting. Personal and homely. I can see myself playing on the rug by the fire, or snuggled up against him on the couch while he reads me a story. I can picture us playing cards at the dining table I caught a glimpse of through the archway behind us, or drinking beers on the back porch.

"You do?"

Chance's vulnerability reminds me of when we were kids. He was always the shy, sensitive one. I was the bold, feisty 'don't give a fuck' guy, even if it was just a mask. Though he's grown up to exude masculinity in ways I never can, I can tell he's still a soft soul at heart. He's still the same boy who approached an ostracized new kid in the cafeteria and offered a hand in friendship, just because seeing other people alone and sad upset him. He's the same kid who would make up excuses to invite me to his place because he knew I was struggling being alone with my mom. The same guy who obviously knew I was more camp than a row of tents, but never pushed me to come out. Not even when he bravely did so himself.

"It's gorgeous," I tell him, moving forward to run my hand over the soft fabric of his couch, squeezing the plush high seat back. "My place has, like, no personality. Yours is full of life. It's a *home*, Chance. Not just a place to crash."

His big, bearlike arms wrap around my waist from behind, and he rests his chin on my shoulder, kissing my neck. "I'm actually really relieved to hear that, Kade. After seeing your place…" he trails off and sighs. "Anyway, I just want you to be comfortable here. Happy."

My heart squeezes and I fight the urge to pinch myself. A week ago, anyone saying such things to me was a pipedream or a fantasy I couldn't allow myself to indulge. But now the guilt is still gone, and I'm allowed to have this. I'm allowed to have the hot boyfriend —a Daddy no less— and to be taken care of. I'm allowed to be happy. I'm allowed to want to be happy.

A rush of giddiness almost overwhelms me.

I've never felt like this before.

Chance must feel the hyperactivity in my posture, because he presses another kiss to my neck and then turns me around to kiss my lips properly, keeping it sweet and chaste, before pulling back. "Let's sit down before you vibrate out of your skin, baby."

I feel the blush crawl up my chest and neck and up to my cheeks and ears as he pulls me around to the front of the couch, tugging me into his lap as we drop down onto the seats together. I avert my gaze. "I don't know what's up with me today," I explain, a hint of that whine creeping back into my tone. My leg bounces with nervous energy and I chew my lower lip before I add, "I've never felt this…unsettled?" That's as good a word for it as any.

"Hmm," Chance smooths a strong hand through my hair and I arch into the touch, "how often do you usually let off steam at the club? Like…Little play or spankings or whatever it is you need?"

I blink at him. I usually visit a couple of times a week. Being able to be myself without anyone else's expectations weighing on me —and without the oppressive silence of my lonely apartment— usually relaxes me, even if I'm not visiting to hook up for a scene.

It didn't feel right visiting without Chance, or at least without having discussed it with him, so I haven't indulged in any sort of kink or kink immersion since last Friday.

"Holy shit," I exhale as the realization washes over me.

Chance swats my butt. "Language," he admonishes.

"Sorry, Daddy," I reply on instinct, then beam at him. "God, that feels good."

"What does?"

"Calling you Daddy." Already the tension inside me is unwinding. "I feel stupid for not realizing how much I rely on the club —on the lifestyle— to get through my work week."

Chance's brows draw together and he shakes his head. "Not stupid. Things have changed quickly for you. You don't feel like you deserve punishment, so I guess you haven't felt to urge to visit for that reason. And, from what you said last weekend, you've never really visited just to let go in Little space, so it wouldn't occur to you that you needed that." He sighs. "That's on me. I should have touched base. I should have asked if you needed—"

Pressing my index finger to his lips, I shake my head. "No. Nu-uh. If I'm not at fault, neither are you. This is new for both of us."

His hazel eyes glint with mischief and that's the only warning I get before his warm, wet tongue darts out and licks my finger, making me squeal and yank it away at the unexpected sensation. Then he's tickling me, those thick fingers finding all of my most sensitive spots with insane accuracy (one of the many benefits of having known me for my childhood, I'm guessing). I'm giggling and squirming and absolutely loving the attention.

"Stop!" I laugh, trying half-heartedly to get away from the playful assault. "Stop, Daddy! Please! I'm gonna pee!"

He laughs and eases off, then tilts his head. "Diapers would take care of that."

My face already felt flushed from laughing so hard, but it burns a little more at those words. "I've never...I mean, I've thought about it. But..."

"You've never had a Daddy or really indulged your Little side, I know." Chance's words are gentle now. His hand rubs up and down my back. "We should talk about that. About the stuff that interests you, the stuff you want to try, and the stuff you already know is off limits. And we should probably do that before you go any further into Little space than you already are." His hand cups my cheek as I feel my skin turn inexplicably hotter and avert my gaze. "Nope. Don't be embarrassed. I've got a few friends who are fluid in their headspaces. I'm good with it, and I'm glad that you feel comfortable enough with me to relax like that already."

"Yeah, well, it's *you*." I have no other way to explain it. "You're my best friend." Even with twenty years of separation. A lump lodges in my throat, and my voice is tight to my own ears when I admit, "I don't *have* other friends. I didn't..." I pause to take a deep breath. "After what happened —and how I thought I'd hurt you— I didn't think I deserved any more friends." I hold up a hand to forestall his sympathy or pity. "But that's changing. Slowly. I know one spanking isn't a magical fix all, but…you really have given me closure and I'm starting to heal. I…I'm thinking of seeing a counselor or a therapist."

After my conversation with Don left me reeling for the week, I decided it was time. I need to properly face my demons and work through my deep-seated issues if I really want to get better. Not for Chance, not for our relationship, but for me.

"I'm so proud of you, Kade," Chance's voice is also thick with emotion, and it reaffirms how much he cares. "And I'm behind you one hundred percent. Whatever you need, I support it."

God, this man. The thought '*I don't deserve him*' tickles the back of my consciousness, but I shake it off.

Giving a slightly watery laugh, I shake my head. "One day we're gonna be a normal couple and *not* start every encounter with a deep and meaningful conversation."

Beneath his coppery scruff, Chance's lips quirk. "Meh," he shrugs, "normal's overrated." Then he cuddles me close and says, "So…Little space?"

The next laughter that bubbles out of me at that is lighter, happier. "Well," I tell him, having thought over all of this during the week, "I like stuffies. I know I only have Teddy—"

Chance snorts. "That's a super original name."

"Shut up," I smack his shoulder, but we're both grinning.

"Sorry," he says, suitably chastened. "Go on. You like stuffies, good to know. What else?"

"Um, I never really allowed myself to explore the fun stuff, but the aftercare after a punishment always felt so good. Like…bath time and cuddles. Bedtime stories. The Daddy re-dressing me. That kind of thing." In hindsight, I know it's because I was so desperate for affection, but being taken care of is something I genuinely crave. Chance seems to get it, because he nods.

"What about play time?" he asks after a beat. "Does anything specific interest you?"

"Blocks," I blurt without hesitation, then I blush. "I like building stuff. Lego…or Duplo, if you wanna really push the age regression. I haven't…I mean, I've probably been more Middle than Little, but…"

"But?"

"I'd like to be *little* little, I think. Maybe like a three year old?"

Chance considers this for a moment, then bobs his head. "That's not a surprise. You like being taken care of. Handing over the reins. Having someone else do all the big things for you. It takes away the pressure and stress, and you get to just be impulsive and joyful for a bit." Smoothing his hands over my back again, he continues, "Which leads us back to diapers. Would you be interested in wearing them? Using them? What are your limits?"

"I'd give wearing them a go," I answer with consideration. Then the rest of my answer practically tumbles out of my mouth. "I don't want to wet, though. But I like the idea of pull-ups and Daddy helping me go to the bathroom." Okay, maybe this is something I've been thinking about for more than just the last week. "And sippy cups are cool. Pacifiers at nap time. Oh, and having my meals cut up for me. That kind of thing." Chance is beaming at me now, but I have to ask, "What about you? What are your limits?"

"Well," he brings one of his hands up to his jaw, rubbing over his beard in contemplation, "I don't have a whole lot of hard limits. No consensual-non-consent or rape play, no cheating role play…no scat play—"

"Okay, eww." I can't help but interrupt, horrified at the thought.

Chance chuckles at the look on my face, then teases, "You're still interested in puppy play, right? Doesn't that include, like, shitting on the rug?" He pokes his tongue out at me to let me know that he doesn't mean it maliciously.

"Gross," I hit at his shoulder again. "But, yeah, I would like to try puppy play one day…if you're okay with that?"

I appreciate that he doesn't agree immediately. That he actually stops to think about it properly. "I'd like for us to be more comfortable with each other first," he eventually tells me, thinking out loud but obviously choosing his words carefully. "I'm not saying no, but it's not something I have experience with, and I'd like to read up on it some more. Maybe talk to people at The Grove or The Center. When —*if*— we do it, I want to set us both up with the maximum chance of enjoyment, you know?"

I don't have the words to express just how much that level of consideration means to me, so instead I lean in and kiss him.

Chapter Eleven – Chance

I've been thinking about Kade's mouth on mine all week. If I'm honest, I've been thinking about our mouths all over each other's bodies. So, as he brings our lips together, mine part readily, *greedily* for him, inviting his tongue to twine with mine.

He tastes sweet like cola, and I can't get enough of it. I can't get enough of him. We've spent the week talking on the phone and via text, but that hasn't been nearly enough for me. Having him in my lap with our mouths moving against each other is *heaven*. There's no other word for it. It's like coming home. This is where I'm meant to be. It's where I've been meant to be since I was fifteen.

Admittedly, we weren't ready then.

But we're more than ready now.

The kiss is turning desperate and needy. There's fire in my veins and I can't help gripping Kade's hips as he shifts to straddle me properly, holding him down against my hardening cock. I ache for him. Last weekend we kept things slow and chaste, the both of us needing to process the fact that we were each suddenly dating our high school crush and best friend. But after a week of reacquaintance, of lighthearted flirting and promises to properly explore our chemistry this weekend, I can't hold back any longer.

Thankfully, it seems like Kade's on the same page. He rocks his hips slowly as we kiss, grinding against me until we're both breathing heavily into each other's mouths.

"You feel so good," he tells me while we part for air, still rocking and writhing on my lap. His eyes are closed, his head tossed back. He's a vision in a polo shirt and black business pants. "Chance...*fuck*...I could come from just this."

Fingers flexing at his slim hips, I groan at the thought. "Do it, baby. Come for me, and I'll clean you up. *Daddy* will clean you up."

Kade's breathing hitches and his rocking loses its rhythm for a beat or two.

I can't help grinning. Oh, I am so playing with this. "You liked that, huh?"

He nods.

"I need words, Kaden."

"Y-yes," he stammers, rolling his hips with a bit more urgency, "yes, Daddy, I...*oh fuck!*"

"Such a potty mouth on my boy," I chuckle, even though I know I caused his exclamation. "What happened to rule number two, baby?"

"N-not during sex," he stammers, then finally glares down at my hand. "And it was your fault anyway."

What can I say? I'm an impatient bastard sometimes, and with his back arched, he gave me perfect access to the front of his pants...and he's not wearing a belt, which made it easier to pop the button, lower his zipper and wriggle my hand inside the soft, rapidly dampening cotton front of his underwear.

"Ch-*Chance*," he whines when I squeeze his length and stroke, rubbing my thumb through the precum at the head of his cock, using it to help slick the way for my palm. His hands scrabble for purchase on my shoulders, and he starts to move frantically now, fucking my fist and breathing hard.

My jeans are unbearably tight over my own throbbing cock now, but my release can wait. I want so badly to push Kade over the edge. To watch him fall apart as bliss washes over his pretty face. I don't think it will take much longer. Not with how hard he's breathing, or the way his fingers are gripping my shirt, fisting the material at my shoulders as he thrusts over and over into my hand, the movement giving me hints of the friction I desperately crave myself.

He whimpers when I let his cock go, but I can't stop myself from grabbing at his hips again, fucking the bulge of my denim-clad erection up against his answering hardness. He slams his lips back down onto mine in a sloppy, heated, desperate, utterly perfect kiss until he starts to cry out his release. I can barely feel it through my jeans, but there's definitely a rush of warmth as he tenses and then pulses against me, coming hard in his underwear.

Even though I haven't followed him over the edge, I gentle my movements, kissing him tenderly as he comes back down from his high, smoothing my hand down his back and over his thighs. His face his flushed pink, his blonde hair mussed, a sheen of sweat under his hairline and down his neck.

He's beautiful.

When he finally opens his eyes, the blue is dark with arousal, but they're hooded with sated exhaustion. Then he shifts and crinkles his nose adorably, looking down towards his crotch with a groan of dismay.

"Jesus," he says, shaking his head as embarrassment creeps over his face, "I actually came in my pants like—"

"Like I told you to," I head off any self-disparaging commentary. "Because you're a good boy who follows his Daddy's instructions. And now," I grin, "I get to clean you up."

As if my words alone are easing him towards Little space, Kade smiles shyly from beneath lowered lashes. "I'd like that," he replies, his cheeks still a bit pink. Then he sucks on his bottom, kiss-swollen lip and looks down between us again, little lines appearing above the bridge of his nose as he frowns.

"What's wrong?"

One of his hands reaches between our bodies, cupping my bulge. I gasp. Kade looks back up at me. "You didn't come."

"This wasn't about me," I try to explain, but he only frowns again.

"We're equals in this, Daddy. Your pleasure *is* my pleasure."

Oh my heart. If he keeps saying stuff like that, I'm going to find myself right back where I was at eighteen: hopelessly in love with him. It's too soon, things are too fresh and too fragile, but…damned if he's not just as loveable as he always was. Maybe even more now that I know the attraction goes both ways.

While my brain scrambles over those thoughts, Kade's hands undo my jeans and slide the zipper down, reaching into my boxer briefs to release my still-hard cock from its cotton confines. The relief I feel is immediate. Then his slender, elegant hand is wrapped around my shaft and I stop thinking altogether.

"Is this okay?" Kade asks me softly, even as I close my eyes and lose myself to the exquisite torture of finally —*fucking finally*— having Kaden McDonnell's hand on my dick. It's *only* something I've been fantasizing about since I was fifteen and it's blowing all those horny, teenaged imaginings out of the water.

Kade's grip is firm and assured, his strokes measured and determined. He squeezes and twists his wrist *just so* on each upstroke, then lessens his hold on every pass back down my length. I force my eyes back open to watch him, and I'm not disappointed by the view.

He's got his own gaze glued to my cock, to his own hand pumping me. There's a tiny smile playing around the corners of his lips, and his eyes are dark with arousal.

"I knew your cock would be big," he whispers. "I can't wait to taste it. To have it inside me."

I hear myself groan, feeling my balls tightening. "Yes, baby…" Words are difficult to form. "I want that, too."

"God, you're so hard for me. So hot and heavy in my hand. You feel so good just like this."

I should have known he'd be a talker.   Tingles begin skittering through my extremities, the ball of tension inside me that precedes an orgasm growing tighter and more insistent.

"K-Kade," I stammer, trying to warn him. It spurs him on, the hint of a smile now turning into a devious little smirk. I'm leaking precum all over myself and his hand, trying not to buck up into him, needing him to have control here. "Baby, I'm close…"

His grip tightens almost imperceptibly, his motions speeding up. "I'm already a dirty boy, Daddy," he says, then looks me in the eye, "make me dirtier. Come on me. Mark your territory."

"Oh *fuck!*" I cry out as his unexpected words tear my orgasm from me. I slam my eyes shut and rest my head on Kade's shoulder. A rush of heat and intense pleasure rockets through my veins and out of my cock. It feels like I come, and come, and come, shooting over his fist, lower abdomen, and his own cum-stained underwear. I practically sob curses through the wave of bliss, a litany of "fuck, shit, Jesus fucking Christ"s on repeat until I'm spent.

My brain is mush for the longest time after that. I don't know how long we sit there, with me breathing heavily, my head still on Kade's shoulder. It's not until I register his squirming in my lap that I start coming back to myself.

"Holy hell," I manage to croak, my mouth dry from all the panting and heavy breathing. I plant a kiss on the hollow of his throat before I pull away. "That was…" I don't have words for it.

Kade's back to looking like butter wouldn't melt in his mouth, nibbling his bottom lip and averting his gaze with an innocence that is completely, utterly fabricated. "Yeah," he agrees almost reverently. "It was."

* * *

I chuckle at Kade's expression when I lead him into the bathroom. This is the only room in the house that I've renovated, needing my creature comforts. Where the rest of my house looks like it's stuck in the 90s, my bathroom rivals the one in his apartment. It's large, sleek and modern, with a deep freestanding tub large enough to fit two grown men comfortably, and a double shower with rainfall showerheads and an inbuilt bench. It's the only bathroom in my three bedroom house, but considering I'm the only one who lives here, that isn't an issue for me. Besides, the toilet itself is altogether separate, so if I do have guests, we don't have to do the 'someone's in the shower while I need to use the bathroom' dance.

I get Kade to wait while I start the tub filling. I set out a washcloth, some body wash, and a selection of bath toys, and I squeeze a healthy amount of bubble bath liquid beneath the stream from the faucet before I turn back to face him. He's adorably rumpled and stained and his pants are still unbuttoned. For someone who hasn't spent a lot of time indulging his Little side, he's sinking into his Little headspace remarkably well.

"Arms up, baby," I instruct and he complies, allowing me to tug his polo up and over his head, tossing it towards the hamper in the corner. Then I unzip his pants, hook my fingers into the waistband of both the business pants and his underwear, and slide the lot down his slim legs, dropping to my knees to help him step out of them.

When we did this last Friday, he was coming out of some semblance of subspace after his spanking, and the bath was more aftercare than it was bonding between a Daddy and his boy. This time, the atmosphere between us is electric. The sex confirmed our chemistry, but I'm still aware that a lot of what we're going to be doing will be new in practice for Kade.

It still upsets me to think that he'd denied himself all the joyful experiences of being a Little, purely out of guilt and self-loathing. Hearing him admit that he needs help, that he's going to talk to a therapist or a counselor, eased a ball of tension inside me that I hadn't even realized was there.

Of course, my thoughts drift to Emmett and I bite back an irrational jolt of jealousy, knowing that Emmett and Kade have interacted at The Grove before. Emmett's a good man, and by all accounts a fantastic counselor, but if Kade were to approach him for help...well. Would Emmett even be allowed to offer his services to someone he's acquainted with socially? To a friend's boyfriend? To a man he's spanked in a kink club?

Probably not. That would have to be a conflict of interest, right?

I'm totally overthinking this. Kade never said that he'd go to The Center or Emmett's private practice. He didn't mention the name of any counselor or therapist, just that he's *thinking* about seeing *someone*.

Getting my panties in a knot over the very hypothetical situation where he *might* want to go to Emmett is stupid and irrational, and I am *not* a controlling ass-wipe like my dad. I have no reason to feel insecure, and I certainly have no right to question who Kade talks to. I trust him.

Besides, I really should be thanking Emmett, because he took care of Kade when Kade was hurting and, if not for Emmett, Kade might never have come along to the auction that reconnected us.

So, yeah, I actually owe Emmett thanks and if Kade wants to see him professionally, I will support that. Or if he wants to just stay friends with the guy. It's not as though Emmett's not already hovering on the edge of our social circle anyway. He's a good guy who has been a good friend to both of us, and I should feel ashamed at having entertained any thoughts of jealousy, no matter how mild.

Anyway, I give myself a little mental shake, *there are more important things at hand.*

Things like giving my boy his first bath purely for enjoyment in Little space.

I should focus on that instead. On what a privilege and honor it is that Kade trusts me to be a part of this. That he's comfortable enough with me to let down his walls and experiment with something he's only ever let himself daydream about.

I smile to myself, hoping that he enjoys the evening I have planned for him. I want to give him everything he's been denying himself. I want to show him how special being little can be.

Having pushed back to my feet, I test the temperature of the bath —which has barely filled— and adjust the faucet accordingly. Then I turn back to Kade and reach for his hand, squeezing it. "Traffic light?"

"Green." His response is swift and sure. I relax a bit more, once again not having realized how badly I needed that reassurance.

"Good boy. If any of this is too overwhelming, safe word out, okay?"

He rolls sparkling blue eyes at me, but it's a playful gesture that reminds me of his teenaged self. "I will, Daddy, I promise." His grip tightens on my hand, and he's back to sounding big when he says, "I trust you. Trust me to know what I need, too."

"Fair point," I concede, tilting my head. "Heard."

"Good. 'Cause I wanna be little now." The declaration is accompanied by a cheeky grin and, just like that, I know things are going to be better than I'd hoped.

By the time he's in the bath, surrounded by bubbles, any lingering doubts about Kade struggling with finally giving in to his desires is well and truly gone. He's crafted himself a long, trailing bubble beard, and a bubble hat, and I jokingly call him Santa, which earns more giggles than the playful teasing

91

honestly deserves.

I pick up my tub of bath toys and hold it out to him from where I'm kneeling beside the tub. "Want to pick some toys?" Usually, I'd set a limit of three, but this is his first time truly playing in a bath, and I'm happy to spoil him.

His eyes widen and he pokes through the tub with greedy enthusiasm, cheering when he plucks out a small blue and white boat and a gray submarine, completely ignoring the bright yellow ducks and the neon-colored fish.

"Look, Daddy," he beams, brandishing his selections, "a boat! An' a submarine! *Pssshhhh!*" The sub is sent crashing into the water, sending up a spray of bubbles and liquid on impact. The boat lands on the surface and bobbles from side to side in the resulting waves. "The sub's an enemy," he explains, propelling the item in question beneath the whitewash of bubbles, "an' the boat don't know it's there."

"Oh no!" I play along, widening my eyes. "What's gonna happen?"

For the next fifteen minutes or so, he zooms the two watercraft through the warm waters of his bath, telling a story of their epic battle, including talk of radar systems, radio calls, and the sub's periscope in action. Naturally, the heroes on the boat win, the bad guys on the enemy sub are taken into custody and the sub is claimed by the winning forces. I'm not *quite* sure that's how things work in the real world, but I'm not arguing with his imagination.

Somewhere along the lines, the ducks and a couple of plastic army men I'd forgotten even existed made their way out of the toy tub to take part in the unfolding story, and I fish them out of the water, my arms to my elbows now dripping wet, making them cheer and celebrate alongside the boat.

Kade's eyes are clear and bright, and his gorgeous smile is wide, and once again my heart seizes with emotion that my brain knows is far too early to feel.

I stare at him for probably a moment too long before I clear my throat and give the toys in my hand a quick shake to rid them of lingering bubbles and moisture, before tossing them back in the plastic tub on the floor beside me.

"Toys away now. It's time to wash up and get ready to get out, baby, Water's getting cool, and your cute little fingers —and probably toes— are getting all pruney." To illustrate my point, I grab one of his hands and gnaw gently on the tips of his index and middle finger, making growly 'nom nom nom' sounds while he squeals and lets out a peal of laughter.

The cuteness overload is too much and simultaneously nowhere near enough. Those three little words hover at the back of my mind again and it's all I can do to stamp down on them.

Too soon. I should not feel this way after a week. Especially when we haven't even *seen* each other over the week.

The splash and crash of the boat and sub being launched out of the bath and into the tub beside me bring me back to my thoughts. Even though it now seems like I have more water on my jeans and shirt than what remains in the tub, I smile at Kade. "Good boy," I praise, delighting in the way he visibly brightens and preens every time I say the words. "Daddy likes it when you follow his instructions."

I know Kade. I know that at some point, when he's more comfortable, he will push my boundaries and be a bit of a brat, and I'm honestly looking forward to that (for all that I tease Josh about his bratty predilections). But, for now, I'm loving this sweet side of him. I'm loving how easily he's embraced the fun of being a Little. I'm loving his adorable smile and his imaginative play. I'm loving that he's comfortable letting me join him in his games.

I've been in relationships with Littles before, but there's honestly something extra special about sharing this with Kade. Maybe it's because of our shared past, or because I used to love him (and, yeah, I'm teetering on the edge of that same feeling again), or because he's really giving it his all without reservations. Whatever it is, I want to savor these moments. Draw them out. Make them last.

Taking up the washcloth, I use the bodywash I grabbed earlier, squirting a dollop onto the cloth and then lathering it into the creamy expanse of Kade's back. He's lean and smooth, but there's firm muscle hidden behind his shoulders and down his flank, and I wonder if he's a bit of a gym rat in his spare time, too. He relaxes into the motion of my actions, his body practically melting into the cooling bath water.

Neither of us speak while I do this, each of us lost in our own thoughts.

I'd love to know what he's thinking. Whether he's enjoyed his bath as much as I have.

I lean forward to reach down deep into the opaque bath-water; the bubbles having dissolved into a thin white foam on the water's surface. My strokes with the cloth are gentle but purposeful as I caress the curve of his perfect ass, dipping into his crack, teasing his hole with the fabric. Kade makes a small sound at the back of his throat —a cut off moan, barely a whimper— as he rocks his hips backwards, seeking more of my touch.

The water laps at the lip of the tub, but I couldn't give a shit if it spills over onto the tiles. It's just water. It'll dry, or I'll mop it up later.

I bring the cloth back out of the water to rinse the lather from his shoulders and back, smirking to myself when he huffs with impatience. Satisfied that his back is clean, I apply another dollop of bodywash to the cloth and move it to his front, trying to keep my pace just as steady and methodical as it was when I cleaned his back. But my swipes over his firm pecs are bolder, broader, quicker. I can feel his beautiful blue eyes burning holes into me as I work, but I keep my eyes on his chest, knowing that once I look at him, I'll lunge for his perfect, pouty lips.

This time, I wash off his soapy chest before taking the cloth beneath the water, rubbing it over his outstretched legs and then up over his lower abdomen and belly. I've deliberately skipped his cock for the same reason that I won't meet his eyes. I'm trying to extend our mutual enjoyment. I want this to be special, not rushed.

Kade's patience runs out first. *"Daddy,"* he grumbles, planting his hands on the base of the tub as he arches his back, lifting his hips towards me in a clear indication of what he wants from me.

Still, I play dumb, pulling the washcloth and my hand out of the water and sitting back on my heels, crossing my wrists over the porcelain edge of the bath. I cock my head and aim for my best befuddled expression, trying not to smile at the affronted, pouty look on his face. "What, baby?"

Sticking his lower lip out dramatically, he rocks his hips some more, the force of the action causing a few little waves of water to crest over the edge of the tub and land with small splats on the tiles. He's oblivious to that, though. "You missed a spot," he sulks.

"Oh no," I play along, lifting the cloth again, "on your back?" Those beautiful blue eyes narrow. "No."

"Under your arms?"

"No."

"Oh, I know!" I watch as relief starts to creep over him as I lean forward, "I missed your cute little face."

"What? No! *Daddy!*" Kade protests through laughter as I swipe the cloth over his cheeks and nose and chin. "You missed a spot...*down there.*" He pulls one of his hands back out of the water, droplets flying as he points emphatically towards his crotch. Affecting widened eyes and that over-the-top pout again, Kade looks up at me through lowered lashes. "It was *very* messy before."

There's my cheeky boy.

Heat lances through me at the reminder of our earlier activities and, though the water is cloudy with the remnants of the soap and bubbles, I catch glimpses of his reddened cock head bobbing beneath the surface, as if it's straining towards me.

"That's true," I eventually find my voice, shaking off my distraction and growing need. "But Daddy's washing you on his own schedule, Kaden. Not yours. Understood?"

I can tell that he wants to argue. That he wants to demand instant gratification. But I can also see when the realization that this is part of the game —of the role play— takes root and he accepts it, albeit grudgingly. There's still a hint of challenge in his gaze when he bites that pouty bottom lip and nods, offering me a soft, "Yes, Daddy."

"Good boy." Only now *I* have to follow through on my own words. Damn it. Looking him over again, inspiration strikes. "Now, I'm going to wash your hair, baby. Just let me grab the shampoo and conditioner." I keep both in the shower, in the inset recess between the two showerheads, so I push myself to my feet with a bitten back complaint about my protesting knees and cross the tiles to grab the two white bottles. When I turn back around, Kade's watching me with the same burning intensity as before, his hand back beneath the water, quite clearly working over his cock. I frown, even though my own plumps up at the erotic sight. "*Kaden*," I growl.

His arm freezes, but his hand stays where it is.

"That's not for you to play with," I tell him firmly. "Little boys don't get to get themselves off unless Daddy says so. Daddy's in charge of big boy touches, remember?"

His jaw drops and he seems to come back to his adult self for a moment. "That's a serious rule?"

We've had plenty of time over the past week to go over the rules and negotiations of our mutual kink, but I chuckle at his disbelief. "It's right up there with no swearing —except for during sex— and no disparaging yourself, baby. You can only touch yourself when I say you can."

"I don't like this rule," he protests, but he makes a show of letting go of his cock, holding his hands up in the universal sign of surrender.

I can't help but laugh at that. "Well, not all rules are meant to be liked."

He thinks over this a bit more, then squints at me. "Can I still touch myself when I'm big? Or is this an all the time rule, like the cussing?"

There's a primal, possessive part of me that wants to say he can't get himself off without my permission. A part of me that wants to be in control of *all* his pleasure. But I'm not that dominating or possessive.

To put that rule in place seems especially unfair when we don't live together and, if this week has been anything to go by, don't get to see each other as often as we'd like. So, I shake my head. "No, baby. This rule is only for fun when you're little." I pause. "You can safe word out of all the rules at any time, you know that, right?"

"Daddy, we talked about this…" he sounds vaguely exasperated, but he's still smiling even as he huffs and tries to glare at me.

"Okay, okay," I drop down in front of the bath again, setting the bottles of shampoo and conditioner on the floor beside me. "I'll stop reminding you."

He's already sinking back into Little space again, making it seem almost effortless. He shoots me one of his cheeky grins and reaches up with a dripping hand to pat my cheek patronizingly. "Good Daddy."

I owe Josh about a billion apologies, I think, marveling over just how much I like the slightly bratty behavior from my boy.

"Okay, baby, let's wash your hair. Water's really cooling down now. Head back, eyes closed."

He complies as I use a small bucket from the collection of toys to wet his hair with the bath water, then lather shampoo through the silky blonde locks. Then I fill the little bucket with warm water from the faucet and rinse the shampoo out before smoothing some conditioner through. I use my fingertips to give him a head massage to let the conditioner do its thing, grinning as Kade turns to putty in my hands. Then I refill the bucket from the faucet and rinse the conditioner out, too.

"Mmm," he says as I card my fingers through his now clean hair, "that was nice, Daddy."

"I'm glad you liked it," I tell him. "And you were so good

for me, that you've earned a reward." At that, I pull my hand away from his hair and plunge it into the water in front of him, finally grasping his cock, which is still hard despite the complete lack of attention it's been shown in the past few minutes.

Kade's eyes fly open at the touch, but he shuts them again and tosses his head back, sighing in relief when I stroke him slowly. "Oh, God, yes," he breathes, rocking his hips into my fist.

I'm so addicted to watching him unravel already. The way he pants, the way his skin flushes —the pink crawling up his chest and neck and over his cheeks— the way he throws his head back with abandon and whimpers as his pleasure mounts. The way his breathing hitches when he's close to the edge. The way his fingers tense, tightening over whatever he's holding (right now, it's the edges of the tub on either side of him), making their already pale lengths turn white at the knuckles. The way he babbles incoherently, muttering praises and cuss words and directions in a jumbled verbal onslaught.

But my favorite part? It's when he goes over, crying out, swearing and calling me Daddy.

His cum spurts into the water, ropes of it drifting in the hazy liquid above my still moving fist, until I've pumped him dry and he flinches away, hypersensitive. Then he's slumping against the end wall of the bath tub, boneless and sated and easily the prettiest thing I've ever seen in my life.

"Come on, baby," I urge him gently, getting to my feet and drying my hand on a big, fluffy bath towel, which I then extend out in my arms, gesturing that I'm going to wrap him up in it, "time to get out, get dry, and snuggle with Daddy."

I had plans for play time —for blocks and cars and stuffies—

but his heavy-lidded gaze tells me we need to postpone them. And that's okay. We've got all weekend. Hell, if my heart has anything to say about it, we've got forever.

But I'm keeping those thoughts to myself for now.

Chapter Twelve – Kade

I wake up on Saturday morning cocooned in warmth, with Chance's heavy arm wrapped over me as he's spooned up to my back, the hardness of his morning wood pressing into my ass in the most pleasant way. Last night was amazing, but the stress of my work week —combined with two intense orgasms— was enough to knock me out for the count, it seems. I feel a little guilty for that. I know that Chance wanted to explore our dynamic as Daddy and Little, and *I* wanted to cook him a nice meal. Instead, we went to bed hungry, but sated in other ways.

My mind drifts back to the bath, cataloging the differences between last night's experience and last Friday's. Both were significant moments for me, both emotional but in contrasting ways. Last Friday was pure aftercare, all sweet and serious. But last night was playful and sexy and fun in ways I've never experienced in Little space before. Not that I have a huge amount of experience being Little at all.

My previous experience, as I've already told Chance, boils

down to a bit of scene play when I first started out in the BDSM lifestyle. I gravitated mostly towards punishment scenes even then, with very minimal time spent playing with toys, unless it was to set up a tantrum or otherwise bratty behavior for the scene. But last night Chance let me go nuts playing in the bath, and I lost myself in an imaginary world for a bit.

It was mind blowing.

I completely forgot my adult woes while I played. I forgot about the pressures of my job. I forgot about Chance's dad and his thinly veiled threats and implications. I forgot about my deadlines and my staffing concerns. Instead, I staged a war where the heroes won and the world was a happier place. The fact that my Daddy joined in and played with me made the whole experience even more enjoyable, too. He shared my excitement. He helped my little imaginary naval guys win against the bad guys on the sub. He had the civilians —in the form of a rubber duck and some fish— celebrate right alongside me.

Not once did he make me feel silly, or like I was wasting his time. If anything, I think he was just as disappointed to put an end to it as I was.

But, oh, the way he washed me so sensually afterwards was worth it.

So fucking worth it.

"Morning, baby," Chance murmurs behind me, nuzzling the back of my neck as he grinds his hard length into me lazily. "I can't believe we slept so long. I thought for sure we'd wake up some kind of hungry in the middle of the night."

I smirk, and roll over so we're nose to nose, uncaring of morning breath. Chance inhales sharply when I rub my erection into his. We're both only wearing cotton boxer shorts, the material a thin barrier between us. "I'm definitely *some kind* of hungry right now," I tell him, my voice roughened with need even to my own ears.

His belly chooses that moment to growl, and he chuckles ruefully, the skin above his beard pinking adorably. "Turns out, so am I."

When my stomach also grumbles, we both dissolve into laughter. I look down at my tummy and then back at Chance, shrugging. "I guess that settles it."

* * *

Chance insists on cooking me breakfast. He sits me on a stool in front of the short edge of his L shaped kitchen —which is stuck in the 90s, decked out in hues of terracotta and apricot and sky blue— as he gets to work cooking bacon, eggs, and waffles. We chat while he cooks, discussing how we both felt about last night (I think it's a relief to us both that we agree it was awesome and that our chemistry is fantastic) and he asks me what I'd like to do today.

"Did you wanna go out on a proper date? Or stay here and play the Playstation like the good old days, or try out some more Little time, or…anything else?"

"I want to do it all," I blurt, unable to choose. Chance turns the bacon sizzling in the pan in front of him and gives me a sideways glance, his eyebrow arched. "Go out on a date as a Little, then come back and play Playstation?" he teases.

I pick an orange up out of the bowl of fruit beside me and toss it at him. He catches it deftly.

"I just meant that it all sounds good. I…" Licking my lips, I take in a deep breath and explain, "Honestly? I just want to spend time with you. In any capacity."

I just want to get to know him properly all over again. I want to reconcile the young man I knew better than the back of my hand with all the changes that have happened over the last twenty years. I know that we still click, that we're still effortlessly compatible, but I want to get to know him for who is is *now*. Every single part of him.

"Oh, baby," he exhales, placing the tongs down beside the burner before he walks away from the pan, rounding the bench to pull me in for a hug. "I just wanna spend time with you, too. But I also want to give you a taste of everything you've been denying yourself over the years. So, go nuts. Think of all the fun shit you've told yourself you don't deserve —but that your heart secretly desires— and we'll do it all. Maybe not all in one weekend…"

There's a playful lilt to the way he trails off and I can't help smiling. "Okay," I answer softly, so overcome by the seemingly endless choices. "Um. Well, I…Um."

Chance snorts. "That was helpful."

With a balled fist, I lightly punch his bicep. "Shut up. It's overwhelming."

Immediately, his mirthful expression morphs into one of concern. "Is that something you'd prefer I do? As Daddy, I mean. Make choices for you?"

I'm flooded with relief at just the thought and I'm nodding before my brain even catches up. "Please. Yes." I spend my workdays being in charge of so many big decisions that handing over the reins for my private life sounds blissful. Chance knows me. He knows what I like and dislike, and I trust that he has my best interests at heart. "Whether I'm big or little, if you could just decide things for me, that would be amazing."

Chance presses a kiss to my forehead, his whiskers tickling my skin. "Sure, baby."

And, just like that, it's like another weight has been lifted from my shoulders.

Chance returns to the bacon, which by now has filled the whole house with its intoxicating aroma, and lays the strips out on some paper towels as he cracks the eggs into the pan. He also checks on the status of the waffles cooking in the waffle iron, muttering to himself about timing.

While the eggs cook, he grabs a gallon bottle of orange juice from the refrigerator, and a bottle of syrup from the corner pantry. Then he pulls plates and cups from the cupboard beneath the bench, right in front of where I'm seated.

I blink when he slides my empty plate and cup in front of me.

He's chosen a melamine set emblazoned with cartoon dinosaurs, and the cup has a lid with a spout. When I look back up from the surprising selection, Chance offers me a tentative smile. "Do you like dinosaurs?"

"Uh…"

"Or would you prefer *Teenage Mutant Ninja Turtles*? Or *Spongebob*?" It looks like he's blushing again. "I *may* have gone a bit overboard at Walmart this week."

"Dinosaurs are great," I tell him, feeling my stomach flip at the wide grin he gives me in return. I hold up the sippy cup. "Do you, um, want me to be little for this? For breakfast?"

I was under the impression that we'd start with scenes and see what works and what doesn't, but Chance seems wholly prepared for a lifestyle Little.

Still, he shakes his head. "Nah. I just thought you might like to try it. I can get a normal cup—"

"No," I hold the sippy cup close to my chest at the thought of it being taken away. "No. I do want to try it." I mean, for Christ's sake, I *just* told him that he was making my choices for me, and the first thing I do is question him? If I'm not careful, I'll have him second guessing everything. "I just wanted to know if that was what you'd chosen we'd do today."

The tension in Chance's shoulders seems to melt away and he smiles, shaking his head. "Right now, we're just having breakfast. I promise, I'll be clear about scenes if that's what we're doing. But," his lips twitch and he juts his chin to where I'm still clutching the cup tightly to my chest, "if you feel like dipping in and out of little space, I'm happy for you to do so."

Feeling my cheeks heating up, I set the cup back down on the hideous apricot colored bench and nod. "Okay. That's fair. I don't know what that's like. To…to just sink into Little space. Usually, I have to convince myself that it's okay. It feels awkward and weird for a bit…until it doesn't."

A flash of sympathy appears in Chance's hazel eyes, but he blinks it away. "There aren't any rules for how you want to explore your kink, Kade. Just do what feels good for you. I'll go with it."

God, he's perfect. It's not the first time I've had this thought. It won't be the last. Chance always was my biggest supporter, so it makes sense that he's the same now. Being little with him last night was easier than it ever was with the strangers in the clubs. So, maybe flowing in and out of the different headspaces isn't beyond my reach after all.

When he plates up my breakfast for me, cutting my food into bite sized pieces before I can lift my knife and fork, those same thoughts resurface. My lips pull upwards and I smile widely at him when he pushes the plate in front of me. "Thank you, Daddy."

He beams back at me, and the fluttery feeling in my belly returns.

Yeah, I really don't think it's going to be too difficult to be little for him after all.

Chapter Thirteen — Chance

I am wholly unsurprised when Katie sits herself down in front of me at lunch time on Monday. I'm back in our usual café, once again attempting to eat my burger and fries in peace, but she's not having a bar of it.

"You disappeared all weekend again," she observes, plucking a fry from my plate. She waggles it in the air between us. "Were you with *Kade* again?"

I sigh as she pops the fry past her hot pink lips. "What do you think?"

Katie grins and bounces in her seat, clapping her hands happily. "Tell me *everything*."

Just to annoy her, I take a huge bite from my burger, chewing it thoughtfully while her face twists with impatience. Then I grab my Coke and suck a generous few slurps through the straw to wash down my food. By the time I've swallowed that, Katie's on the verge of a conniption.

"*Chance…*" she whines at me.

"It was good," I tell her, stifling a laugh at the affront on her features. "Okay, okay: it was better than good. It was awesome."

I think back over the weekend just gone. Over the time spent playing with Kade in Little space, over the thrill of introducing him to the simple joys of building with blocks and coloring in. It was satisfying to watch him truly relax and let himself go.

I also think over the more adult activities we shared. More hand jobs and frotting, rocking against each other in bed and in the shower until we both shouted out our releases. The spectacular blow job Kade gave me when we woke up this morning: 'Something to remember me by this week', he'd said cheekily. (Like I'd ever forget anything we did together.)

I think about taking Kade out on a real date, sitting across from him at one of my favorite restaurants in the city, learning about the past twenty years of his career and sharing my own. It was like Katie said it would be: I am getting to discover the parts of him that have changed and grown over adulthood, while already knowing who he is at his core. Learning that Kade has developed a genuine passion for marketing filled me with pride for the kid I'd known, the one who had resigned himself to a minimum wage job he knew would make him miserable, but who just had to get on his feet any way that he could.

I think about how much more comfortable he is in his own skin now. How the feisty teenager was more a front than his actual personality. How the man he's become has a quiet confidence that doesn't require him to put on the same act from our youth...though he's still fiery when it suits him. I think about how fucking hot he is, especially when he's wearing a suit tailored to his lithe, trim frame.

I think about just holding him and breathing him in.

I also think about everything else we've talked about, including his repeated interest in talking to a professional to help him work though the past twenty years of depression and guilt. Even though he has made huge strides in trying things that make him happy, the past couple of decades have certainly left their mark on him. From there, I think about his request that I take control of all the little decisions when it comes to our time together. I understand that it takes the stress of having to choose away, but I want him to be able to express what it is he wants to try together, too.

Puppy play. The words ring in my ears, even though he hasn't repeated them since last week. He's definitely liked being little: he loved the toys, especially when I brought out the brand new stuffies I bought just for him, and he loved sprawling out on the rug in front of my fireplace, playing and drawing without fear of judgment or derision.

But would he prefer puppy play to being little?

"Alright, where's your head at?" Katie prompts me, two more fries now held captive between her manicured fingers and thumb. "Because as awesome as you just said your weekend was, your face just did that whole overthinking thing."

"That whole overthinking thing?"

"...Well, it's either that or you're constipated."

I throw a fry at her and she laughs, catching it and munching down on it with relish.

"So," she prods again, "what brought that look on?"

"Kade's curious about puppy play," I find myself answering truthfully, before I can stop myself. It's probably not fair on Kade to air his secrets like this, but I suddenly desperately need to talk to someone about it. Someone I trust. Someone I know won't judge or, despite her hyper personality, tell anyone else.

I could call Spencer, but Katie is sitting right here, and I've already spilled the beans. So, I keep going. "And I've never even thought about it, you know? Like…it's not my kink."

"Huh." She sits back and frowns, lines forming between her eyebrows. "So…you're not into it? Or you just *think* you're not into it?"

"Well, I mean…"

"Because," she continues on, steamrolling over my attempted response, "I don't think there's that much difference between role playing as a Little and role playing as a Pup."

That gets my attention. "Wait. What?"

Grinning smugly, Katie holds up her left hand and starts counting down, pointing at each hot pink nail with her right index finger as she lists her arguments. "Both are about balancing playtime and discipline. Both involve moments of hyperactivity and desperate desire for affection. Both require treats and positive reinforcement. Both involve activities like bath time and cuddles. Both can include house training of sorts, *if* you're into that sort of thing. Both—"

"You've run out of fingers," I interrupt, my mind already reeling because she's right. There *are* parallels. How did I not see that before?

Katie gives me *the* finger, then switches hands, speaking primly as though I never cut her off. "Both can involve non-verbal cues, especially if your Little side is more infantile. Both involve cute dress-ups and accessories. Both rely on a dominant partner to set rules and help guide or train the submissive role. Both—"

This time, I hold my hand up to stop her. "Seriously, Kate," I breathe, shaking my head. "Stop. I get it. Point made. I'm an idiot."

"Hey," she leans forward, her hand outstretched towards me, clearly wanting to offer comfort. "You're not an idiot. You've never been interested in puppy play because, as a Daddy, you've had your itches scratched through age play. Why look elsewhere when you know what you've already had experience with works for you?"

"But—"

"But now it might be worth looking into, hmm?" Once again I'm struck by how knowledgeable she is. She's a Little, sure, but Katie is a strong, smart woman who won't take shit from anyone. "Because if Kade's had the courage to tell you there's something he's interested in trying, you owe it to him to at least research what it might include, to maybe negotiate some things that you can try together that interest you both. And, if it turns out you really can't get into it, at least you've tried it and haven't just assumed that because it's different, it's not for you."

I let a few moments of silence pass as I mull her words over. "God damn it, Kate," I sigh, but I smile at her. "I hate it when you're right."

"When will you learn?" She chirps back, her smug, self-satisfied smile back in place. "I'm *always* right."

* * *

London and I stare at each other in surprise, each of us with a handful of items we're planning on purchasing, but neither having anticipated bumping into someone we know. Which, in hindsight, is kind of dumb because it's not like either of us have vanilla sex lives, and this *is* the best adult store in the city.

"Uh," he says, a little color creeping up the back of his neck,

"Chance. Hey." He surreptitiously tries to reorganize the stuff he's carrying, which, of course, draws my attention directly to it. A flash of hot pink lace catches me off guard and puts images in my head that have no place being there.

But also...*good for you, bro.*

"Hey," I force an easy smile, suddenly understanding his momentary embarrassment, even though he should know by now that none of the guys in our group would ever judge him or be dicks about it. London's still young, and I'm guessing he's got hangups like any of us do. He's a stocky guy, a little taller than me, utterly no-nonsense and the *last* person I would have imagined would be into wearing anything lacy or feminine. And I know for sure it's him and not Matt, because Matt's into onesies and diapers and makes no secret of it. Glancing down at my own kinky selections, I shoot him a rueful look. "Guess I'm busted, huh?"

London blinks at me for a moment, then seems to be overcome with relief that I've diverted the attention to my stuff instead. His eyebrows raise when he sees the paws and ears and tails.

"I have so many questions," he chuckles, looking back up to meet my gaze. "Are you trying something new? Like," he waves his hand over the stuff in my arms, "you're a pup now?"

There's zero judgment in his tone, just curiosity. I shake my head. "Nah," I answer honestly. "I've, um, met someone. And we're...he's...I mean, *this*," I give my soon-to-be purchases a little shake, "is new for us both. But...why not give it a go?"

Ever since my chat with Katie the other day, I haven't been able to stop thinking about it. She was absolutely right: there's not a huge difference in the role play. I can still buy Kade toys. I can still sit on the living room floor and play with him. I can

113

still bathe him and cuddle him and call him a 'Good boy'. It's just the costume that's different. And, yeah, he probably won't use words as a pup, but I've been with boys who were into full on infantilism, so I've done the non-verbal cues before.

London's lips pull into a big, genuine smile. "Is this the same guy you've been ditching the group chat for? The one you fled the auction with the other week?"

"I didn't *flee*," I correct him. "I was *bought*, remember?"

"Yeah, and Charlie and Ted said—"

"Oh, God, I don't need to know what they said." They caught me and Kade in such an emotionally charged position, and I should probably take the time to explain it to them. Hanging my head I huff, "Kade and I have a history. I was surprised to see him, and it was…an intense moment. But, yeah, we've reconnected and…" I shrug, knowing that I'm smiling goofily. "Things look like they're gonna go well."

The amusement on London's face morphs into something softer. "I'm glad to hear that," he tells me. "With everyone else paired up…" he trails off and shakes his head. "Not that I think everyone should be in a relationship just for the sake of it, but…well, we just want to see our friends happy."

"Ash has been conspiring again, huh?" I can't help but laugh.

"Dude, you have *no* idea. Just be thankful that Matt's a stabilizing influence on him and Zephyr."

I think of my Little friends and snicker. "And here I was thinking Josh was the one whose behavior I needed to watch out for."

As if by unspoken agreement, London and I fall into step beside each other and continue our way towards the registers at the front end of the store – where we were both originally headed before we bumped into each other.

"Josh might like to play the brat, but he has *nothing* on Ash and Zeph together," London assures me. "Without Matt and now Tony, they'd be getting themselves into a world of trouble."

Hearing Tony's name reminds me that I've been neglecting my friendship with Spencer lately, too. I feel a bit guilty that, instead of turning to him for advice, I asked Katie, but I know Spence will understand. He's super chill and not the kind of guy to get upset over a couple of weeks of radio silence. Besides, when he and Tony first got together, he fell off the grid with the group as well.

When I don't reply to London, he bumps my shoulder with his. "So, when are we gonna get to meet this mystery boy of yours, then?"

"Things are still new and tentative," I explain, "so...give me a couple more weeks, okay?"

"Hey, no pressure. Just...maybe don't be a stranger in the chat? Matt and I can only hold the more enthusiastic guys off for so long before they wind up on your doorstep."

Considering that very situation actually happened for Matt and London, I don't doubt him at all. Nodding, I reply, "Got it. I'll reassure everyone that I'm still alive as soon as I get home."

And that's what I do. With my promise to London in mind, I decide to bite the bullet and finally check in to the group chat. Unsurprisingly, I've been tagged about a billion times, and I can't help smirking at some of the taunts and teasing that accompanies them.

Josh has added a bunch of gifs in increasing ridiculousness, while Charlie and Ted have sent me private messages asking if everything is okay.

I respond to Charlie and Ted privately, assuring them that

I'm fine and so is Kade. I thank them again for giving us privacy and space during our reunion, and give them a quick run down of what they witnessed. Then I open up the group chat itself and brace myself as I type:

Chance: I'm alive. Call off the search party.

As expected, a flurry of replies come in at once.

Ash: Yay! We've missed you!

Matt: I'm more interested in *where* you've been. He adds a winking emoji.

Cherie: I'm with @Matt on this one. At least she refrains from mentioning the fact that the last time she saw me was when I first laid eyes on Kade.

Josh, on the other hand, has no such restraint.

Josh: @Ted said you left the auction with a Little, then you ghosted us for ages. When @Spence vanished, he found himself a Forever boy. And when @Matt did it, he'd found himself a Forever Daddy. So...

A string of emojis follows, including a pair of ghosts and some LOL emojis, then a gif of two arguably handsome men kissing in bed. Then another gif of those same men in a much pornier situation. I snort, then snort again when Charlie takes the bait.

Charlie: Oh, come on! Really?! Delete that shit, @Josh. Also I'm glad you're alive, @Chance. Beers soon?

Tony: LOL @Josh. @Spence had himself a forever boy the second I met him, we just didn't know it yet. But @Chance, I told you so! I told you doing the auction would land you a boy you couldn't resist.

He did, actually. As a budding romance writer, Tony decided months ago that the auction was my ticket to a happily ever after. And, while it's too soon to call it, I'm starting to think that maybe he was onto something.

Chapter Thirteen — Chance

Chance: @Charlie Beers are a hell yeah. @Tony, you said it would be a meet-cute, but I have a plot twist for you!

I know I'm stirring the pot a bit, but he's my best friend's boy and I know he'll bite.

Of course, so will the rest of the group. A flood of questions and demands to know what's going on follow my teaser, but then my phone rings.

Spencer's name flashes on my screen. I grin, press the green answer icon, and bring the phone to my ear.

"You've got to learn to type faster," I taunt him by way of greeting.

"Shut up. Talking is faster. And if *anyone* should get the scoop first, it should be me."

I laugh. "Oh, really? Because I remember someone else not giving me first dibs at his good news."

Spencer half-squawks, half-laughs. I can picture his mop of dark hair flying as he shakes his head in refutation. "Excuse you? You were there when I met him. You had a front row seat to *our* meet-cute."

Yeah, I think back with amusement, *and I might have teased you mercilessly at the time, too.* Its this thought that has me softening and confessing, "Kade was my high school best friend."

"No way!" Spence sounds suitably surprised and impressed. Then he sobers. "Hang on, is this the one you came out to?"

As my best friend, we've discussed all sorts of things over the years, and coming out is obviously a deep and meaningful subject among them all. I'm not surprised that he remembers my story. Back when I met Spence —almost fifteen years ago now— the whole situation felt fresher, the hurt still somewhat close to the surface, even if I had privately forgiven Kade in my own head and acknowledged that we'd been kids unable to handle such big feelings at the time.

"Yeah," I answer, "that's the one."

He's quiet for a moment, his soft breaths over the phone line the only evidence that he's still there. Eventually he asks, "And you're okay?"

"I am," I tell him truthfully. "It's been a bit of a mindfuck, but…I didn't realize how badly I missed him, y'know? Not until I held him in my arms and it hit me like a tonne of bricks."

A vague hum of understanding follows. "So…you're together now? Just like that?"

"I know it sounds crazy," I tell him, "but, yeah. In some ways it feels like the last twenty years didn't happen. That we were just apart for a few weeks or something."

Another hum. "And he's a Little? What are the chances?"

"I know, right?" I can't help laughing in my own bewildered delight. "It's like we were always so *right* for each other."

Spencer sighs. "It sounds great on paper, but—"

"It's fast," I finish for him.

"Hey, it's not like I can talk: Tony and I moved fast, too. And we didn't have a history like you guys."

I appreciate that he's being understanding and supportive, even while he's clearly concerned for me. For all the shit I give him, this is why he's my best friend. He gets me. We've got each other's backs.

"But it's that same history that's got you worried, right?" I ask him.

"*Ding-ding-ding!*" Spencer replies, sounding every bit the animated voice actor that he is, "Got it in one!"

I can't help smiling. "It's that same history that makes this feel right," I insist. "And I think we can be happy, Spence. I really do. He's spent two decades beating himself up over the way we went our separate ways and if that doesn't show how much he actually cares, I don't know what does."

"Okay, okay," I can picture my best friend holding his hands up in surrender, "I believe you. And there's no such thing as no risk of heartbreak when it comes to relationships, whether you've got history or just met, I guess."

"No, there's not," I agree, feeling another wave of affection for my best friend. He's always been one of the calmest, most rational people I've ever known. I hadn't realized just how much I needed his unspoken backing until just now.

Not that I need his approval, but knowing he's in my corner and doesn't think I'm crazy settles any remaining doubts that might have been lurking in my subconscious.

"Well then," he says, as if that's that, "when can we meet him?"

Chapter Fourteen — Kade

T hankfully, the week passes without any additional veiled threats from Don, which has me hopeful that he's no longer keeping tabs on Chance. Or me, for that matter. On Wednesday night, Chance comes over to my place and we have dinner, then he changes me into my pjs and reads me a bedtime story. The short, sweet indulgence of my Little side helps get me through to the weekend without a repeat of last week's build up of stress and energy, though I do wish that Chance could have stayed the night.

Still, it's a much more relaxed version of me that pulls up in Chance's driveway on Friday night. This time the anticipation buzzing beneath my skin is pure excitement to see my boyfriend, to reconnect with him and spend time with him however he chooses.

"Hey, baby," he greets me at the front door, having opened it and stepped out before I'd even shut off my engine. He takes my bag, tosses it just inside the entryway, and then yanks me into his arms for a deep, delicious kiss.

"Mmm," I murmur when we separate, my fingers curled around his belt loops, "I could get used to that."

"I hope so." Chance smiles and brushes a floppy lock of hair out of my eyes. His expression is doting and warm and...I have to stop myself there. It's only been three weeks. I should not be getting ahead of myself.

And yet, as Chance leads me into the living room and sits me on the couch, my heart flutters anyway.

"So," he says, rubbing the back of his neck, a curious expression on his face. He looks almost nervous, but excited, too. "I...uh, I've been researching...um...stuff. And, look, there's no pressure, but I bought some things and, well, I hope you'll be interested in trying them? Not right now. But...maybe we could talk about them and how you feel about it and...yeah."

My mind races with possibilities. "Is it diapers?" I ask him. "Because I already said I'm happy to wear them, just—"

"No," Chance cuts me off, and it is equal parts concerning and amusing to see him so flustered. "Here," he says, pulling a nondescript black plastic bag out from the other side of the couch, "why don't you just, y'know, look at them and, uh, tell me what you think. But, remember, there's zero rush or pressure or..."

He trails off as I arch an eyebrow at him and open the bag wide. The first thing I see is a long, furry...*something*. I reach for it, pulling it out from the bag and hear myself breathe, "Whoa."

It's a tail. Not of the butt-plug variety, but the kind that attaches via a harness or a belt. It's super soft, a tawny blonde color, and kind of addictive to run my fingers through.

Setting it aside gingerly, not wanting to ruin the pretty faux-fur, I dig back into the bag with gusto. This time I come out with a pair of soft ears that match the tail, set on top of a headband rather than into a restrictive hood or mask.

Still standing in front of the couch, Chance fidgets. "I didn't want to get the hardcore stuff yet. I thought maybe you'd prefer to start light and just…see what it feels like first, you know?" He clears his throat. "Although, the second tail *is* a plug, but you don't have to use it." He pauses, seemingly rethinks his words, and rushes to explain, "Not that you have to use *any* of it, but—"

"Breathe, Daddy," I demand, then look back down at the ears in my hand. I stroke over the soft fur with my fingertips, excitement and anticipation zinging through my veins. "This is…these are…" I pause to gather my thoughts. "I love them." My eyes meet his and I swallow. I'd mentioned my interest in puppy play once. *Just once.* Weeks ago, and during an otherwise insanely emotionally charged evening. But he remembered. Not only did he remember, but he's also gone and made this really sweet gesture. "I love you."

Those last three words are spoken softly as my heart hammers in my chest. I know it's early, but at the same time it's been twenty-odd years in the making.

"*Kade*," Chance says my name on a reverent exhale, crossing the small space between us and dropping to his knees in front of me. "I love you, too. I don't think I ever stopped."

Suddenly, the remaining contents of the bag are forgotten, unimportant in comparison to the desperate need to have my arms around Chance's neck and his lips on mine. As our mouths crash together, I pour over twenty years' worth of longing and love into it. Our tongues move together, our breath mingling, our hands clutching and holding on to one another's bodies as though we're both equally terrified that we'll be separated again.

Chance breaks away first, pushing to his feet and pulling me up from the couch. "C'mon," he says gently, "let's have dinner."

I know I'm frowning back at him, a bit incredulous. Other parts of my anatomy are demanding attention, and one look at the bulge in Chance's jeans says he's in the same boat. "Dinner?" I echo.

He chuckles and cups my cheek, stroking his thumb across my skin in a gentle display of affection that never fails to have my legs go a little wobbly beneath me. "Dinner," he repeats. "And after we eat, I'm gonna take you to bed."

The sentiment sounds so similar to our activities on Wednesday night, but the heat in his delivery leaves no question to his intentions.

I grin. "Dinner it is."

* * *

"Oh, yes, *Chance*," I say his name like a prayer as he lays me out on his bed, kissing and nuzzling the crook of my neck while his fingers pluck at my belt.

We teased the ever loving fuck out of each other over our meal, playing footsie under the table like teenagers, reaching out to touch each other and share kisses between bites of the delicious chicken parmigiana he'd had baking in the oven. It was all either of us could do to even make it to the bedroom by the time we'd cleared our plates.

"I'm not gonna last," I warn him with a self-conscious huff of laughter, my fingers carding through the slightly curled hair on top of his head. "Not with you edging me over dinner."

Chance leans back from where he's been doing his best to give me beard rash above my collarbone, and smirks. His gorgeous whiskey-hazel eyes seem to twinkle with mirth. "Baby, that was just flirting. If I'd really been edging you, you'd be incoherent right now," he promises.

I whimper.

He returns to his duel tasks of kissing and undressing me.

By the time he has me naked, I'm a writhing, babbling, despairing mess. My cock is hard and leaking an almost embarrassing amount of precum, and I can feel my whole body blushing pink. And Chance is still wearing pants.

I managed to tear his shirt off him somewhere along the lines, and he kicked his shoes off before we even made it to the bedroom, but all of my attempts to get those damned jeans off him have been futile.

"Oh, God, *please*," I beg when he takes my cock in hand, stroking me the way he's discovered I like it best, firm at the base and twisting on the upstroke, palming the weeping head before easing back down the shaft to repeat the motion again and again and again. I rock my hips up into his fist. "Please. Please fuck me. I need you inside me."

"You sure?" He asks, the tightness of his voice and the intensity of his gaze giving away just how badly he wants this, too.

"Fuck," I pant, my balls tingling. I don't want to come like this. Not tonight. "Yes." I toss my head sideways, staring towards his nightstand. "Tell me you've got lube in there. Otherwise, I'll send you out into the kitchen for oil of some kind. I don't even care right now."

I feel the tickle of his whiskers against my belly as he peppers the soft skin there with butterfly kisses. "I do indeed," he says, then releases his hold on my dick and gets to his knees on the mattress. "I've got condoms, too."

"I get tested every two months like clockwork," I tell him. It's something I've been mildly paranoid about, if I'm being honest. Even though I've *always* used condoms. They can break. Shit happens. "Last test was last week. Results were negative. I can show you...." I trail off. "Not that we have to...I mean, if you'd rather..."

Planking over the top of me, Chance silences my ramblings with a soft, sweet kiss. "I haven't been with anyone in months," he says quietly, "but I got tested last week, too. All negative."

"Are you comfortable going bare?" I ask him. "I never have. But...it's *you*." I run my hands up and down his sides, and I don't know if I'm soothing him or me. "I wanna feel all of you." Then, understanding that I'm probably coercing him, I hurry to add, "But only if you're okay with it. There's no pressure."

He doesn't answer right away, and I don't know whether to be relieved that he's thinking it over, or afraid that I've made things awkward.

"You're absolutely sure?" he eventually asks me, gaze flickering over my face as if he's searching for any hint of hesitation. "Because I want it more than anything."

And just like that, I'm desperate for him all over again.

"Face to face," I demand once he's fished the lube out if the drawer in his nightstand and has told me to roll over. "I want —*need*— to see you when you come."

"Oh, God, baby," he moans, positioning himself over me, rubbing our flushed, aching lengths together while he captures my mouth in a messy, sexy, needy kiss. Then he starts easing down my body, licking and sucking a trail down my heated skin, his beard tickling and scratching even as his tongue creates a wet, cooling trail. It's erotic as fuck. "You're gonna be the death of me."

He mumbles the words into my upper thigh, and I swear I can feel the vibration of his voice in my thigh, so close to my cock. My own grasp of the English language —of *any* language— vacates me when he closes his lips over my erection, fireworks exploding in my nerve endings. I thought that our serious moment was enough to back me down from the edge of coming, but it wasn't. It *really* wasn't.

"Oh fuck, oh fuck, *oh fuck*," I pant, clutching at the sheets beside me, curling my fingers into the cotton so tightly that my fingers start to hurt.

Chance's mouth is a hot, wet haven of suction and tongue. He takes me all the way in, demonstrating his lack of gag reflex, and it's all I can do to not thrust upwards. Then a lubed finger is circling my hole, loosening the rim with patience I'm both jealous of and irritated with, and I have to clench my eyes and jaw to not spill down his throat like this is my first ever blow job.

But, fuck, it *feels* like it's my first time. Maybe because it's been a while. Maybe because it's Chance. Maybe because I'm so keyed up and he's everything I've ever wanted and I can't actually believe this is happening.

I whine when Chance eases up off my cock, suckling gently at the head while he eases his finger inside me. Then he crooks it, finding and caressing my prostate, and I just about arch right off the bed, crying out.

"N-no," I almost sob, my voice hitching and causing me to stammer, "don't wanna come yet. Need you in me. Please. *Fuck*. Please."

His lips press soft, affectionate kisses on my lower belly.

"Shh, baby. Easy. Breathe for me."

I don't want to breathe. I want him to fuck me already. But I can't form the words, whining plaintively instead. The sound turns into a moan when his single finger becomes two, scissoring and curling and stretching me. The burning starts at three fingers, but it's a *good* burn. A sign of good things to come.

I'm begging and blathering nonsense by the time Chance finally moves over me, hoisting my thighs to wrap around his hips, notching the head of his cock at my hole. It feels searingly hot, and I marvel at just how intense this feels without the usual barrier of thin latex.

We lock eyes, the only sounds in the room coming from us, sounding almost amplified in the silence. I bear down as Chance slowly pushes in, biting my lip against the initial pain of the intrusion.

"Breathe, baby," he reminds me, whispering the request while his hands squeeze my hips and he guides himself inside me in one long, slow movement. "That's it. Good boy."

He bottoms out and stills, waiting for me to adjust.

"I'm good," I tell him, my eyes fluttering shut despite how badly I want to watch him, "you can — *oh, fuck.*" I drag the curse out, finding myself right on the precipice of coming again when he starts to rock back and forth, stimulating my prostate with accuracy that is most certainly not fair.

"*Kade,*" my name is a benediction on his lips. "Baby. You feel so fucking good. So tight. So hot. Sucking me in. Gripping me. God, if you could see yourself…"

I'm not used to this. To the talking. The intimacy. The adoration in my lover's tone. Usually, my sexual encounters are short, fast, and impersonal. Get in, get off, get out. This is the opposite of that.

Chance is taking his time, drawing this out, pushing me to the edge and then refusing to let me go over. He's worshiping me, gently running his large, warm palms over whatever stretches of my skin he can reach before he spreads himself out over me with elbows planted just above my shoulders. He kisses my chest, my collarbone, my neck and my jaw. His breathing is heavy and warm against my skin.

I'm pretty much delirious with pleasure at this point. I have never felt so connected to someone else. Never so important, or cared for, or...loved.

That's what this is.

It's not fucking. It's making love.

I can feel hot tears welling up in my eyes and spilling down the sides of my face, into my hairline and trickling into my ears. The top of Chance's forehead brushes against them as he nuzzles me and he freezes instantly, pushing up with his arms.

"Kade..."

I force my eyes open and try to impart everything I'm feeling with a tremulous smile. My arms are wobbly and heavy, but I bring them up to cup Chance's face. "I'm good. I'm better than good. I promise."

He does not appear convinced. "Did I hurt you? Did we go too fast? Is this too much, too soon?"

I lock my ankles behind him when I realize he's about to pull out. "Nuh-uh," I inform him, rocking my hips up, trying to encourage him to move again. "I was just," I pause, struggling to explain, "overwhelmed with happiness. I've never...I mean, sex has never been like this before."

I feel a little weird having this conversation while we're still intimately connected, while I'm still rock hard and leaking trails of precum onto both our abdomens. But I'm with Chance, so I'm safe and comfortable in a way I've never been. I can tell him anything at any time, and it's okay.

His eyes light with understanding and his expression gentles away from concern. It turns more indulgent. Sappy. I love seeing this look on his face.

"Well," he says, slowly thrusting his hips again, "enjoy it while you can, 'cos I'm close." He shuffles his position as I groan with his movements, and winds up back on his elbows, leaning his weight on his right arm so he can wriggle his left hand between our bodies to stroke me in time with his renewed thrusts. "So fucking close. And Kade?"

"Hmm?"

He ducks his head, kissing me softly, as if the sweet expression on his face moments ago hadn't already told me what he pulls back to say. "This is special for me, too."

With his hand on my cock, and the delicious feel of him moving inside me, I nod my agreement. "I know," I tell him. Then I swallow roughly, "And I'm close, too." He closes the small gap between us and kisses me again, and that's enough to finally tip me over the edge. "Oh," I moan into his mouth, "Oh, oh God, I'm...I'm..."

He swallows my cries with a deep, hungry kiss, groaning right back into my mouth as his hips still and he floods me with his release, pulsing inside me. Then he rests his forehead on mine while we catch our breaths before he slowly and carefully pulls out.

I miss him almost instantly, but I don't love the feeling of his cum trickling out of my ass.

"Shower?" he suggests after chuckling at what is undoubtedly an unimpressed expression on my face.

"God, yes."

Chapter Fifteen — Chance

S aturday dawns gray and depressing. Storm clouds hover overhead, and it's such a juxtaposition to how amazingly bright and chipper I feel. Kade told me he loved me, and the sex that followed was life changing. After our shower, I coaxed Kade into relaxing into Little space, reading him a bedtime story and snuggling him to sleep, giving him the experiences he's confessed to craving but rarely ever indulging.

After whipping up a quick breakfast of toaster waffles, syrup and some strips of bacon, Kade and I sit side by side on the stools at the kitchen bench and discuss the plan for today.

With a glance out the kitchen window, I cut my gaze to my beautiful boy and offer him a rueful smile. "Looks like today's gonna be best spent inside," I tell him.

He nods around a mouthful of food —which I insisted on cutting up for him— and swallows before he speaks. "So… what do you wanna do, then?"

He's cute like this, all sleep-ruffled and riding the line

between headspaces. Even though I'd love for him to choose where he's most comfortable, he waits for me to decide. I swish the last bite of crispy bacon through a puddle of syrup and pop it in my mouth, chewing contemplatively.

"Can we talk about the puppy play stuff?" I ask him. "I know you were happy with the things I bought, but we got a bit distracted…"

His cheeks flush adorably and he pushes his food around on his *Spongebob* plate with his fork. "We don't have to."

"*Kaden*," as always, bringing out Daddy voice gets his full attention and he looks up at me immediately, those liquid blue eyes of his wide and earnest, "we *do* have to." I push my plate forward so I can lean on the countertop. "We have to talk about whether it's something you do want to try and, if it is, we have to talk about what kind of scenes you're comfortable starting with. Just like with being Little. We need rules, safewords, all the things to make sure we're looking after ourselves before we play."

His nod is a bit more reluctant this time, but he gives it anyway. "I just…" he sighs and pushes his half-eaten meal next to my empty plate. I frown at it, thinking I'll just have to make sure he eats his entire lunch before he continues speaking. "When I brought it up, you were kinda' freaked out by it?"

"I was taken by surprise," I correct him gently. "But a good friend recently—"

"You *told* someone?" He sits back, panic splashed over his features.

"She's a Little," I try to justify, thinking that I should ignore accidentally clueing London in as well. "She's a Little, and all I said was—"

"Oh, God, your friends are going to think I'm—"

"What, Kade? Kinky like them? Because my friends are all in the lifestyle, too."

I know it doesn't exactly justify telling anyone about his interest in puppy play, but it was something I desperately needed to get off my chest. And, if Katie hadn't given me her perspective, I'd still be confused and stuck in my own head about it. Besides, everyone confides in their closest friends about their relationships, don't they?

Kade shakes his head, a few locks of his blonde hair flopping down over his forehead and into his eyes. "It's just really personal information, Chance."

"I know," I try to assure him, feeling guilty but still justified in talking to Kate. "I wasn't giving out sordid details or anything. I was just…in need of a bit of guidance."

He sighs. "You should have asked me first."

"Yeah," I concede, "I probably should have. But…I didn't know I was going to say anything until after I did, and by then it was done." I hang my head. "I'm sorry. Maybe I should have looked online, or gone to The Center for help, but I had no idea where to start. I just…I really wanted to be able to give you what you wanted and I didn't know how *I* felt about it, and Katie's like…well, she's got this magical power that makes it so easy to just talk to her, y'know?"

Snorting, Kade repeats, "Magical power, huh?"

"I swear, she casts a spell or something."

It's a relief to watch his lips twitch with amusement. "I thought you were immune to women's charms?"

"Katie's all sorts of awesome," I shrug. "You'll love her."

His eyes widen all over again. "You really want me to meet your friends?"

I'm confused now. How can he possibly have thought

otherwise? "Uh, yeah? I mean, I love you. You're a big part of my life. They are also a big part of my life. At some point, I'd like to be able to wrap it all up with a nice big bow." I grin to myself, imagining him in his Little headspace, playing with the other Littles and being doted on by my Daddy and Mommy friends. I can also picture him big, debating pop culture with Zephyr and Josh, or discussing gaming with Matt and London, or books with Tony and Spence. "The whole group is gonna love you, I'm sure of it."

He bites his lip. "Even if I'm a Pup and not a Little?"

My heart thumps almost painfully in my chest. I reach for his hands and hold them tight. "Baby, you could be into anything —or *nothing*— and they'll still love you for you." Then I cock my head and smile, giving his hands a little shake. "And who's to say you can't be both a Pup and a Little? There aren't any rules here. You're not giving up one for the other. Hell, if you wanna be a baby pup, you can. Or a Little who barks. You get to decide what you're comfortable with."

He practically flings himself off his stool, wrapping his arms around me, tucking his face into the crook of my neck. "You're too good to me," he mumbles and it somehow both breaks my heart and makes it soar all at the same time.

"There's no such thing," I insist, kissing the top of his head. Then, after another moment or two has passed, I ask, "So...can we talk about the puppy play now?"

* * *

In the end, I don't know which of us was more anxious to try the new role play. We talked about the things Katie had mentioned: the parallels she saw between Littles and Pups.

We discussed all the 'beginner' scenes I've researched online, and the other accessories I bought just in case he still wanted to play. We went back over safe words and how he felt comfortable communicating and even moving around as a Pup.

We even talked about what Kade would like to wear as a Pup, and he shyly informed me that he wants to wear a body suit or a leotard —something soft and breathable, that covered his arms and legs— with the wearable tail and ears, as well as a set of paws. He drew the line at a masked hood, not liking the idea of covering his face, but said that he'd love to be gifted a collar if our first few scenes turn out to be as enjoyable as he hopes.

I even confirmed that he didn't want me to get any pee pads or do any housetraining scenes, which made him blush bright red and shake his head vehemently. Kade was equally against gags, which is just as well. He also refused to let me rename him something ridiculous like 'Fido'. Just as when he's little, he's still Kade.

In turn, I expressed that I don't want to call myself 'Master'. I'm still Daddy, even when he's my Pup and not my boy, and that's how I'll refer to myself (even if he can't, because he doesn't want to use words when he's in Pup space). I also told him that while I'm okay with sexual exploration during Little play, I'm still not sold on the idea of sex during puppy play. It's not wholly off the table because who knows how we'll both feel once we're more comfortable doing scenes together, but…I don't think it's my thing.

And that all led us to this moment: with Kade wearing sweatpants, a long-sleeved cotton t-shirt, and the soft, floppy ears and matching tail I bought him, kneeling in front of the couch with his head cocked to the side – the picture of a curious pup. In my hand, I hold a soft yellow stress ball.

We're starting off easy. A light scene including some ball play, pets, and —if he follows my commands— treats. For now, those treats are little gummies shaped like dog bones (one of the other items I found at the adult store in the section dedicated to pet play), but if Kade enjoys this as much as I suspect he will, I'm going to bake cookies in the shape of dog bones for a more immersive experience.

"Okay, boy," I tell him, holding the ball up so he can see it properly. His tongue lolls out and he starts waggling his butt, despite being seated. It's adorable. "Let's see how good you are at fetch."

I gently toss the ball across my living room, with barely enough force to send it past the rug's edges. It would be better to do this outside in the yard, but without the proper pads for Kade's hands and feet —and with the rain setting in today— we have to make do with inside for now.

Kade doesn't seem to mind the limited area, though. He scrambles after the ball on all fours, yipping and whining excitedly. His fluffy tail swings with his movement and, when he pounces on the ball and grips it between his teeth, his ears flop about wildly when he gives his prize a shake.

"Good boy," I praise, patting my thigh. "Now bring the ball back to Daddy."

He doesn't hesitate, trotting over with his head held high. He drops the toy at my feet and wags his tail, whining for a repeat. I scratch the top of his head with my fingertips before I pick the ball up and throw it again.

We continue this game for a few more minutes, and I can't get over just how quickly and easily Kade sank into his pup headspace. There was no hesitance —not like there was for his Little headspace— and even though I've seen him enjoy playing as a Little, it doesn't seem to compare to the unfettered exuberance of his puppy side.

He growls playfully at the ball at one point, batting it with his 'paw' before leaping on it with his teeth bared. I can't help but think it's the cutest damn thing I've ever seen.

When he brings the ball back for what has to be the tenth time, I stroke his head and reaffirm that he's been a good boy. He seems to be tiring of the game, so I tell him we're going to have a little break, and he can either jump up on the couch and rest with his head in my lap, or sit by my feet while I pet him and get some work done. Little does he know, the 'work' involves trawling websites on my phone, looking for pet play toys and accessories, because it's clear to me that Kade's loving his time as a pup.

He looks at the couch, then at my face, then at the couch again before he hoists himself up onto the seats beside me in a very canine-inspired way, his front 'paws' coming up first before bringing one leg and then the other up behind him in quick succession. It takes a little maneuvering before he's lying on his belly with his knees tucked in underneath him, his arms folded next to my leg and his chin resting on top of my thigh. He looks up at me with big, doleful eyes and I grin and scritch the top of his head again, feeling my heart flip as his eyes drift closed and he lets out a happy chuff of breath.

"Good boy," I murmur, then use my free hand to start scrolling websites.

Today has turned out to be better than I'd hoped, and I'm even more interested in seeing how much further we can explore this new dynamic.

Chapter Sixteen — Kade

At this point, I'm fairly sure I've had a psychotic break and the life I'm living is not real. It can't be real. It's too good.

Chance and I have been dating for a couple of months now. We've fallen into a routine of spending Saturdays as Daddy and boy or Daddy and pup, depending on which mood strikes us both, and Sundays going out on proper dates. On Wednesday nights, he comes to my place after work, we cook dinner and then spend the night cuddling or fucking —or fucking and *then* cuddling— and often indulge in some light age play, too.

I've met most of his friends over the past couple of months as well. Chance didn't want to overwhelm me with the giant get-together his friends kept pushing for via their group chat, instead wanting me to meet them in smaller doses.

First it was Katie and Cherie: a Mommy and Little couple who were super sweet when we met for lunch one Sunday. I recognized Cherie from the auction, but she was kind enough not to mention watching the moment Chance set his eyes on me for the first time in twenty years. She earned herself so many points for that.

After them, I was dragged along for a night of bowling and drinking beer with Tony, a kind of shy Little, and his Daddy, Spencer, who Chance sheepishly explained has essentially been his best friend for the past decade or so. I expected to feel jealous when he said that, but I wasn't. How could I really be jealous, when I know that Chance loves me, and what he and Spencer have as friends is nothing like what Chance and I have together? The relief on his face when Spencer and I got along like a house on fire, the two of us ganging up on him with our banter, was definitely worth meeting the guy.

Following that, he took me to meet Ted and Charlie, and their respective boyfriends (and, unsurprisingly, Littles), Zephyr and Asher. We met the group at a gorgeous mansion home which, it turned out, belonged to Ted. Ted and Charlie were also familiar, but unlike Cherie, they did bring up the night of the auction. However, instead of being too inquisitive or judgmental, all they said was that they were glad to see me looking happier and that they were sorry if their intervention on the night was awkward or irritating. Then Zephyr and Asher dragged me into conversation —and a playful interrogation about myself— and I felt oddly accepted and welcomed.

Finally, last night I was introduced to London, Matt, and Josh. I had to do a double take on the latter, because he looks a hell of a lot like Charlie, but he's younger and apparently a Little, where Charlie's all Daddy. Matt is sweet and gentle, even though he looks like he'd fit right in with a motorcycle club, and London is young but possibly one of the most mature guys in the whole friendship group. I instantly click with these guys, falling into easy conversation about what they each do for work and just going from there.

Through all of this, the thing that really strikes me is how the entire friendship circle are so endearingly open about their kinks and relationships. I can understand now why Chance reached out to some of them to discuss the puppy play thing. And, having met them all, I no longer mind that they know. In fact, after I was added to the group chat, play dates were suggested and not one person seemed weirded out when I asked if I could play as a Pup instead of a Little. If anything, the entire lot of the Littles got super excited about the idea of playing with me, and that made me want to wag my tail and start playing immediately.

We've even started having Emmett over for dinner occasionally, because I feel as though he's the first real friend that I've made myself in a long time. The fact that Chance already knew him, even if they weren't close, made it easier to turn their acquaintanceship into something more of a friendship. It's not quite the same as when we're with Chance's original social circle, but we've been talking about asking Emmett to join the larger group more often anyway. It's not like he doesn't already know them all through Charlie and The Center.

So, yeah, everything seems to have fallen into place and it feels surreal. Don still hasn't mentioned Chance again, so I've stopped stressing that he's surveilling either one of us, and work (while still stressful because of the nature of my job) has been good, all things considered.

And with today being another Saturday, I'm looking forward to more of the same.

I've started dropping into Little space for breakfast every Saturday. Chance loves it, and the more I do this, the more

I enjoy it, too. It's genuinely relaxing to let go of my adult concerns and to let myself be taken care of. The therapist I've been seeing —a woman Asher referred me to, who is kink-friendly, warm and kind— is impressed with how far I've come. I have a praise kink a mile wide, and I no longer seek out punishments (except for fun). I'm a very good boy, as a Pup and as a Little, and Daddy's affection and reassurance is far better for my mental health than any spanking ever was.

When I'm little, I generally hover around a mindset of four or five. I'm beyond potty trained, so there are no diapers in my lifestyle, but Daddy has me wearing training pants 'just in case'. Some part of me wonders if he *wants* to experiment with an 'accident' scene or two, but until I'm sure I'd be okay with it, I'm not going to suggest it myself. Besides, between my woeful lack of experience with Little scenes and our mutual new exploration into puppy play, we have so many more things to entertain ourselves with for the time being.

"Look at you," Daddy declares in a tone of mixed amusement and exasperation. "You're covered in syrup, baby."

I've taken to eating my bites of waffles —or, in today's case, pancakes— with my fingers. Daddy loves cleaning me up, and it turns out messy eating is a lot of fun. My fingers are sticky and I know I have syrup smeared over my mouth, chin, and cheeks, too. I beam at him.

"I love syrup," I proclaim, before running my index finger through a puddle of the gooey, sweet substance on my plate and ramming it into my mouth. "Yum."

Daddy shakes his head and pushes off his stool. "I'll get the cloth. Stay put."

I wriggle on my seat, licking more syrup off my fingers with childlike glee. I barely even notice Daddy's returned from grabbing a washcloth and running it under the faucet until he's grabbed my wrist and is wiping the stickiness off while I struggle and giggle against the sneak attack.

He cleans my hands to the best of his ability, then wipes over my face. Once he's done, he peppers my cheeks with kisses. "Come on, let's get you washed up properly and do our teeth, too."

I groan. "I don't wanna brush my teeth. I wanna keep tasting syrup, not yucky mint."

"Too bad, sunshine." He pulls me from the stool and gives my ass a playful swat. "Brushing teeth is non-negotiable."

I grumble all the way to the bathroom where Daddy makes me wash my hands and face properly before he squeezes toothpaste onto my Avengers themed toothbrush and arches an eyebrow when I hesitate with it halfway to my mouth.

"Kaden, don't make me brush them for you. You know that will also earn you corner time."

Corner time is *not* fun. Not like spanking is.

I sigh dramatically and pop the head of the brush in my mouth, scowling at the spicy mint taste while I scrub.

Daddy smirks and cards his fingers through my hair. "Good boy."

The words light me up inside, filling my tummy with butterflies, and it makes brushing my teeth worthwhile.

* * *

"So, do you feel like Pup or Boy today?" Daddy asks me when we're back in his bedroom. He's standing in front of the closet expectantly.

"Pup." I don't even hesitate. I have no reason to. Not

anymore.

I love that, even though I want Daddy to make most decisions for me, he still asks me to tell him where my head is at. He genuinely doesn't seem to prefer boy over pup —or vice versa— and I can't express just how much more I love him for that. I know he had misgivings about being 'Master' to a pup, but we've talked about it over the past few weeks and, because he's still Daddy, those worries have been allayed. He just has a fur baby instead of a human one sometimes. That's a thing, right? Even if it's not, we're making it one. Like he said all those weeks ago: we get to set the rules on what works for us. And this works for us.

"Perfect," Daddy says, then points towards the bathroom. "Go potty, get undressed, then come back here so we can get you all dressed in your puppy clothes."

I obey, putting my pajamas in the laundry hamper before scampering back out to the bedroom to find Daddy sitting on the edge of the bed with one of my pup costumes all set out beside him on top of the covers.

A few weeks ago, he surprised me with a selection of long-sleeved body suits designed specifically for puppy play. I'd already told him I wasn't into pleather, vinyl, or leather, so he found a company online that made softer, cuter outfits and ordered me three. One of them is a dalmatian print, another a tawny golden color in a slightly furry texture, and the third is the one we call 'the mutt', because it's got longer fur in random patches of color. All three are soft and warm —the dalmatian a breathable cotton which will work better in summer time— and have a specially designed crotch/ass area, so if we decided to use the butt plug tails, or I wanted to start marking my territory in the backyard, we would just need to unzip a couple of hidden patches of material and take them off. It's really quite clever, and I've been wearing my belted tail under my costume and slipping it through the specially designed patch at the rear (intended for plug tails) to make my whole look sleeker.

Today, he's chosen the mutt, which is my favorite costume. He helps me climb into it and situates my tail, then zips the whole suit up using the hidden zip that starts just below my navel and travels up to the collar of the body suit. Next he helps put on my front paws, and finally my ears. By the time it's done, my head is in pup space.

It's not a whole lot different to Little space. Fuzzy and floaty and relaxed. Admittedly, I find it harder to focus on long strings of words when I'm in this headspace, so Daddy usually communicates in simple words and phrases. And touch. He's always affectionate, but when I'm a pup it seems even more pronounced. He's always petting the hair on my head, stroking a hand on my back, or tapping out a gentle, pleasant rhythm on my hip or my butt cheek if we're sprawled out and resting. He scritches behind my ear or rubs my belly when we wrestle play. It's the absolute best.

"Come on, boy," he says once I'm dressed and on all fours, waggling my butt in anticipation of whatever fun he has planned for us, "outside. I've got something new for us to try."

I bolt for the hallway, my knees —acting as rear paws— slipping on the tiles in my current furry costume. But outside time is the best, so I right myself and continue to race for the back door.

This is one of the many perks of Chance living so far out of town. His backyard is large and private, with his house set further back from his closest neighbors. He also has high timber fences and lots of trees around the perimeter, providing additional coverage, too.

I was surprised to discover that Chance is one of those 'lawn proud' kind of guys. He's meticulous about lawn maintenance —mowing, weeding, keeping the soil healthy or whatever— and it shows. His house might need work, but his yard is like something out of a magazine. The grass is pristine and soft under foot. He's got a little oasis down the far end of the yard, complete with wooden decking and a pergola and sun loungers, surrounded by plants and blooming flowers. On this end, off the back of his house he has an outdoor entertaining area set up with matching timber decking, a grill and a large outdoor table and chairs.

But, instead of the wide expanse of grass I'm used to seeing between the two spaces, the space now contains a variety of obstacles – the kind you see on those dog competition shows. There's a ramp constructed of two wide planks of wood set at forty-five degree angles, a large tunnel that looks *just* big enough for me to crawl through, a series of plastic cones set out in a straight line on the ground, and…are those little hurdles?

I stop short on the deck, just outside the backdoor as I take it in, sitting back on my butt and cocking my head up at Daddy, making one ear flop over the top of my head.

He chuckles. "…like it?….obstacle play…little boys play too…"

I know he's actually speaking in sentences, but only half of his words really filter through to my puppy brain. Still, I get the gist. I bark and bounce on the spot, excited to try out new toys with my Daddy.

"Stay," he instructs with a firm tone that has me sitting up straight and still. "Good boy." He strokes my head, then brandishes a collar and leash. They're made of a light blue colored leather with diamantes inset, and I instantly love them. I try not to wiggle too much in my happiness when Daddy bends to secure the collar around my neck. The leash is already clipped to it.

"Now… walking…leash…" he explains, again using more words than I actually hear, and all my mind focuses on is 'walk'.

I spring up and surge forward towards the yard, tugging Daddy along behind me.

"Kade!" He gives the leash a quick tug in warning. "Sit! Stay!"

It's hard to follow the command. I want to explore the yard, sniff the grass, stretch my muscles. I want to run and frolic and play. But Daddy's commands are firm and he tightens his hold on the leash.

"Slow," he instructs, starting to get into the habit of smaller instructions. "No pulling. Now, come."

We set off around the perimeter of the yard at a slower pace than I want to take. But Daddy lets me stop to sniff at things, laughing when a nose full of pollen causes me to sneeze. We practice basic commands while we walk, with Daddy randomly telling me to 'Sit', 'Stay', and, at one point, 'Lay down'. By the time we make it back to the spot where we started, he's praising me for being a good boy and making me sit again before digging into his pocket and pulling out a little ziplock bag of…TREATS!

Treats! Treats! Treats!

I yip at him, wagging my tail so hard that my entire body moves with the effort.

"Sit," he warns again, but he sounds happy. It's all I can do to obey, whining as he holds a bone-shaped cookie out in front of me. "Now, remember – *gentle*, Kade."

Okay, so I might have gotten excited and accidentally bitten him once.

Just once.

It wasn't even a hard bite. Just a nip to his fingers as I took the treat.

But that meant I had to sit and be still and quiet for *forever* afterwards, so I'm super careful nowadays.

I take the proffered treat with exaggerated caution and crunch it happily between my teeth. Daddy scratches me behind the ear and I lean into the touch.

"Okay…water…obstacles."

Again, only a few words out of his actual sentences filter through the fog in my brain, but I let Daddy lead me over to the table, where he pulls down a gleaming porcelain dog bowl and pours water into it from a fresh bottle he'd grabbed from the refrigerator before we came outside. I drop and lap at the offering happily, washing down the last of the treat, uncaring of the mess I'm making.

Daddy waits until I'm done and then tips the remaining dregs of water out of the bowl and onto the grass, placing the bowl back on the table before picking my leash back up and leading me towards the ramp.

He stands at the side of the construction, making sure the leash is lax so I can climb without being accidentally tugged towards him. The side of the ramp we start on has built in rungs running horizontally across its surface. They're *just* bumpy enough to give me leverage to climb, but don't stick out enough that you could call them footholds or handholds. It takes me a while to work out the best way to climb: when I'm on the ground, I use my human knees as my rear paws, but for this exercise I need to use my socked feet. Even though it's not a big ramp, nor is it that high off the ground, my front paw pads mean I don't have fingers or grip, and it takes longer than I thought it would to make it to the top of the obstacle.

Daddy praises my efforts the whole time, though. Even when I slip backwards and need to reattempt it.

I hesitate at the top with my front paws scrabbling for purchase on the slippery ramp down. An unconscious whine escapes from the back of my throat when I realize that heading down is going to be faster —but more difficult— than climbing up.

"It's okay," Daddy strokes his hand down my spine, starting at the top of my head and ending at my tail. I concentrate a little harder on what he's saying. "You've got this. Good boy. Good dog."

The praise bolsters me, and I launch forward over the apex of the ramp, slipping and sliding paws first to the ground below.

I land in an ungainly heap at the bottom no worse for wear. Getting to my paws, I give my whole body a shake.

"Good boy!" Daddy praises, dropping to his knees beside me on the grass. He rubs my sides with both hands, petting and scratching and praising. "Good job, Kade."

I flop to the ground in front of him, rolling onto my back, letting my tongue loll out as he rubs my belly.

Yeah, life is good.

* * *

Forget *good*. Life is fucking excellent.

These are the thoughts I have an hour or so after our scene in the yard, when Chance has me pressed against the cool, white tiles in his shower, his cock teasing in between my cheeks. His mouth is trailing wet, open mouthed kisses over my shoulders and up my neck, and his hand —his magical, glorious hand— has managed to wriggle in between the tiles and my body, squeezing and stroking and teasing my cock.

The water from the shower is deliciously hot as it rains down on us, and Chance doesn't seem to be in a hurry for us to clean up and get out. If anything, he's intent on making us dirtier.

I'm down with that.

"Did you have fun today, baby?" he whispers huskily into my ear and his whiskers tickle my jaw.

I almost don't understand what he's asking. I'm too distracted by the hand on my dick, and the feel of his hard shaft rubbing in the cleft of my ass, so damn close to where I'm starting to desperately need him.

"Nnngh," I answer, nodding. The movement shifts some of the lusty haze from my brain. "Yeah...oh, *fuck*, Chance."

He chuckles. With his lips brushing my earlobe and his back pressed up against mine, the rich sound envelopes me. "I meant the pup play, baby."

"Oh," I say, still not entirely present in the conversation. "L-loved it." And I did. I loved how immersive it felt, and how much effort Chance has gone to to set up his yard, fully investing in this part of me, literally building it into his lifestyle. "Love *you*, Daddy."

Chance groans and pushes me even harder into the wall as he curls around me, trying to capture my mouth with his. I turn my face under the water's spray to meet his kiss. It's hungry and raw and I love it, even if it is uncoordinated and sloppy.

"Wait here," he demands as he pulls away, and I frown and complain when the warmth of his body leaves my back. Even though the shower is hot, I'm bereft without him.

Over my shoulder, I watch him leave the shower and rummage through the cabinet under the bathroom sink, heedless of the water he's trekking all over the floor. When he cries out victoriously and brandishes a bottle of silicone-based lube, I grin and spread my legs invitingly.

"Good boy," he praises, stepping back in under the spray, his treasure in hand.

I preen, brace my forearms against the slick tiled wall, and push my ass out further towards him, watching as his eyes, already blown wide with lust, seem to darken with his want. His cock is hard and straining towards me, and I can't help but lick my lips as I eye it.

Chance's large palm slaps one of my round butt cheeks lightly. "Not now, baby."

I pout, but I can't hold the expression for long, because Chance isn't in the mood to drag things out right now.

He drizzles lube over his fingers, then down the cleft of my ass, and brings his fingers to my hole almost immediately, rubbing circles over the ring of muscle, encouraging me to loosen up for him. I can't help but close my eyes and lean my forehead against my folded arms on the wall, giving in to the rush of sensation.

It doesn't matter how many times we've done this together now, every time still feels special. It's like I still can't quite believe that Chance wants me like this. That *Chance* is taking care of me. Stretching me open. Loving me. And every single time, I vow to savor it. I try to memorize every second, to burn it into my brain, because it's *Chance* and I will never take another second with him for granted ever again.

Even though he was in a hurry before, he still takes his time prepping and teasing me, crooking his fingers and searching for that spot that makes me see stars. It's only once I'm writhing on his fingers, slamming back onto them and begging for his cock, that he finally deems me ready.

There's a pause as he slicks himself up, and then his hands are on my hips and he's slowly sinking inside me and it's just as perfect as the first time. I pant through it, listening to his bitten off moans and the litany of praises that unconsciously fall from his lips as he fully sheathes himself.

"*Move*, Daddy," I urge, "Fuck me. I need—*oh*."

Chance sucks on my shoulder and the base of my neck as he starts to thrust, setting a punishing pace. I know that I start to babble, telling him how good he feels inside me, how much I love his thick, hard cock, how only he has ever made me feel quite like this.

None of it is a lie or embellishment.

I've obviously had good —even great— sex over the last twenty years. But nothing like what I have with Chance. There's something extra special about having the emotional connection, about sharing the pup play and being his boy. It's added intimacy that I've never known before and, yeah, even at times like these, where I'm being railed mercilessly in the shower, it's still somehow tender and loving.

He's going to leave impressive hickeys over my skin, but I don't care. I'll wear the marks with pride, and I'll remember exactly how I got them. Each and every one.

Chance starts to repeat my name like a heady, desperate mantra. "Kade," he pants on every hard slam into me. "Kade, Kade, *Kade*."

"Yes, Daddy," I answer, crying out when his hand —bruising fingerprints into my hip— slides around to grip my cock. I hadn't even noticed that he wasn't stroking me yet, too far gone on how much I was enjoying just having him in me. "Yes!" I shout again.

"Come for me, baby," he begs, his voice rough and ragged. "I need you to come, Kaden."

I don't need any further encouragement. A few more squeezing, slippery strokes of my dick is all it takes before I fly over the precipice of bliss, coating the tiles in front of me with my release.

"Oh fuck, oh fuck, oh *fuuuuuck*," Chance practically bellows, his hand having returned to my hip to hold me in place as his own orgasm crashes over him. His voice reverberates off the tiles and his cock spurts and twitches inside me.

And it's perfect.

Everything is perfect.

Chapter Seventeen – Chance

J osh: *When's the next official get-together/play date? The Grove's not bad, but I miss you guys.*

That's the message that kicks off an hours-long thread in our group chat about availability, work schedules, and the questions about when we all got so old and boring.

I can't help circling back to Josh's message, though. It's not often that he reaches out like that, and my not-so-inner Daddy is on alert. Even though we've all finally agreed to catch up next Saturday afternoon, I can't stop worrying that my younger friend might need support or something, so, when I finish work for the day, I pull out my phone and call him, not bothering to leave the office yet.

"Walker," he answers on the third ring.

I snicker. "Come on, man, you would have seen my name on the caller ID."

There's a pause before he says, "Yeah, look, I'm at work, so…"

"Oh, shit, sorry." He recently made Detective, so I cut to the chase, knowing that, all joking aside, he takes his job seriously.

"I just wanted to check in, make sure you're okay."

Another stretch of silence spreads between us over the line, and that's got me even more on edge. When he does answer, his words don't do much to resolve my concerns. "I've just got some stuff going on is all," he tells me, and I can feel myself frowning. But he can't see that. I can't see him, either, but I can picture the fake grin on his face when he forcefully chirps, "So a day with all the guys is just what the doctor ordered."

"Josh…"

"Listen, Chance, I've gotta run. Duty calls. I'll see you next weekend, okay?"

The line goes dead before I can reply.

I pull my phone away from my ear and stare at it blankly for a minute. I'm even more worried about Josh now than I was before I called him. And, no, I mightn't be his Daddy, or even a regular caregiver, but he's one of my friends, and he's Charlie's little brother, and —all jokes about his attention seeking aside— this is all out of character for him.

Before I can make up my mind about whether or not to call Charlie, my phone starts to ring in my hand. Kade's face lights up my screen —a shot I took of him a few weekends ago, smiling and relaxed on a date at a local restaurant— and I grin as I answer, "Hey, baby."

My stomach plummets at the sound of his sniffled, "H-hey."

"What's wrong?" I sit bolt upright in my chair, all thoughts completely focused on my boyfriend.

"Can you come over? I…" It sounds like he swallows a sob. "I know it's only Tuesday, but I need you."

With my laptop already packed away in my satchel, it takes me less than five seconds to toss the remaining detritus —a couple of pens, a notepad and some sticky notes— in with it. Then I'm patting down my pockets with my free hand, checking for my keys and wallet as I tell Kade I'm on my way.

Chapter Eighteen – Kade

Tuesday starts like any other day. I park in my executive spot in the garage beneath our office building, I ride the elevator up to our company's floor, I greet Rhonda, the receptionist, with a smile and a wink, and I head over to my glassed in corner office, ready to dive into a mountain of sales reports and data analysis.

Things start feeling different as soon as I power up my laptop and open my email application. The very first email to grab my attention is one that arrived moments after I clocked in. It's from Donald Baker, and it is marked with a bright red exclamation mark.

Urgent.

What could Don possibly need from me that's urgent? We only had our most recent meeting last week. He has the same reports to sift through that I do. We haven't had any notable changes to any of our contracts with our suppliers or franchisees, and there aren't any major sales campaigns scheduled to start this week.

Something is up.

I can feel it deep in my gut. The tense, churning sensation only increases as I click on the email and open it to find three simple words: 'See me immediately.'

I don't know what it is that inspires me to do so, but I methodically and systematically wipe any passwords stored in my computer, my browsing history and any personal files from my laptop. I don't use my work computer for personal tasks often, but the odd copy of a receipt or photo of a meal has sneaked in over time. I also make sure to download any of the excel files filled with complicated formulas and macros that I've built myself to streamline my job, saving them to my personal thumb drive before I delete them from the work server.

Call it paranoia, but I have a feeling I won't have access to my office for long after I've spoken to Don, and I'll be damned if I make it easy for him to replace me or my hard work. Sure, IT can probably recover the excel files from backups from the server, but only if they know about them in the first place.

After one final sweep of my laptop, I shut it down and then make sure my briefcase has any of my minimal personal effects already stored away. If my gut is right —and it's rarely ever wrong— and I'm going to be forced to leave, I'll be doing it with dignity and as minimal fuss as possible.

With that settled, I tuck my phone into my hip pocket, my wallet into the other, and stride out of my office and back through the catacomb of cubicles. I nod and smile at my colleagues, those working on my team and those I've barely spoken three words to, and follow the hallway that curves around past the break room and bathrooms towards Don's office. The door is open when I arrive, and he spies my reflection in the glass of his window, which he was staring out of as I approached.

The man turns his high backed leather chair slowly, and I can't help but liken him to a cheesy Bond villain. All he needs is a fluffy white cat to stroke menacingly, but I wouldn't want to subject an innocent kitty to this man's personality.

"Close the door, Kade, and take a seat."

His voice is oily as ever, and that dread I was feeling earlier solidifies in my belly. Still, I do as he says, even though I desperately want to head back out into the office proper so I can grab a witness.

Don sits silently and observes me from across the glossy timber desk, and I know he wants to see me squirm. I refuse to give him the satisfaction, so I force myself to sit still, appearing as calm and patient as possible.

"I thought we had an agreement, Kaden," he finally says, after God only knows how much time has passed in strained silence.

I arch an eyebrow at him. "An agreement?"

Don rolls his eyes and slaps his palm on the surface of the desk. The harsh sound makes me flinch, despite my best efforts to appear unruffled. "Don't play dumb with me. I told you to stay away from Chance, did I not?"

That solid lump of dread seems to increase in size. My thoughts drift back to his threats from weeks ago, and his intimation that he's been keeping an eye on his son. If it's an ongoing thing, of course he'd know about our relationship: I've been spending enough time at Chance's place lately, that's for sure.

I have a momentary, fleeting thought that I want my Daddy, but I shake it off and narrow my eyes at my boss. "I don't recall agreeing to anything, Don."

His resulting chuckle is dark and condescending. It's an unpleasant sound. "Well, let me make things clear to you. I won't have you fraternizing with him. Is that clear?"

"With all due respect, Don, you can't control who —or what— I do in my private life."

The old man's lips curl into a sneer. "I'm well aware. However, you have a choice to make. You can continue to undermine me, and I'll remind you that I am the entire reason behind your success and your ability to enjoy your...*lifestyle*," the word is spat out, like it's distasteful, *"or,"* he takes a breath, and I can see a perverse sense of enjoyment in his expression, "you can keep your job. You can't have both."

Even though I knew it was coming, the words hit me like a sucker punch to the solar plexus. "That's illegal," I breathe before I can think better of it.

Don scoffs and reaches into the top drawer of his desk, pulling a wad of glossy papers —*photos*— out and dropping them in front of me. They fan out as they land and the dread in my stomach turns to revulsion. I feel sick.

The photos are all of me and Chance, indulging in puppy play —and Little time— in his yard. I'm not stupid enough to think that these are the only copies in existence, either.

"Why..." I start, gaping, unable to formulate words.

Don nods solemnly. "I asked the same thing when I saw this. It's beyond disgusting, you realize that."

No, I want to scream, *it's not. It's proof that we love and trust each other. It's proof that Chance takes care of me.* But I don't bother and the words refuse to come anyway.

I know how it looks to an outsider. I know images like these would make Chance and my lives much more difficult. Even though discrimination based on sexual preferences is illegal, I'm sure Chance's boss or his clients could find other reasons to justify letting him go. And future employers? They'd laugh us both out of interviews. Our reputations would be ruined.

"Now," Don takes my fuming silence as invitation to repeat his ultimatum, "you can continue with this perversion, or you can keep your position here. Which will it be?"

Chapter Nineteen – Chance

Kade's beautiful blue eyes are rimmed in red when he opens his apartment door and I pull him in for a crushing hug. "What happened, baby?" I ask, smoothing my palm over his head.

He mumbles something unintelligible against my chest.

"You...lost your dog?" I try to parse it out, thoroughly confused.

He shakes his head then turns it to the side, resting his ear over my heart. "Job," he repeats sullenly. "I lost my job."

I can feel my jaw dropping, even as I tighten my hold on him. "What? How?"

He's damn good at his job, I know that much. Despite all the things I said when we were kids, my father got himself a smart, analytical, driven employee when he hired Kade. The fact that Kade climbed the corporate ladder all on his own merit —when I'm sure my father would have rather seen him fail— is proof of that. Then there's all the advice he gave Charlie and Cherie —and, to a lesser degree, Tony— about how best to market their businesses. He knows his shit.

Kade huffs. "It doesn't matter."

Daddy instinct kicks in. Whatever happened, he doesn't want me to know, which means he either did something wrong, or he's protecting me.

I scowl over the top of his head. "What did my dad do, Kade?"

I know I'm right when he tenses in my hold. "It doesn't—"

"Yes it fucking does. This is your *career*. You were on track for promotion. You—"

"He gave me an ultimatum." Kade cuts me off, still clinging to me just inside the doorway of his apartment.

The words don't really compute. "He…what?"

With a sigh, my boyfriend pulls out of my arms and shuts the door behind me, trudging into his living room and plopping onto the couch listlessly. It's only now that I take him in properly. He looks disheveled, his usually pristine business shirt rumpled and untucked, and his hair a mess, like he's been running his fingers through it over and over again. There's a tumbler of amber liquid sitting on the coffee table with a ring of condensation puddled beneath it on the glass surface.

"Kade…"

He leans over his spread legs, resting his forearms on his thighs and hanging his head. His messy blonde hair flops over his forehead and over his face, but he doesn't brush it away. Kade speaks to his shoes when he starts to explain, "He gave me the choice. My job and reputation in the industry, or…" Trailing off, his eyes flit towards me for only a second, but I hear the message loud and clear.

"Or me."

He nods miserably.

Rage fills me, starting low in my gut and spreading outwards to my extremities. I clench and unclench my fists while I process the information.

I haven't spoken to my father in twenty years and he's still trying to get under my skin. Only this time, he's brought the man I love into it.

A red haze seems to settle over my vision, and I want nothing more than to get back in my car, drive to my parents' house, and confront the man. I know well enough not to do that, of course, but the urge to attack him —physically, verbally, in *any* way possible— is strong.

I *should* be comforting Kade. I should be calling Ted and asking what kind of legal avenues we can pursue here. I should be reaching out to my professional contacts to see if anyone needs a sales or marketing guru...but I'm too angry to do any of that.

Then it hits me. "How did he know we were together?"

I don't love the fact that he winces and averts his gaze completely.

"Kaden," I press, slipping into Daddy voice without meaning to, "how did he know? I haven't spoken to or seen him since I left home."

Kade mumbles his response under his breath, but I'm pretty sure he just said "He's been watching you" which is creepy as fuck.

"He's...*what?*"

"The asshole has kept tabs on you," Kade suddenly snaps, taking me by surprise. It's like he's suddenly a different person, no longer hovering on the edge of Little space. His face twists unpleasantly and I don't mention the cussing rule. For now, there are more important issues at hand than our kinky relationship and the ongoing games therein. "He...he had

163

photos, Chance."

The way he emphasizes the word tells me that they're not just photos of us holding hands at a restaurant or kissing chastely in the park. The blood rushes from my face and I actually feel woozy.

I own my kinks, but the idea that my privacy has been violated like that in a place where I'm supposed to feel safe is horrifying. Not to mention what might happen if my father were to send those kinds of photos to my boss, or my clients, or my competitors.

"I'm sorry," Kade sniffs. His voice cracks. "It's my fault."

That's enough to snap me out of whatever anxiety attack was just building. "No, baby," I force my feet to move and I drop down on my knees on the rug beside his legs. I reach for his hands, squeezing them tight. "It's his fault. Only his."

"He told me to stay away from you. When we first got together. Made veiled threats..." Kade's lip quivers when he forces himself to look at me. His eyes are wet, little red lines starting to appear in the whites as he works himself up. "I ignored him. I thought he was talking shit, just being Don, you know? And I should have told you. I should have. I just didn't want to stress you out unnecessarily when I thought he was just talking crap."

I don't even have it in me to be upset that he didn't say anything. At the time, we had so much more to talk through than throwing my dad's crap into the mix. And, honestly, who would have thought the old man would follow through on what any normal person would assume were idle threats?

"I know, baby." I push off the ground, groaning as my knees protest, and squish myself up beside him on the couch, pulling him against me in another hug. "And that still doesn't make any of this your fault."

"I know. Rationally, I know. But if I'd listened to him…"

It hurts to hear the man I love hypothesize about not being with me. "And, what? Broken things off with me? He would have won."

Kade snorts. It's a bitter, ugly sound. "Because he hasn't won now?"

"Nope." I kiss his temple and nuzzle the side of his face. "Because we're still together. Because we love each other, and love *always* wins. You'll find another job. A better job. And we'll sue him for…for invasion of privacy and blackmail or some shit. Take him for every fucking thing he's got."

Kade lets out a watery giggle. It's only a half-hearted sound, but it calms something inside me. "I don't think we can do that."

"I'm going to talk to Ted anyway."

He exhales and shrugs. "It's not worth it. I'd rather walk away and let him think he's won."

Except we'll both live in fear that those photos will surface at some point, but I don't bother saying this out loud. Not right now. It's all too raw and we're too emotional.

Unwilling to talk about it anymore, I ask, "Do you want to be Little for a bit?" I think a scene or two would do us both good. "Or my pup?"

Kade doesn't need more than a second to consider it. His answer is quiet, but decisive. "Little please, Daddy."

As much as I've come to love our pup play, I'm relieved that he's chosen to be my boy tonight. I want to be able to use proper words with him. I want to snuggle him and kiss him all over. I want to read to him and reassure him that he's loved and precious. Sure, I could do a lot of that with my pup, but

I feel like he's more likely to fully understand when he's my boy.

Besides, puppy Kade is a bundle of energy and pure joy. I don't think either of us wants to experience miserable puppy Kade or bring sadness into our pup play at all. Not that I want my boy to feel miserable, either, but I feel I'm better equipped to comfort a sad boy than a sad pup (and I don't care if it's role play and it's the same person – there's a difference, damn it.)

We order Chinese food and, while we wait for it to be delivered, I take Kade into his bedroom and help him change into a pair of training pants emblazoned with a race car, and a set of soft blue pajamas covered in cartoon dogs. Ideally, I'd like the pants to match the outfit, but most of Kade's Little stuff lives at my place and beggars can't be choosers.

Twenty minutes later sees our food delivered and I suggest we eat out of the cartons while we watch a movie. Kade picks the original *Space Jam* and we settle in to watch it together. I can't help but think of the first time we did this exact same thing. We would have been ten or eleven years old, and we hired the VHS from Blockbuster, then got pizzas and had a sleepover at my house. Even back then, I think I loved him. Though, at the time, it was more platonic than romantic.

Tonight, we find ourselves positioned the same way we were all those years ago, with Kade sprawled out across the couch and his head in my lap, my legs propped up on the coffee table in front of us. Empty food containers litter the previously pristine surface, but this time my mom isn't going to come in and pitch a fit about the mess. Instead, I'll clean it up because *I'm* the responsible adult.

"Daddy?" Kade asks me midway through the movie. His voice sounds sweeter and younger than I've ever heard it.

When I look down at him, I can't help but gently brush his hair out of his eyes.

"Hmm?"

"Do you 'member when we first saw this?"

I can feel the grin splitting my face. "I was just thinking about that, baby."

"You said you was gonna be a basketball star." He giggles. The sound is a balm to my lingering agitation from earlier.

"To be fair, it was the 90s. *Everyone* said they wanted to be basketball stars." It was a huge fad at school. Kids wore their team jerseys to school, had team branded pencil cases and other merch, and *Space Jam* was one of the most popular movies for kids our age, even if we did pretend that we were too old for cartoons. It had Michael Jordan in it, damn it. How could that *not* be cool?

Kade scrunches his nose. "I didn't wanna."

"No, I know."

"I wanted to be a astronaut."

The lapsing of proper grammar is so insanely adorable. I know it's the stress of the day sending him so deep into his headspace, but I can't help enjoying it.

"I remember," I smile softly, waving a hand towards the TV while I speak. "So, while I liked watching this for the basketball, you liked it for all the aliens and spacey stuff."

He turns his head back towards the screen and nods. "Yup."

God, I love him.

Just chilling on the couch like this, not doing anything even remotely sexual or even all that romantic, and my heart can barely contain just how strongly I feel about him. I adore everything about him, from the softness of his naturally blonde hair, to the elegant slope of his nose, to his fine jawline, and further on to the man behind the pretty features. He stood up to my dad and lost his job over it. If that doesn't prove how strong and good he is, I don't know what will.

I spend the remainder of the movie watching him. Watching as the stress of the day takes its toll and makes his eyelids heavy. Watching as he drifts off to sleep, snuggled in my lap, trusting me to keep the inevitable nightmares at bay. I pick up the remote from where I'd left it beside me and click the power button on the TV, plunging the living room into darkness, illuminated only by moonlight the twinkling lights from the city outside his window.

"Come on, baby," I murmur gently, easing myself out from under him as he grumbles in his sleep. "Let's get to bed."

He cracks bleary blue eyes open. "Bed?"

"Uh huh. Potty first."

I can't help chuckle as he scrunches up his nose and complains, "Don't wanna. Comfy here."

"You won't be comfy if you stay here, I promise. Couches aren't great for backs."

He grizzles some more as he pushes himself into a seated position, then up to his feet, but then I surprise him by picking him up and forcing his legs around my waist. He's petite, and I'm stronger than I look. Sure, I can't carry him far, but the way he clings to me and hides his face in the crook of my neck is worth the effort of getting him down the short hallway and into his master bathroom.

I set him down in front of the toilet and turn him to face it, smothering a laugh when he just blinks at the waiting porcelain bowl owlishly.

"Need help, baby?"

Kade nods, his cheeks going pink.

We've done this before, but I still feel the need to check in. "Color?"

"*Gween*, Daddy."

My heart stutters. I hadn't thought he could get more adorable, but he proved me wrong. Even though I love his usual headspace, there's something special about seeing him sink lower, to something even younger, and more vulnerable. This isn't for anyone else. This is what he needs, and I'm beyond grateful that he trusts me enough to let me be here for him.

In a practiced move, I tug his pajamas and training pants down before I step up behind him with my front pressed to his back. He reaches distractedly for his penis and I hold my hand over his, helping him aim properly over the toilet. He does his thing, and I help him give himself a couple of quick shakes before he grabs a couple of squares of toilet paper and dabs himself completely dry. Then I praise him while he flushes the toilet and I help tug his underwear and pajama bottoms back up.

Kade hums a little song as we wash our hands together at the sink, with me taking up the same position as I had at the toilet, soaping, lathering and washing both our hands under lukewarm water from the faucet. He giggles when I shuffle our bodies, still pressed together, over to grab the hand towel so we can dry off our hands.

Business done, I usher him back towards the bedroom, climbing in beside him as his eyelids droop again.

"I love you, Daddy," he murmurs sleepily, snuggling deeper into my embrace. "I'm never letting you go again."

I didn't need to hear that last declaration because, honestly, his actions today —choosing me over the life he's known for the past twenty years— spoke more about his intentions than words ever could, but I'm suffused with warmth and affection anyway.

I kiss the top of his head. "I love you, too, baby," I reassure him, feeling myself choke up with emotion. It's not the first time we've shared these words, but today it feels new and special all over again. "And I'm not going anywhere."

I cuddle him to sleep but, once he's out, I get out of bed again, go to the bathroom myself, and then head back out into the living room in search of my phone.

Regardless of what Kade said, I'm calling Ted for advice.

Chapter Twenty — Kade

C hance is frustrated when Ted tells him what I knew all along: there's nothing we can do about the pictures Don has of us. I didn't get a great look at them, but they appear to have been taken from the public space of the forestry behind Chance's home, which means it's not illegal. Even if the photographer had to use a drone or climb a tree to get a line of sight into Chance's backyard.

Currently, Ted is sitting at my dining table, sipping at a mug of coffee. Chance called him last night while I was asleep, and it's a testament to how close their friendship circle is that Ted rearranged his morning meetings to talk to us.

"But isn't there, like, an expectation of privacy or something like that?" Chance argues with him.

Ted shakes his head, the gray streaks at his temples glinting silver with the sunlight pouring into my apartment. "Not in a backyard. You have a right to assume privacy in spaces like your bedroom or bathroom, but an outdoor space —especially one backing on to public land— isn't likely to be considered private."

Chance scowls and folds his arms across his chest. "Even when I have fences that are six feet high and a border of even taller trees besides that?"

Ted shifts his head from side to side, the physical equivalent of umming and aahing. "Look, this isn't my specialty, so take my advice with a grain of salt. I guess you could *potentially* argue that you had an expectation of privacy, and it does look bad for your father if the photos were taken via drone or from an angle not easily achieved by standing in the forestry, but I wouldn't bet on it working out in your favor. Besides, we'd have to be able to prove the photos exist, and that he intends on using them for whatever nefarious purposes suit him."

My Daddy huffs and waves one of his hands in my direction. "What about firing Kade because he wouldn't dump me? *That* has to be something we can fight, right?"

"But I don't want to," I speak up before Ted can answer, and they both turn to look at me. I sigh and reach for Chance's hand. "Even if I did take legal action and win, do you honestly think he wouldn't retaliate by sending those photos to your boss? Or posting them online? Or *something*? They're insurance for him right now. Yes," I continue, holding up a hand to stop Chance from arguing, "it sucks. Yes, it means he wins. But I'd rather that than the alternative where those photos ruin both our lives and reputations."

Ted smiles at me. It's a gentle, understanding expression, laced with sympathy. "Unfortunately," he says slowly, "I agree with you. The safest bet is to walk away right now."

I startle as Chance slams a fist onto the table, making the mugs rattle on the glass surface. "Damn it," he seethes, "I want that asshole to pay."

"I know," Ted reaches over and pats his shoulder consolingly. "My parents were dicks, too. But sometimes *not* giving them the reaction that they're trying to provoke is even more of a punishment. Think of how frustrated he'll feel when you guys ignore this and move on with your lives."

"And what if he decides to push us further then? He's got those photos, he can—"

"Call his bluff, then," Ted leans back and folds his arms, shrugging as though it's simple. "You really think he wants to be connected to the kink he's shaming you for? After all, estranged or not, you're his son, and Kade was one of his top employees. If he does send those photos out to your bosses or whatever, he's still associated with you. Would he risk that?"

I watch as my Daddy thinks that over. "Huh," he muses, a wry smirk twisting the corners of his lips. "I hadn't thought of it that way."

Ted nods. "I still don't think it would be worth pushing the issue, though. He'd be more likely to do it out of spite if you sued him rather than just to get your attention."

There's a moment of silence before Chance exhales heavily. "Fine. But I want it on record that I'd prefer it if the old man suffered."

"You say the sweetest things," I tease him, and he laughs.

* * *

I spend the rest of my week applying for new jobs. It's stressful but oddly liberating. Even though I worked hard to climb the corporate ladder at Don's company, I hadn't had to work to get my foot in the door. Now, as I write cover letter after cover letter, I realize that this is the first time I've really had to consider what I want and what I can offer a company.

I know I'm unlikely to find another executive role and, while I'll miss the income and perks, I'm okay with that for the time being. I can always work my way back up to it again, assuming I land a position in a large enough corporation. Otherwise, I decide that I'd like to work in a role based in marketing and advertising. That's where I thrive. I don't mind the merchandising and operational tasks that came with the job I've just left, but they're not where my interests lie. So it won't be the end of the world if I have to shift gears a little.

I have plenty of savings, courtesy of never allowing myself to truly indulge my successes, and the mortgage on my apartment is low, given that my downpayment was substantial. Despite my initial hesitance to move back to this city, I'm glad that I took the step to buy my place when I did, rather than to lease an apartment as a temporary measure. No matter what happens with my career, I'm not concerned that I'll end up homeless, but Daddy did suggest that I could move in with him if things became dire, which was sweet. Not necessary, but sweet.

Speaking of Daddy, though, he's been distracted for the past few days. I can understand why: his father really did a number on us —on *him*— and I know our agreement to turn our backs and move on without a fight is still niggling at him. I don't know how to make it better, and I can only hope that time will help. Plus, if I find a job that makes me happy, I might even be able to convince him that this was all for the best. Not that being under surveillance can ever really be 'for the best', but it is what it is, and I refuse to let Don win here.

He can think that he's won, but our happiness will prove otherwise.

So, I do what I do best: I come up with a plan to remind Daddy of just that.

On Friday night when he opens his front door, I grab him by the hand and start dragging him towards my car.

"Wait," he protests through chuckles. "Baby, where's the fire?"

"Come on," I urge, planting my feet and tugging fruitlessly at his arm. He's bigger and bulkier than me, and he doesn't move far. "I've got a reservation for us."

His rusty-brown eyebrows wing upwards. "A reservation?" he asks. "Where?"

"That's for me to know and you to find out." I try pulling him forward again. "Please, Daddy. Trust me."

Chance's expression turns all soft and indulgent, the way it always does when I call him Daddy. It makes my belly all fluttery and warm. "Alright," he agrees, "but let me lock up first." He turns back to the door, then pauses and looks back at me over his shoulder. "Is what I'm wearing okay?"

He's in his usual Friday night outfit of jeans and a Henley —this one dark red— and I nod, but then think it over. "Well, actually…"

Chance arches an eyebrow.

"Maybe business pants and matching shirt?"

His nod is slow as he looks me over. I'm dressed casually, so it's not like I'm telling him to change for a dress code. Smirking, all I offer him is, "I'd like to see you looking all corporate, Daddy."

This time his eyes widen with understanding. "I'm very much Daddy tonight, then?"

Not wanting to give anything more away until we get to our destination, I roll my eyes and motion with my hands for him to hurry up. Chance chuckles and goes to change.

* * *

"I should have guessed," Daddy ponders out loud as I make the turn towards the industrial area that houses The Grove. I focus on the road, but I can see him turn in his seat beside me, and I can hear him grinning. "What have you got planned, baby?"

"You'll see," I respond coyly.

We've spent a lot of time as Daddy and boy, and as Daddy and pup, but we've done all of that at home. Next weekend, we're meeting with the entire social group for a get-together and play date, but I honestly think Daddy and I deserve something a bit special and different to our usual routine. The Grove provides a safe space for that while giving us the illusion of being out in public. I think we both need this to recenter and regroup after having our privacy violated by his father.

I pull my car into the carpark at the rear of the large warehouse building, finding a spot near the rear of the lot. The front end of the lot is insanely busy with patrons of the club lined up at the food truck that Chance's friend Tony owns. I don't know much about my fellow Little yet. He seemed quite shy during our first meeting, but it was obvious that he and Spencer —Daddy's best friend— are in love.

Tony's manning the grill inside the black food truck and doesn't see us as we pass. Chance leans in and explains that Tony prefers cooking to dealing with people, so he's hired a couple of other staff to take orders and help out on busy nights like these. That makes sense to me and, as we pass by, I wonder whether he's considered other marketing and sales strategies for the truck outside of its longstanding position here at The Grove. It's named *BDSM* —Burgers, Dino-nuggets, Shakes & More— and is a glossy black beauty of a truck, with a cheeky logo comprised of a cartoon burger dressed in bondage gear, holding a limp fry like a whip. While it seems niche, I think it's kitsch enough that even vanilla folk would be drawn to it.

"I thought we were here for pleasure," Daddy purrs in my ear, making me jump. We've reached the entrance door, an unassuming thing with an olive tree logo the only sign that we're in the right place, and I shake my head.

"Am I that obvious?"

"Nah," he answers, pulling the door open and guiding me into the bright white lobby ahead if him, "I just know you well enough to know that's your work face."

Those words fill me with love and warmth as we step up to the reception desk to check in. It's a quick and easy process as we're both members, but Chance cocks his head when I tell Meg that I booked a room for us.

She hands the key over, as well as the bag of items I asked to be set aside when I came here and made the reservation, before she goes over the general rules and expectations of use, and then tells us to enjoy our night.

As always, when we open the big, soundproofed double doors, we're met with a blast of bass and sound. The ground floor nightclub and bar space is already busy, which is unsurprising for a Friday night, but this is not where I intend to spend our evening.

Chance peppers me with questions as we take the hallway which wraps around the lefthand side of the club space, and I laughingly remind him that I'm supposed to be the excitable boy, not him. The light tease does nothing to stem the flow of his questions, even as we make our way up the grand staircase at the rear of the building. It takes us up to the second floor, with two parallel hallways spread out in front of us once we reach the top.

This part of the building feels like a classy old hotel. It's all golden wood paneling and red carpeted floors. The doors that line the halls are soundproofed, as are the rooms within, but they still look like unassuming hotel rooms, with gilt numbers around eye level on their lacquered surfaces.

Where we would usually take the hallway on the right to head down towards the playroom, I lead Chance down the one on the left, to the door marked 207. I use the key to unlock it and I step inside with Chance on my heels. As Chance moves into the room proper, I make sure the door is shut and locked.

I watch Chance as he takes in the themed room I reserved for us, from the oversized mahogany desk and leather desk chair, to the matching leather three-seater couch along the right side of the room, to the large embedded screen on the wall which is designed to appear like a window, showing a view of a non-descript city beyond, as though the office that we're standing in is situated in a high-rise building. The carpet beneath our feet is a dark forest green, and the walls are painted cream. It's like an executive's office from the late 80s or early 90s, the vibe authoritative and marginally imposing. On the far side of the room, behind the desk, there's a door that leads to a little washroom, tiled in dark green, with a toilet and sink.

Chance turns to me with a corner of his lips lifting upwards. "Daddy's bringing his boy to work tonight, huh?"

I love that he gets it immediately. Except I have a very specific scene in mind. "That's the setup, yeah," I tell him, and then I tell him the scene I have in mind. I can tell by the darkening of his eyes that he's on board.

"Let's get you dressed into your play clothes," he says, taking the bag that's currently slung over my shoulder. He unpacks it on the couch, setting aside the toys and crayons and paper I'd packed while I take off my adult clothes. Then he helps me into the training pants, shorts and t-shirt I packed yesterday, and I start to settle into my Little headspace.

"Very cute," he declares once I'm all dressed to his satisfaction. The shorts are a soft, stretchy cotton-elastane blend in dark blue, and the shirt is a pale pink, decorated with blue text across my chest which reads 'Daddy's Boy'.

I beam at him. "Thank you, Daddy."

Daddy presses a kiss to my forehead and his beard, grown out and soft, tickles my skin. Then he cups my cheek and smooths his thumb over my jaw, looking me in the eye. "Okay, now Daddy has some very important work to do, so I need you to sit over here in the playtime corner and entertain yourself quietly, okay?"

Already feeling kind of giddy, because we both know I'm not going to do that, I smile sweetly and nod. "Yes, Daddy. I be good."

I'm not going to be good. I'm going to be naughty.

Up until now, we haven't revisited spankings. Certainly not for fun. But after the week we've had, I can feel how desperately I need one. I don't really feel like I need punishment, though. Between therapy and talking to Chance, I don't pile as much guilt on myself as I used to. But I still feel a tiny bit responsible for the crap that's happened, and a spanking will help me deal. I also feel like Chance might need to get his own frustrations out, not that I believe he blames me at all. But smacking something, *someone*, might be therapeutic.

More than that, though, I'd like us to experiment with spanking for sexual enjoyment.

So I'm going to push boundaries today with the intent on earning a light spanking, and I'm going to have fun doing it.

Chapter Twenty-One — Chance

Settling myself at the big, dark desk, I pull out my phone and decide to trawl through my emails while occasionally glancing over at Kade. Anticipation bubbles in my gut, and I'm curious to see how he's going to play this.

I'm so damn proud of him for knowing that this is something he needs, and for asking for it. While I would have been happy to play with puppy Kade tonight, I have to admit that I'm curious to see what he's like when he's pushing boundaries in Little space. He always was feisty when we were kids, demanding of my attention. I can't wait to see how that manifests during this scene.

I lose myself in actual work for a little while, responding to emails and chasing down reports. I wind up getting so engrossed in actually working that I jump when Kade whines, "Daddy, I'm bored."

Instinct tells me to put my phone down and go play with him, but he's already told me that is not what he needs from me tonight. So, I sigh and set my phone down on the desk before I look over at him.

He's sitting in the corner near the 'window', toy cars, crayons and paper strewn around him. He's got his arms folded across his chest and he's pouting at me.

"Kaden," I aim for a tone of warning, "Daddy's working."

That plump bottom lip of his juts out further. "Work is boring," he huffs.

It's the cutest display of temper I've ever seen. I just want to kiss him stupid.

"It is," I acknowledge, "but it's necessary. Daddy needs to work so he can spoil his baby boy."

Kade grizzles and picks up one of his cars, throwing it across the room. It hits the couch with a *thwack*.

"Kaden," I admonish. "We don't throw toys." I point at the car now lying upside down on the floor in front of the couch. "Pick it up and play nicely for a little longer."

"Don't wanna."

"*Kaden,*" the warning is a bit more serious now. "This is your last chance. Go pick up your car and behave, or you'll be going over my knee."

He narrows his eyes at me, as though he's considering his options, before he exhales loudly and stands up, stomping over to pick the car up as instructed.

So he's in the mood to really push boundaries tonight, then.

Smothering a smile, I suggest, "Why don't you do some drawing, baby? I'll be finished soon."

I half expect him to throw a tantrum, but he does as I ask. When he's settled back in his little corner on his belly on the carpet, scribbling on the paper with his crayons and humming to himself, I force my attention back to my emails.

A few minutes later, the humming stops.

The hair on the back of my neck bristles.

A quiet bratty Kade is *never* to be trusted.

I look up and I can feel my jaw dropping as I take the situation in.

Kade is kneeling in front of the wall, his tongue poking out of the side of his mouth in concentration while he creates a beautiful picture with his crayons.

On the office wall.

Clever boy. It's the sort of behavior that will obviously get him in trouble, but The Grove invests in easy wipe-down paint for obvious reasons, so clean up when the scene is over will be super easy. Not that I give more than half a second's thought to that as I take in what he's doing.

"*Kaden!*" I'm on my feet and rounding the desk before my brain catches up. "*What* are you doing?" I demand as I cross the space towards him in a few long, purposeful strides.

He startles and gasps, dropping his crayons as he swivels at the hips to face me with wide blue eyes. His guilt is written all over his pretty face, but he still attempts to rally by batting his lashes and saying, "Pretty picture, Daddy?"

He's going to be the death of me, but what a way to go!

Planting my hands on my hips, I do my best to frown at him even though I want to eat him all up. "Are you allowed to draw on walls, Kaden?"

My boy makes a show of biting his lip and looking away, his cheeks turning pink.

"I'm waiting," I prompt.

"No," Kade mutters, keeping his eyes downcast.

"So," I prod, "why did you choose to draw on Daddy's office wall? Was that the sort of thing good boys do?"

"Da paper wasn't big enough," he argues petulantly, and it's all I can do to keep a smile off my face. "An' I was *bored*."

"We talked about this earlier, didn't we?"

Kade's blonde hair flops into his forehead as he nods, but he's still refusing to look at me.

"Look at me, Kaden." He complies with reluctance. I tilt my head to acknowledge that he did as he was asked. I still just want to scoop him into my arms and cuddle him, but he was clear about what he needed from tonight, and I'm going to deliver. With his blue eyes on mine, I gesture to his artwork — bright pink and purple scribbles on the otherwise pristine cream wall. "What did I say would happen if you continued to misbehave?"

Shaking his head, he refuses to answer.

"Kaden, don't make this worse for yourself."

There's an undeniable flash of heat in his gaze before he responds to me, playing the scene out just like we discussed it, "Daddy spanks naughty boys."

"He sure does," I agree. "And this was very naughty, wasn't it?"

"It's pretty," he protests, still sounding sulky.

God, he's too cute when he's bratty.

"That's it," I tell him, unwilling to draw this out any further. "Up. Go wait in front of the couch."

Kade pushes to his feet and makes all the appropriate protests one might expect from a four-year-old about to be punished, but he trudges over to the couch dutifully anyway. I follow and sit down on the leather surface.

"Pants down," I instruct, and he hesitates for only a second before he does as asked.

I have to swallow at the evidence of how excited he already is at the prospect of what's about to happen. He's not completely hard but well on the way, and I have to fight the urge to wrap my hand around his cock and stroke him.

Planting my feet, I spread my thighs a little further than strictly necessary and pat my right one. It's only as Kade positions himself, his hardening dick a hot brand on the outside of my thigh, that I consider the fact that I'm still wearing my business pants and this is going to become both messy and uncomfortable for me.

However, I have no intention of stopping now, so I shake off those thoughts and make sure Kade's situated comfortably and safely.

"Standard safe words," I remind him softly before rubbing the creamy, pale skin of his perfect ass to warm him up and get the blood going. His cock twitches against me.

"Yes, Daddy."

"Now, you're going to get five smacks for disobeying Daddy and being naughty," I inform him, and I wonder if the strangled sound he makes at the back of his throat is disappointment or excitement. "I want you to count them. Then, once it's done, that's it. You're not in trouble anymore."

Even though we both know his bratty behavior was a setup just for this purpose, I don't need his guilt complex kicking in after the fact. This is for pure enjoyment. For both of us. It's also why I've gone for a set number of spanks. I don't want his ass to be too sore, after all.

"Yes, Daddy."

I indulge in a little more rubbing of his rounded cheeks for my own pleasure before landing the first stinging slap to the fleshy center of his left cheek with an upwards motion. He jolts forward in my lap, stifling a gasp.

185

"*One*," he breathes out belatedly, remembering that I asked him to count.

"Good boy," I murmur, low and soothing. Then I land a matching blow on his perfect right cheek.

"T-two."

I gaze down at my handiwork so far, smirking at the pretty pink flush to the previously pale skin. In my pants, my own cock strains for attention, and I ignore it in preference of giving my boy what he needs.

I deliver another smack to his right cheek, just where his ass curves over and leads towards his thighs. Kade's fingers curl tightly into the fabric encasing my left leg.

"Three!"

His voice is tight. Needy. I love it.

On "Four," he jerks forward again, then follows the movement with a couple of short thrusts against my thigh.

"Uh-uh," I still him with my palm outstretched over his lower back, "what's the rule about grown up touches?"

"D-daddy says when it…when it's allowed…" Kade is practically vibrating out of his skin, sounding so wrecked despite me barely touching him. I can feel my own precum seeping into my underwear and I know that, once I land this final swat, neither one of us will last long.

"That's right," I say, drawing the tension out. He whimpers, trying so hard to stay still, to not rock his leaking, aching cock against me. I wait a bit longer because I can't help being a little bit evil. "Good boy." I lift my hand again.

He braces himself for the fifth swat, but when I bring my hand back down it's to gently stroke down his spine.

This time he's unable to keep still. "*Daddy*," he whines, jerking his hips forward again, even as he still clutches at the leg of my pants, his fingers twined tightly into the fabric.

"*Kaden*," I bring out the big guns, my Daddy voice low with caution. I take my hand away entirely and it sounds like he bites back a delirious sob.

It's clearly an effort for him to hold himself still again, but I make no move to continue until he's doing just that, even if he is quivering with anticipation now.

This time, I don't say anything or give any indication that the final spank is coming. My palm lands on the pretty pink flesh in the meaty middle of his butt, catching both cheeks with the motion, and he cries out, "Oh! Fu—*five!*" and jolts forward again, grinding his dick into my thigh, surprising us both when he comes.

As the warm wetness of his cum seeps into the material at my thigh, his hips moving involuntarily with each spurt, I can't help but chuckle. "Holy shit," I muse, stroking his back through the aftershocks of his release, "you really did need that, huh?"

Kade mumbles something unintelligible against the outside of my left thigh, where he's pressed his face tightly. I give him time to come down from the high, petting the smooth plains of his back from the nape of his neck to the top of his ass. When he finally sits up beside me, I ignore the smeared mess over his crotch and my pants, noticing that his cheeks are bright pink.

"Sorry," he says, averting his gaze. I grab his wrist when he attempts to escape and I pull him in for a cuddle, even though I'm aching to come myself.

"What for?"

"I broke the rules."

I blink. "What—"

"I wasn't s'posed to come," he mumbles, a hint of his previous petulance returning with his embarrassment.

It's still fucking adorable.

"Oh, baby, you think I'd actually be mad at that? I made you come without even touching your dick. I'm feeling pretty proud of myself, all things considered."

After a few seconds of contemplating my words, he looks up at me. A small smile begins to creep onto his face. "Well, you should. Feel proud of yourself, I mean. That was exactly what I needed." His gaze drops to the bulge in my pants and his smile turns devious. "And now I think you should get what you obviously need."

Kade's intentions are clear when he climbs off the couch and nudges my knees further apart before settling on the carpet between them. His fingers deftly undo my belt and whip it through the loops, tossing it onto the couch cushion beside me. Then I help out by popping the button above my fly, lifting my hips off the seat after he undoes the zip and curls his fingers into the waistbands of both my pants and underwear. He eagerly tugs them down over my butt and down my thighs, and there's some grumbling and awkward shuffling as they get pulled off at my ankles and discarded in a heap over the top of my belt.

But then his hands are spreading my legs wider, and his beautiful blue gaze is zeroing in on my cock, which is flushed dark with arousal, arching up towards my shirt-covered belly. I watch him lick his lips as a fat, pearly drop of precum spills over from my tip.

"Can I suck it, Daddy?"

It's all I can do to not thrust upwards with expectation and desperation. "Yes, baby. Please."

The look he shoots me is almost coy, all batted lashes and faux innocence, before he leans forward, his palms splayed over the fuzzy tops of my thighs, and ever so gently takes the head of my leaking prick between his perfect pink lips.

Unable to contain my groan, I fight to keep my eyes open so I can watch him pleasure me.

It's unlike any blow job I've ever received before, even from Kade himself.

He suckles the tip of my cock like it's a lollypop. It's exquisite torture, and when he swirls his tongue and then teases the slit, I have to clench my hands against the unyielding leather at my sides. It's simultaneously too much and not enough. Nowhere near enough.

Kade tears a gasp from the back of my throat when he takes his fingers to my balls and taint, tickling the sensitive area with just the pads of his fingertips, a touch so featherlight I'm almost convinced that I'm imagining it. There's something insanely erotic about this. I'm being driven to the edge with the barest hints of attention, my shaft neglected, the head of my dick bathed in the heavenly warm, wet suction of his mouth.

He continues to nurse on the head of my cock like it's the teat of a bottle, but the tickling over my balls gradually shifts to more decisive fondling until he's rolling my balls in his palm and moaning around the tip of my dick. Then he brings his other hand to the base of my cock, wrapping long, elegant fingers around the shaft. I lose the battle to keep my eyes open, throwing my head back with another groan as I surrender to the absolute bliss of his ministrations.

Kade starts to bob his head and I feel it as he slowly starts to take in more and more of my pulsing length, finally letting me feel his mouth the way I'd originally anticipated I would. He uses his hand to pump what doesn't fit, and his other hand continues to stimulate my balls.

When he starts to moan around my shaft, the delicious vibrations do me in. My balls tighten and tingles race up my spine and to my extremities.

"Fuck, baby," I manage to find the ability to speak, to warn him even though I'm sure he knows my body as well as I know his now, "I'm coming, I'm—" My words are choked off with a shout as my orgasm rockets through me. I shoot in jets down Kade's throat and he takes every last drop, swallowing and licking at my spent, hypersensitive cock until I'm forced to tell him to stop because it's just too much.

He sits back with a satisfied grin while I smile groggily down at him through hooded eyes. "That was…" I don't even have the words.

"Yeah," he agrees. Then his expression turns soft. "Thank you for doing this for me, Chance."

"For us," I correct him. "We both needed this, and I think you knew that."

"Yeah. I did."

And, in that moment, I'm once again blown away by just how perfect he is for me. Now I just need to make sure I take care of him half as well as he takes care of me.

Chapter Twenty-Two — Kade

"Come on in," Ted says a week later, opening the door to his mansion and stepping aside as he greets us. "Some of the guys and gals are already out back."

He and Chance hug, exchanging thumps on the back, and I shoulder my duffel bag while I wait to follow my Daddy through the beautiful abode.

I'm a little nervous about today. Even though I've met the whole group, and I'm a part of their insane group chat, this is the first time I'm spending time with the lot of them en masse, and it's a playdate to boot. Daddy packed my Little things *and* my Puppy things, and I'm still not sure which way I'm going to go...if I'm going to play at all.

Chance's hand on my lower back brings my nerves back down to a simmer. "You okay?" he asks me softly.

I nod. "Yeah. Just...anxious. I've never done anything like this before."

I'm not just talking about the playdate, either. I'm talking about being included as part of a big circle of friends. At school,

Chance and I were pretty much it for each other. Yeah, we had other kids we sometimes hung out with, but we weren't exactly popular and we were generally happy to just do things as a pair. As an adult, I threw myself into work and denied myself the comfort of friends because I didn't believe I deserved them after how I'd treated Chance. So now this feels new and a little overwhelming.

"You don't have to do anything you're not comfortable with," Chance reminds me in a low murmur, pressing his lips to my temple sweetly. "Everyone here has been through the same thing in one way or another."

That is a valid point. I've gotten to know the guys, having even been included in a separate group chat for just the Littles, and I know a bit about their backstories. I feel like, of all of them, I relate to Matt the most. He explained that he came to Age Regression play through his ex, and then after a decade with the guy, found himself alone and too old for most Daddies he encountered. He said that he wasn't used to the club scene, having mostly experienced Age Play at home, and it wasn't until he met Ash that playdates even became a thing in his world, let alone having a circle of friends in the lifestyle. I was able to empathize with all of that, in my own way.

I was also able to relate to Ash and Tony, too, though. Ash never had a Daddy before Charlie, and Tony's brand new to the lifestyle in the same way I feel new to it. Even if I previously identified as a Little, I realize now that I'd barely scratched the surface of all the things I hadn't tried.

Besides, they've all already told me that they would love to see my Pup side just as much as they want to meet Little Kade. I know I'm safe with them. This is just nerves and nothing else.

Reassured by this reminder, I take a fortifying breath and smile at Daddy. "You're right," I tell him. "Let's go say hi to everyone."

Ted leads us out to the back outdoor entertainment area, which is a beautiful, tiled deck off the back of his house, covered by an extension of the roof and surrounded by perfect green lawn and a stunning swimming pool. In summer, I'm totally telling Daddy to beg Ted to let us come over for a dip in the sparkling blue depths.

In the middle of the space, two large, square, timber outdoor dining tables are pressed together lengthwise, providing enough seating for the large group assembling here today. There's a state-of-the-art outdoor kitchen off to the left side, and café style patio heaters set up in the corners for when the weather turns really chilly.

Around the table, a few of the others are already nursing drinks and nibbling at a spread of snacks. Katie squeals and pushes back her seat when she sees us, racing over to hug Chance and then me. She's all sunshine, her ample curves emphasized by the bright yellow dress she's wearing, and the wide, genuine smile on her round face instantly sets me at ease.

"It's so good to see you again, Kade," she says, grabbing my arm and pulling me over to where she and Cherie have staked their spots at the table. "You'll sit next to me, won't you?"

"Give the poor boy a chance to breathe, Kate," Cherie admonishes, but her tone is warm and fond. She smiles up at me from under the whisps of her honey blonde bangs. "Hi, Kade. How are you doing today?"

The whole group knows about my current work situation, of course. It's been a topic of discussion in both group chats.

The fact that it was Chance's dad who fucked me over has made the whole thing even more of a hot topic. But it's not something I want to dwell on, so I shrug.

"I'm fine. I've done some freelance stuff on Fiverr and Upwork this week, and that's been cool." It's actually been nice to set my own hours and dabble in new industries.

"Oh?" Ted asks, handing me a beer. "Are you thinking about freelancing fulltime?"

"I've been giving it some thought, yeah," I admit, twisting the top off my bottle with a satisfying crack and hiss.

"You should talk to Tony and Spence, then," he advises. "And Ash and Charlie. They know a bit about starting your own company and working for yourself."

That's not a bad idea. But, before I can say as much, another voice speaks up behind me. "Who's starting up a new company? Is Cherie *finally* taking my advice?"

I turn to find London and Matt walking through the glass sliding doors, clearly having let themselves into Ted's home as though it's something they do every day. Chance did warn me that the guys are all basically like family and tend to make themselves comfortable in each other's lives. Thankfully, none have just let themselves into Chance's place yet. At least not while I've been there. After having our privacy violated once, I don't want it to happen again. Not even by well-meaning friends.

Matt's tattoos are mostly covered by a long-sleeved Henley today, and to look at him and London together, you'd think Matt was the Daddy. But London, younger and a tiny bit shorter, radiates Daddy vibes. He's carrying a duffel not unlike mine, and presses a kiss to Matt's bearded cheek. "Come sit, sweetheart," London instructs his boy.

Matt rolls his eyes but does as he's told. "Yes, Daddy."

Then London turns piercing blue eyes back on the rest of us expectantly. "So?" he prompts. "Is my bestie finally seeing the light?"

Cherie rolls her eyes at him, waiting until he takes his seat before she picks up an olive from the charcuterie board in front of us and lobs it at him. "I'm not starting a company selling Little wares," she informs him primly. "I'm happy working for Charlie."

"*With*," the man in question corrects her as he and Ash saunter through the door. He's not quite as broad or muscular as Matt, but he's about as tall, and has one of those Hollywood pretty boy faces, all chiseled features and artful dark scruff. His boy, Ash, is shorter with an athletic frame and floppy brown curls. They're a very pretty couple. "You work *with* me, not *for* me." Charlie makes his point clear before he drops what can only be described as a diaper bag over by the door. It's pale blue, covered in cartoon lambs, and is absolutely adorable.

A quick glance over at Asher confirms that he's wearing a diaper beneath his outfit. The tell-tale padding around his butt is obvious, even under the loose denim jeans he's wearing. This doesn't come as a surprise to me, though, because he's been very open about his fluidity with Little space, and how much Charlie is into the whole diaper change thing.

Cherie and Charlie are still debating semantics when Spencer and Tony arrive. Tony hurries over to sit with Ash and Matt, his shyness as obvious as the diaper he's also wearing. From where he's manning the grill, Zephyr gives the newcomers a friendly wave. Meanwhile, Spencer pulls Chance away, animatedly talking, and I still wait to feel jealous, but it never comes.

I thought it would be difficult to reconcile the fact that, where I was once Chance's only best friend, Spencer shares the title now. He's been there for a lot of Chance's adult life, while I was only there for our formative years. Instead of being bitter about it, I'm glad that Chance found someone —a whole group of someones, even— to fill that void.

Yes, I can admit that there is a tiny, possessive part of me that misses those early years where I was his go to for all things, but what we share together now is something nobody else does. Sure, Spencer is a Daddy and relates to Chance in that way, but there's nothing romantic between them. That part of Chance is all mine, and only mine.

So I'm not jealous that Chance has a new best friend, even though I thought I would be. What Chance and I have together now is so much more than that.

"Hey, newbie," Josh greets me, shaking me out of my thoughts as he drops into the chair Chance had been sitting in. He looks so much like his brother, Charlie, it's uncanny, though his eyes are brown to Charlie's blue, and he's more muscular up top.

"Hi, Josh," I answer easily.

He grabs a handful of snacks from the platter in front of us and starts munching down on them in no particular order and with very little finesse. "How's the job search coming?"

I shrug and repeat my earlier answer about the freelancing. This time, the others around the table who have started their own businesses offer me advice and suggestions, and I have to admit that it's kind of nice to have this group of relative strangers be so supportive and helpful. In turn, I follow up on some of my previous suggestions about marketing strategies for their own businesses, and that leads to London leaning forward and asking if I'd be interested in consulting with the landscaping company he works for. Before I know it, I have an appointment lined up on Wednesday and Chance's hand on my shoulder, squeezing as he leans down to tell me that he's proud of me.

"Well, now that's settled," Josh declares through another mouthful of deli meats and cheese, "We gonna have playtime, or what?"

I'm not oblivious to the looks shared around the table. Littles and Daddies alike seem to be surprised and concerned that Josh is pushing this so heavily, but Josh himself just dusts off his hands on his jeans and looks around expectantly. "Well?"

"I'm already halfway there," Ash answers him when nobody else does, swinging his legs under his chair, his sneakers scuffing over the tiled floor. "So I'm down."

"Me too," Tony says quietly. He wriggles in his seat. "Daddy, do I gotta wear my jeans?"

Spencer shakes his head, an indulgent smile tugging at his lips. "Nope. You've got your onesie on, so the jeans can come off."

With wide, brown eyes only for his Daddy, Tony claps his hands and cheers.

"I'll go get changed," Zephyr declares with a bright smile. "Daddy bought me a new dress last week. It's got rainbows on it."

"I've got to get changed, too," Matt says and pushes his chair back. "Daddy, help?"

As London and Ted take their boys inside the house, Josh beams and turns to Kate. "What about you, Kate? Are you playing?"

She nods. "Uh huh. I'm already dressed up, but I'll get

Mommy to do my pigtails."

Josh's attention finally shifts to me and he cocks his head. "You in?"

This last thirty seconds has been kind of overwhelming. The sudden shift in all these adults to varying degrees of Little is unlike anything I've been a part of before. Even at the club, by the time I've entered the playroom, everyone is usually in their headspaces. But to be in a private home and watch my new social circle go from adult headspaces and into Little ones so easily is kind of jarring. It's not bad, in fact it's reassuring and sweet, but it's new and it will take some getting used to.

I bite my lip and look up at Chance. He drops down into a squat beside the chair and smooths his hand over my hair. "If you just want to sit out and watch this time, nobody'll mind."

"What if…um," I look down, twiddling my thumbs in my lap, feeling my cheeks burn. "What if I don't wanna be *Little*, but I wanna…" I cut my gaze towards the duffel bag that Chance dropped down beside Asher's diaper bag.

It's silly asking the question out loud when they've already told me that they're cool with it. I know it is. But I've never been a pup around other people before. It's still so new. At least if I chose to be little, I've done that in front of strangers before and I know how to behave. But as a Pup, this is entirely new territory for me and for Daddy.

"I'm sure everyone will love that side of you, too, baby," he assures me, "no matter how you wanna show it."

"What side?" Katie asks curiously. It's fairly obvious that she's been using the last minute or so to sink properly into Little space. There's just something about the expression on her face, more open and *younger*, somehow. She looks between us and then her eyes go wide with excitement. Clapping her hands together, she squeals. "Puppy?!"

"*Katie*," her Mommy chides, but Chance chuckles.

"Yeah," he says, shrugging as though my additional kink isn't any different to the rest.

She bounces in her seat. "I wanna play with the puppy!"

"No, *I* wanna play with da puppy," Ash says from the other end of the table. He looks at me with unbridled curiosity. "*Pwease?*"

Suddenly, I can't help but get excited myself, much like I did when it was first discussed in theory. I remind myself that a bunch of Littles might provide a whole different level of play time for Puppy Kade than Daddy can on his own. "Yeah," I nod, decided. "Okay."

Katie and Ash cheer and Chance pushes back to his feet to go and grab the bag with my outfit and accessories. As I move to get up and follow him, Josh gently clasps my wrist. "If it gets too much, you can safe word. Nobody'll judge you, okay? We're, uh," he rubs the back of his neck after he lets my wrist go, his expression a little bashful, "a rowdy bunch of Littles."

Josh confuses me.

Daddy says that he's a brat, but none of our interactions have shown him to be anything other than empathetic, thoughtful, and considerate. Yeah, in the group chat he's a bit of a shit stirrer, but it's good natured. Maybe when he's Little he's naughtier, though? I wonder if I'll notice when I'm in pup space.

Smiling at him, I thank him for the heads-up and follow after Daddy to get changed and settled into my headspace.

* * *

"Look at the puppy!" Ash cries when Daddy leads me outside on my pretty blue leash. He points in my direction and soon enough all eyes are on me.

I'm solidly in pup space, though, and the attention makes me wag my tail in anticipation of pets and play time.

Unsurprisingly, it's Katie who first wanders over. She abandons the game of outdoor Jenga she was playing with Matt, appraising my soft golden 'fur' with a wide smile. She looks up at Daddy for permission before she reaches out to fondle the soft, floppy ear attached to my head, then she gently scritches my scalp with her neatly trimmed nails. I lean into the touch, whining softly for more when she stops.

She giggles and strokes the top of my head. "Is puppy Kade still called Kade?" she asks Daddy.

"He sure is," Daddy tells her in the same tone he uses for me when I'm Little. "I wanted to name him Fuzzlebutt, but I was outvoted. He also didn't like Killer, and then I was all out of ideas."

I cock my head up at him and growl my annoyance, and that sends Katie off into a fit of giggles.

"Can we play with Kade, Uncle Chance?" she asks him, once again petting the top of my head, as though she's apologizing for laughing at Daddy's stupid joke name.

"Sure," he agrees readily. When he was getting me ready, we discussed my comfort level, and I admitted that I was excited to play with the others and to see how different it felt. "Don't be too rough, though. He's just a puppy, okay?" He squats by my side and unclasps the leash from my collar, giving the leather around my neck a tiny tug to make sure I'm focusing on his words. "And you play carefully, too."

Feeling bold, I lick his bearded cheek before bounding across the grass towards the group of Littles with Katie at my side.

Chapter Twenty-Three – Chance

Matt laughs as he's tackled to the grass by an enthusiastic pup hellbent on stealing back his ball. Matt had been faking throwing it for a good thirty seconds, so as far as I'm concerned, he had the attack coming.

"You gonna call your pup off my boy, Chance?" London asks me, but there's no real demand in the question. Still, I can't help taunting him.

"You gonna teach your boy that teasing a pup is likely to get him pounced on?"

London chuckles and jerks his chin over to where Kade is still sprawled out over Matt's much wider chest, snapping his jaws and whining in the direction of the ball, which Matt is easily holding well and truly out of Kade's reach. "I'm pretty sure he's learned that lesson now."

As predicted, the whole group has been super cool and inclusive of Kade's kink. If anything, the Littles have gone nuts for a different kind of playmate, and the other Daddies have enjoyed doling out pets and playing fetch and tug-of-war with my pup, too. Kate was right on the money when she said there were parallels between Littles and Pups, and today has completely cemented that.

With everyone else paying Kade so much attention, I've been surreptitiously focusing a bit more on Josh. Considering he was the one who said he needed the playdate to relax, it's been a surprise to watch him basically hover on the edge of the group. He's been joining in on the play, dressed in short shorts and a t-shirt with a teddy bear decal right over the front, but he hasn't been as boisterous or attention-seeking as I'd expected him to be. If anything, his expression has been wistful bordering on sad whenever he's stepped back from the group, and that sets off all sorts of alarm bells in my head.

I'm distracted from my musings when Matt finally throws the ball, sending it rolling half-heartedly across the grass, and Kade scrambles off him to chase after it. But, once he's got it between his teeth, he trots over to where Josh is sitting cross-legged beside Tony, dropping it into Josh's lap and pawing at him to toss it.

I wonder if Kade's noticed my concern for Josh, or if this is his way of showing his own. Either way, I'm filled with pride that he's making an effort to connect with the other Little. Whatever's going on with Josh, he needs to be reminded that he has a support system here.

"And that's my cue," London says, setting his half-empty bottle of beer on the table before he pushes from his chair. I follow his gaze to where Matt has gotten to his knees and is holding out his arms and calling out for his Daddy. London helps him up and then pats the front of his onesie over his crotch, and Matt flushes adorably, averts his gaze, and then nods at whatever question he's just been asked. I'm guessing it involves a diaper change or potty time.

London takes his boy by the hand and leads him past me, confirming my suspicions by grabbing their duffel bag from the pile by the door, and I turn back to watching the group playing, only to notice that Josh was focused on London and Matt with that same wistful expression, his gaze glued to the doorway they just walked through.

Huh. I'm not sure what to make of that.

I know he's close to Matt, of course, but is it more than that? Does he have feelings for Matt or London? Or am I misinterpreting the wistfulness?

Could it be Josh wants more than just the odd scene or playdate? He's always maintained that he's just a scene Little, but the fact that he reached out to us to organize a get-together for his Little time instead of venturing to The Grove to let off steam is telling.

I watch as he seems to shake himself and then smiles down at Kade, who has just yawned widely and curled up on the ground at Josh's side, his head resting on Josh's thigh. Josh cards his fingers through the soft, blonde hair on top of Kade's head and pets him like one would a real dog or cat, and I'm tempted to pull out my phone and snap a photo of the moment.

"That's the most relaxed I've seen Josh in ages," Charlie tells me, taking London's vacated seat at my side.

"What's going on with him?" I ask, unable to keep my curiosity veiled. "Reaching out and asking for today was kind of out of character. But I'm glad he did," I rush to add.

Josh's older brother nods and shrugs. "He's a stubborn ass and won't actually tell me what's wrong. But I think being a Detective is more intense than he thought it would be and," Charlie sighs and turns his head to look me in the eye, "I think he's lonely. I mean, we're all paired up now, and he's the odd man out."

"Because I'm sure it's hard for him to find dates looking the way he does," I scoff sarcastically.

Charlie rolls his eyes. "He's in his thirties now, Chance. And he's a big, buff dude with an authoritative job. He won't say anything, but I think he's starting to come up against the same issues Matt had. Daddies don't want Littles like him. They want..." he trails off and looks towards his husband, who has dragged Tony off to play with a couple of stuffies that seemingly appeared out of nowhere. "Well. I can't talk, can I?"

He's got a point. Ash, like Tony and Kade, is smaller and more 'boyish', for lack of a better word. He's still got a masculine, athletic vibe about him, but he's slender and lean where Josh is built and broad.

Still... "You can't help who you're attracted to, man."

Charlie shrugs. "Yeah, well, you gotta admit, except for London, the rest of us Daddies have been kind of stereotypical in our tastes."

"Josh wasn't interested in any of us, anyway. That'd be weird. He's like family. Hell, for you he *is* family." I make a face. Charlie laughs.

"That's not what I meant. I'm just saying..." he scrubs a hand through the scruff on his jaw, "I don't know what I'm saying. He just...I think he's lonely. Stressed and lonely and finally realizing that he wants more out of age play than the odd scene to blow off steam."

I nod, because these are the same conclusions I was coming to. "Well, if anyone can get him to talk, it's you and Ash. Or Matt."

"Believe me, we're all trying."

"That's all you can do." I look back over and smile again at the sweet scene between my pup and Charlie's brother. It hasn't changed. "And if today is any indication, I think he's starting to loosen up and reach out for our support."

Charlie follows my line of sight and nods, but the concern furrowing his brow is palpable.

Needing to lighten the mood, I add, "He'll be his bratty self again before you know it."

Charlie groans, but he's fighting a smile. "God help us all."

* * *

Life falls into a relatively easy to manage pattern again after our first all-group playdate including Kade. He's really embraced friendship with the guys better than I could have hoped, often arranging his own little catch ups with Ash and Matt, and surprisingly Josh. It turns out he and Josh are both NHL nuts (I prefer NFL), and they've even gone to attend a couple of games together.

But, for as happy as we are together, I can't let go of what my dad did to him. What he threatened to do to me. To *us*.

It festers in the back of my mind for weeks. Even while Kade's freelancing really seems to take off, I'm still pissed as fuck that my dad pulled the rug out from underneath him the way he did. All to hurt me. Me – the son he hasn't spoken to in twenty years.

The asshole can't let go.

Then again, I can't let go of this, either, so I guess it runs in the family or something.

Ugh. To think I'm anything like my old man makes me feel sick.

Despite Spence's urging me to cowboy up and talk to Kade about it, I just can't bring myself to do that. I know that communication is important, but this is *my* hang-up, not his. And with everything else going so well for us, I don't want to ruin things.

Especially when there's nothing either of us can do to make the lingering anger and resentment go away. Or the ever-present fear that my dad will decide to share those photos after all, just to fuck with me, his own reputation be damned. Hell, for all I know, he could always play the victim: the poor old man with the perverted son.

"You're dwelling again," Spence says with a rueful twist of his lips before he sips at his milkshake. We're currently sitting on one of the four picnic tables outside Tony's *BDSM* food truck at the back of The Grove, meeting for lunch while Kade's off at yet another game with Josh.

I bite into my delicious burger to buy myself some time to compose my answer. I can't even properly enjoy the decadence of the grease and salt and meaty-cheesy ooziness over my tongue because Spencer just arches an eyebrow, well aware of my tactic.

"You need to talk to Kade, man. This shit isn't healthy."

I groan and swallow. "I know, okay? But telling him isn't going to do anything but make him worry about me."

"For fuck's sake," Spencer huffs. "Dude, *I'm* worried about you right now. Something's gotta give."

"Yeah, well, what's Kade going to be able to do about it anyway? He's just going to feel guilty all over again and that's not fair on him. He's *happy* now. He's building up his career on his own terms and things are good. I refuse to shit all over that by saying 'hey, so, I'm still messed up over what my dad did to you."

Spence's curly hair flops around as he tilts his head back and mutters, "Give me strength" to the sky. Then he takes a deep, steadying breath and looks back at me with a firm glare. "He's your partner, Chance. You'd want to know if he was all 'messed up' about something, wouldn't you? And don't give me that crap about it being different because you're his Daddy. You're equals together."

I hate it when he makes a valid point. Stupid, logical asshole. I take another bite of my burger to spite him.

"Chance…"

"I know," I mumble out through a mouthful of food, wanting to chuckle at the look of disgust on his face. Still, I finish my bite and wash it down with a slurp of Coke before I speak again. "You're right. I just figured I'd get over it."

"But you haven't."

I nod, conceding defeat. "But I haven't."

"So…" He prods, munching on a fry. "What are you going to do about it?"

God, he's *such* a Daddy. Even though I am too, he treats me like a boy. I can't be bothered calling him on it, though. This is just who he is. He just cares a lot about everyone, and that's really quite sweet. "Guess I'm going to have to talk to Kade, aren't I?"

My best friend's whole countenance brightens and his shoulders sag with relief. "Thank God. The next step was going to be an intervention."

"Oh, fuck you," I scoff, laughing. "Dramatic, much?"

"I'm serious. I've been *worried*, man. You've got a good thing going with Kade. Don't blow it because you're a stubborn ass."

I try to dispel some of the discomfort I feel at those words with humor. "You're channeling your books again."

"No, I'm channeling common sense again."

I lob a fry at him. "Asshole."

Spencer just shakes his head, smirking. "Shut up and finish your heart attack on a plate."

I give him the one-fingered salute before I do just that.

* * *

I do not, in fact, go directly home after lunch. Instead, I find myself driving towards a neighborhood I've avoided for twenty years. I know that what I'm about to do might be a huge fucking mistake, but I *need* to do it anyway. I wanted to do this weeks ago, back when Kade first told me what had happened. I haven't been able to shake the urge off.

I need the closure. I need to look my father in the eye and tell him exactly what I think of him. Once this is done, I can go home to Kade and tell him what I've been struggling with and, hopefully, explain that I've resolved it…or potentially fucked everything up in an epic way. How this is going to all end is yet to be seen, but at least I'll know.

I pull my car into the driveway of the large two story brick and tile home I grew up in. Despite not having been here in two decades, it feels almost as though I only left a week ago. Memories —good and bad— assault me as I turn off the ignition and take the place in.

It hasn't changed.

Sure, the shutters appear to have been repainted in a bright white, and the tiled roof looks like it's also been given a refresh, but the dappled red brickwork is the same as it always was. Mom's garden beds are still neatly trimmed with little blossoms of white flowers popping out amongst the green foliage of the low hedges. The cobblestone path leading to the front porch is still scratched and scuffed from my years of crashing matchbox cars along it.

With a deep breath, I peel myself out of the driver's seat and close my car door quietly, locking it with a click of a button. I stuff my keys, and then both hands, deep into the pockets of my jeans before I force myself up the path.

At the front door, painted white with a stained glass rose design inlaid into the middle of the top panels, I tug my right hand back out of my pockets and press the doorbell, smirking as the familiar strains of Beethoven's 5th ring out through the house.

God, my parents were pompous assholes. What's wrong with a generic ding-dong, anyway?

It's not long before I can hear the click-clacking of heeled footsteps down the tiled floors I know are behind this door. I'm momentarily struck by the thought, *'What the fuck have I done?'*, but I'm powerless to do anything about it when the handle turns and the door swings inward, revealing my mother.

She gapes at me, her jaw dropping, while I take her in.

The house might not have changed, but she has. Where once her hair was auburn, it's now gray and dull. Where once it sat at her shoulders, it's now a neat concave bob cut that cradles her weathered face. The past twenty years have added more lines than I'd anticipated, and her once taut cheeks are beginning to sag with age. But her eyes —currently brimming with tears— are as bright and blue as I've always remembered.

An overwhelming pang of regret threatens to make my knees weak. "Hey, Mom," I croak, surprised by just how terribly I've missed her.

We were never super close, but she supported me when I came out, even though Dad didn't. She wasn't the overtly emotional kind of mom, but I always knew that she loved me. Hell, her calls on holidays and my birthday every year prove that she's never quite given up on me.

"Chance," she breathes, clutching so tightly at the door that I can see her age-spotted knuckles turning white. "Sweetheart, what...? Why...?" She stops and gives herself a shake, brushing away the gathering tears in her eyes with her free hand. A watery laugh escapes her and she steps back, pulling the door open wide. "Come in, come in."

Hesitating only for the briefest moment, I take another steadying breath and cross the threshold, wiping the soles of my shoes on the mat inside the door. Mom waits for me to step aside and then closes the door behind me.

"Oh, Chance," she sobs, throwing her arms around me in an uncharacteristic display of both affection and emotion. I'm not exactly tall, but the top of her head only reaches my chin. As I tentatively wrap my arms around her shaking frame, I'm startled by how frail she feels. She's only in her early sixties, but I'm suddenly worried about her health. "I'm so happy to see you."

I almost miss those last words, muffled as they are by my shirt and chest, but she's beaming as she pulls away to wipe at her now reddened eyes.

I feel like a dick for having pretty much cut her out of my life when I left home. Dad deserved it. Mom did not.

"I'm sorry," I tell her, but she shakes her head.

"No, sweetheart. I understand. I do. But," curiosity steals over her features, "what brings you home now? After all this time?"

I lick my lips, surprised that Dad hasn't ranted and raved at her about my kinky love life. In his eyes, I'm certain it just reaffirmed all the ugly things he spat at me when I came out to them. Maybe Ted was right. Maybe he is too embarrassed by it to actually use the knowledge. Even with Mom.

"Can we sit, Mom?" I lift my chin and direct it towards the formal living room, a space filled with antique timber furniture set against lush cream carpets and floral wallpaper.

"Of course." She leads the way into the room, and my heart pounds in my chest.

I tell myself that, regardless of her reaction, I'm going to be fine. I've made it twenty years without her in my life so, if she's disgusted, I will manage to survive without her. Still, my palms are sweating and my stomach roils as I settle myself down on the cream leather couch with the scrolled timber armrests; the same couch I was never allowed to sit on as a child.

Mom perches on the edge of one of the two matching armchairs, in the one kitty corner to the end of the couch where I'm now seated. I swallow and decide to just drop all the information straight up, like ripping off a Band-Aid.

"I'm into kinky role play," I tell her, which I'm sure comes off apropos of nothing, so I forge on. "Like, pet play and age play. With my boyfriend. Uh, Kade. Do you remember Kade? It doesn't matter." I shake my head. "Anyway, we, uh, we role play at home. My home. Which is supposed to be private." I can't look her in the eye, never having imagined that I'd have to make such a confession to my prim and proper mother. "Like…I don't have close neighbors and my fences are six feet tall and there's forestry…Well, you get the idea. So, imagine my horror to find out that Dad has had my place under some sort of surveillance. That he's apparently got photos…" I trail off as Mom gasps.

"*What?!*" She sounds utterly horrified, but whether it's at the idea of my kinks, or at the last bit of information I dropped, I'm not sure.

I glower across the room at the ornate fireplace which is unlit. The weather's nowhere near cold enough to need it yet. "So, yeah. That's, uh, why I'm here. He…he threatened Kade with the photos. Told him to dump me or lose his job. Kade chose me. But those photos are still out there somewhere and—"

"I'm going to kill him," Mom seethes, which startles me enough that I snap my gaze over to her.

She looks livid. I think the only other time I've seen her so angry was the time I accidentally spilled a bottle of her nail polish over the carpet in my bedroom. (I was thirteen and I was going through a phase.) Her cheeks are mottled pink with her ire, and her scowl is only deepening all those new lines on her face.

"Wha—?" I attempt to ask, but she pushes out of her chair and storms out of the room, hollering for my father. I scramble to my feet, but I can't make myself follow her.

My mother *never* yells. Not even during the nail polish incident. Her anger has always been delivered in an icy, clipped kind of way. Until now.

There's a muted clatter from somewhere further in the house, most likely Dad's home office. Then I hear his heavy footfalls and the muffled sounds of his voice, presumably asking her what's wrong.

Mom's screaming blue murder at him by the time I force

my legs to move, and I leave the living room and head into the house proper, making my way down the hallway where the noise is resonating from. As I step around the corner, I stop short at the sight in front of me.

There's my diminutive mother, holing my father up against the wall and screeching at him almost indistinguishably while he holds his hands in surrender, utterly bewildered.

"Mom!" I shout, worried that she's going to give herself a heart attack or something. "Mom, calm down."

I step forward and put my arm around her shaking shoulders, pulling her away from him. "But he—"

"I know," I say calmly, still a bit shell-shocked at this turn of events. "But we're going to talk about it like adults." Even though I'd come here with the intention of tearing into him myself, seeing Mom do it for me is satisfying enough. Now I just want to put it all behind me and get his guarantee that those photos will never see the light of day.

Dad's blustering now, demanding to know what I'm doing in his house.

"It's my house, too, Donald," Mom hisses at him, and I tighten my hold on her just a little in case she decides to go into attack mode again. "And he's our son."

Dad scoffs, "He stopped being our son when he walked away twenty years ago, Deb. And if you knew half the depraved things he's doing—"

"In the privacy of his own home," she snaps at him, taking the words right out of my mouth. Before I can stop her, she's marching forward again, poking a manicured nail into his chest. "Or what *should* have been considered private. What kind of lunatic are you, Donald Baker? Who violates their own child the way that you have?"

I'm in awe of my mother at this point.

Dad stammers, clearly never having seen this side of his wife either. "I…I…"

"You will get those photographs and destroy them, do you hear me? You'll destroy any and all evidence of their existence. *Then* you will sign a document to promise that you've destroyed them, and that if any should somehow turn up unexpectedly to cause trouble for Chance and Kade in any way, you will forfeit your shares in the company to Chance and turn over the deed to this house to him. Am I understood?"

Holy shit. Can she even do that?

"Mom…"

She continues to stare Dad down, holding a single index finger up in my direction. "No. I'm handling this. I've lost two decades with you because I was too meek and mild to stand up to your father, but no more. He's gone too far this time."

Dad's face is turning purple with some combination of rage and indignation. "Deborah," he pleads, "be reasonable."

"You will do exactly as I've said, Don, or not only will I divorce you, I will destroy you."

"Mom!" I feel like I've walked into a soap opera. *Days of Our Lives*, eat your heart out.

But she just keeps on glaring up at my father. "And, *darling*," the word is practically snarled, dripping with sarcasm, "I'm not bluffing. I'm well aware of your *extramarital* activities: I have my own photographs stashed away for a rainy day. It turns out, you and I are more alike than you know."

Dad has gone pale now, and I'm speechless. Did Mom just say she has photographic evidence of him cheating? Gross. And, also, why the hell would she have stayed married to him knowing that he was cheating?

Then I look around at the grand home I grew up in, the shining diamonds in her earrings and on her fingers, and the lifestyle which she has generally become accustomed to, and I mentally shrug. She'd walk away wealthy if she divorced, but she's wealthier if she stays. It's not the choice I would personally make, but to each their own.

And, just like that, the fight leaves my father entirely. He nods curtly. "Fine," he tells my mother, curling his lip in a sneer. "You win. I'll have my lawyers draft a document meeting your terms. Happy?"

"Ecstatic," she answers drily. Then she finally turns to me. "And you'll have your own lawyer look it over before you sign, too."

It's not a question, but I still nod, knowing that Ted won't mind reading over it for me. Dad's expression twists, but he stays mercifully silent.

Mom steps back and smooths her hands down her polo shirt and linen pants. She rolls her shoulders back and then pins me with a blinding smile, reaching out to hook her arm with mine. "Well," she starts, sounding every bit the prim and proper woman from my memories, like the last few minutes never happened. "Come along, sweetheart. Let's have a coffee and catch up properly, hmm?"

I have no choice but to do exactly what she says.

Chapter Twenty-Four — Kade

I t's late afternoon when I hear the key turning in the lock of Chance's front door. I look up from the book I've been reading on the couch, arching my eyebrows at him. He'd texted earlier to tell me that 'something' had 'come up' and that he'd be home late, but the super vague messages had my Spidey senses on alert.

The past weeks have been great. I feel well and truly included in Chance's social circle now, to the point where I consider it 'our' social circle. Even if he and I were to break up —not something I foresee happening, but you never know— I would still have these new friends to lean on and talk to.

Josh, in particular, has become someone I really value. It goes beyond our mutual appreciation for hockey, too, or the fact that he's a Little like me. We have similar senses of humor, and I've come to discover that he's every part as hard on himself as I have been on myself. He puts on this bratty façade, but behind it, he's definitely lonely. Seeing all of his friends settling down really hasn't helped, either. Not that he has said as much to me, mind you. But I can tell. Like knows like and all that jazz.

So, yeah, I've made an effort to hang out with him whenever possible. It's not romantic in nature, but I think it is helping him to feel less alone. Even though he could reach out to any one of the other guys, Josh is stubborn and independent, and I also suspect he doesn't want to impose on them. So, instead, I've been shoving my excess attention his way. I'm considering suggesting that we go and enjoy Littles' Night down at The Grove next month, the whole group of us Littles. With or without our Daddies. I think Josh would enjoy that, and I wouldn't mind another group playdate, especially if I get to introduce the group to Little Kade, too.

But right now, I'm more interested in whatever is going on with my boyfriend.

"Hey, stranger," I greet him with a teasing lilt as he steps into the room, having shut the door behind him. "Did you have a good day?" I feel a *tiny* bit like a 1950s housewife asking the question, but the warm smile Chance gives me is worth it.

"It was…eventful," he eventually replies, clearly having considered his phrasing carefully. He crosses the room and stands behind the couch, bending to brush our lips together.

"Mmm," I can't help but murmur, closing my eyes and enjoying the sweet kiss. But when he pulls away, I push, "Good eventful, or bad eventful?"

Chuckling, Chance moves around the couch and drops into the seat beside me, pulling my socked feet into his lap. He starts to rub them. "Good eventful."

I'm distracted by the impromptu massage, moaning a bit before I remember that I'm trying to carefully interrogate him. "Hmm?" I ask, then force myself to focus. "What happened?"

I know he met up with Spencer for lunch, but beyond that I'm clueless. The sheepish expression on his face worries me, especially when he looks down at my foot in his hands, unable to meet my eyes.

Those worries increase tenfold when he finally confesses, "I, uh, went to my parents' place."

"You went…?" I start to repeat, then stop, shaking my head. I'm confused, and also surprised to find myself feeling a bit angry with him. "Why?" I demand.

Chance's expression turns apologetic. "So," he licks his lips, carefully considering his explanation, "I haven't been able to get over what Dad did to you…"

I want to know why this is the first I'm hearing about it. Why, in all the time that has passed, he hasn't told me. Hasn't let me in. He's my boyfriend. We love each other. Aren't we supposed to share stuff like this with each other? Wasn't he totally against me bottling stuff up when we got together? Why is he allowed to do it, but I'm not?

Frustrated, I tug my feet out from his grasp, trying not to feel guilty at the wounded look that passes over his face. "Why didn't you say anything?" I ask, curling my legs underneath me on the couch.

"I thought it would just disappear," Chance says ruefully. He exhales and leans his head back to stare at the ceiling, as if that's going to help him better verbalize his shitty decisions. "But it didn't. So, in a last-ditch effort, I went to their place for closure, I guess." He finally looks back at me. "I was going to tell you tonight, no matter how that ended. I just wanted to try and fix it for myself, first."

Well, I can't exactly begrudge him that, can I? Even though I'm still a bit upset that he was struggling with those feelings and I had no idea, I understand where he's coming from. We're equals, but he sees himself as Daddy all the time: somewhere in his mind he's the one who fixes problems, not makes them.

Coming down from my burst of indignant frustration, I recall his earlier words. "And it was…good?"

He chuckles now, and in a tone tinged with disbelief, says, "My mom read Dad the riot act. I told her what happened —all of it— and she…Jesus, Kade, I've never seen her like that. She stormed down to his office, bailed him up against the wall and threatened to out his affair and divorce him if he didn't destroy the photos and sign paperwork guaranteeing that if he fucks us over, I get everything he owns."

I can feel myself gaping at him. "You…*what*?! And he agreed to that? Just like that?" I snap my fingers. "That easily?"

"Dude, you should have seen Mom. She went full-blown 'I will destroy you' on his ass. I'm pretty sure she even said those exact words." Chance sounds awed, but there's a hint of melancholy creeping in now, too.

"You really miss her, don't you?"

From what I remember of the woman, she was nice. Maybe a little cold and aloof, but she was always perfectly pleasant whenever I'd visit (which was often). Even distant, she was still a better mom than mine was.

Chance's shoulders fall and he nods. "It didn't really hit me until I saw her. And she's so different, you know? Not just physically, even though she's aged a lot, but I've never seen her so…so…"

"Emotional?" I offer.

He nods emphatically. "Yes! Emotional. And that made me feel bad for being out of touch for so long."

"Except maybe it was that time apart that helped her see the way she was before wasn't healthy for your relationship with each other." I shrug and smirk. "I mean, not that I know what I'm talking about. I don't have a psych degree or anything."

"No, no. That kind of makes sense."

"Yeah?" I ask.

"Yeah," Chance nods. His smile turns thoughtful beneath his beard. God he's handsome. "Like…even though the time apart sucked, we both needed it to grow as people, or some shit."

"Or some shit," I echo with a laugh. "Well done, Doctor Phil."

Chance reaches for the cushion beside him and tosses it at me. "I was being deep," he pouts.

Having caught the cushion deftly, I throw it back at him and then shuffle my butt over to snuggle up against his side, sighing happily as his arms wrap around me. "I'm still a little mad that you didn't tell me you were struggling with what he did. We're still not great with the communicating thing, I guess." I murmur into the warmth of his chest.

"Mmm," Chance agrees. "I'm sorry. I'll work on that, I promise."

"*We* will work on it. Together." Beneath my cheek, I'm soothed by the steady *thump-thump-thump* of his heartbeat. "But I'm glad you got your closure."

He squeezes me tight for a moment. "More than that," he replies softly, "I'm glad that he's not a threat anymore. Just the idea that he could have tried to ruin our lives with those photos any more than he already had…" I feel Chance shiver uncomfortably. "But he won't now. Mom took care of that."

"And she was okay with…y'know…our, uh, lifestyle?" Not that it matters to me, but if Chance is starting to realize how much his mother means to him, her opinion could definitely hurt him.

He huffs out a laugh and my head bounces with the move-ment of his chest. His large palm smooths down the back of my head and down my spine, almost like when I'm in my pup headspace. "Yeah," he eventually answers my question, after presumably contemplating it. "Strangely enough, she is. And she says she always knew we were meant for each other." I crane my neck back to look at him, only to find him smiling down at me, his eyes sparkling in the dim lighting of the living room. "And, for the record, so did I."

My heart soars and I grin at him, stretching up for a sweet, chaste kiss. The soft hairs of his beard tickle my skin, and I breathe in the spicy, warm scent of his cologne. "Me, too, Daddy," I tell him. "Me too."

And that's all that needs to be said.

* * *

Words aren't everything.

We might have talked out our feelings and promised to work on our communication skills, but when we get ready for bed the way we always do, with Chance dressing my in my pajamas and helping me brush my teeth, I can't help but feel like we need actions to really underline our earlier conversation. And, because Chance is oblivious to my growing need, I decide I have to take matters into my own hands.

Feeling cheeky, I wait until he has turned away to leave the bathroom before I strip out of the cute super hero themed pajamas he only just dressed me in a few minutes ago, and then I follow him back down the hall and into his bedroom.

He turns to say something —perhaps ask me about which

bedtime story I want to hear— but his whiskey-hazel eyes widen and his jaw drops.

I stand in front of him, stroking my hard cock slowly, not taking my eyes from his.

I delight in the way he seems almost frozen with surprise, and I relish the building heat in his eyes as his brain seems to come back online.

"Well now," he says, his voice having dropped into Daddy voice, sending delicious shivers up my spine, "*someone's* being a bit naughty, aren't they?"

Tucking my chin, I look up at him through my lashes, still slowly pumping my erection. "I don't know what you mean, Daddy."

Beneath that insanely sexy beard of his, his lips curl into a smirk. His eyes sparkle. "I just got you dressed, didn't I? And what's the rule about touching yourself, hmm?"

"But I'm not feeling little," I argue, biting my lip and sounding coy, totally belying my argument.

"Is that so?" Chance is grinning now, his hands already hooking into the waistband of his own pajama bottoms. He pushes them down and steps out of them shamelessly, then whips his t-shirt off and tosses that to the ground, too. My eyes are drawn to his cock which is plumping to life in front of me, seemingly twitching at having caught my attention.

"*Daddy*," I whine.

"Yes, Kaden?" How he can stand there and sound so unaffected while his dick is saying quite the opposite, I have no idea.

I step closer. "I need…" Everything. I need everything. My seduction plan is shot to hell and I just need for our naked bodies to be pressed together immediately.

Chance huffs out a laugh and reaches for me, tugging me against him, almost as though he read my mind. I squeal as his large palms slide under my ass and then hoist me up, forcing me to wrap my legs around his hips. Then I'm whimpering, because our cocks are brushing together, the heads now wet with precum, and it's so good and nowhere near enough.

He carries me the few feet remaining to the bed and sets me down carefully, leaning over me and kissing me soundly. I whine into his mouth as our cocks rub together.

"What do you need, baby?" Daddy asks, rocking his hips in a gentle but steady rhythm.

"Anything. Everything. I honestly don't care as long as it's with you." Cheesy and sappy though they might be, the words have come straight from my heart. I've never been more sure about anything in my life. No matter what happens, no matter what I do —sexually, kinky, or otherwise— I need it to be with Chance.

My answer seems to spark something inside him, too, because his expression softens and he pulls away, moving up the bed properly and gesturing for me to follow until we're stretched out in our usual sleep positions but lying on our sides and facing each other. We're so close that I can feel his breath ghosting over my lips, and I can feel the warmth of his body almost touching mine. Chance's left arm is stretched out beneath my pillow, and he brings his right hand up to caress my skin with a reverent touch.

His big palm smooths down over my shoulder and down my side to my hip, where he then reaches behind me and cups my ass cheek, squeezing gently.

"You know," he says quietly, a tiny smile hiding beneath his beautiful beard, "at times like this, I can't quite believe this is real. That I've got you in my bed. In my life."

My heart thumps a bit harder, because it's almost like he can read my thoughts. I still feel that way whenever we're together, and it is kind of mind boggling to hear that he does, too.

"I love you so much, Kade. You know that, right?"

I nod, feeling tears prickle at the back of my eyes. "And I love you," I answer, my voice cracking just a little bit. My hand reaches up to cup his hairy jaw and cheek of its own volition. "I always have."

Chance's smile is almost blinding before he dips his head a fraction to finally bring our lips back together. But the kiss remains slow and deep. By some unspoken agreement, we seem to have decided that we don't need the hot, frenzied fuck that I was initially angling for.

Instead, we kiss languidly and passionately, breathing each other in. Chance pulls me in until our bodies are flush against each other, his big palm still on my ass, but then we just rock against each other while our tongues tangle.

There's no sense of urgency, and I have no idea how long we remain like this — a puddle of pure adoration. We murmur sweet nothings as our kisses alternate from deep to soft and sweet and back again, gasping into each other's mouths as our cocks continue to rub together in the most erotic experience I've ever had, and I'm only dimly aware of how close I am to coming, despite how unhurried and gentle this whole encounter has been.

Our cocks are sticky and slippery against each other, evidence that we're both insanely aroused, and there's something ridiculously hot about the fact that we can affect each other like this with so minimal an effort.

"God, baby," Chance breathes a shuddering breath. He's

whispering, but his words sound loud in the silence of the room. "Please tell me you're as close as I am."

Just the thought of him coming between us untouched —save for the unbelievably slow frotting— has me almost toppling over the edge. "So, so close," I confess in an answering whisper, even as my hips falter in their slow, rolling rhythm. "You're so hot, Daddy. I'm gonna come."

"Thank God," he chuckles quietly, then kisses me deeply again. The kiss turns into a groan into my mouth and his fingers dig into the flesh of my ass as he stills and comes.

The additional sensation of his wet, warm release over my cock does me in and I follow him as the wave of pleasure inside me crests and breaks.

We're sticky, oddly sweaty considering our lack of exertion, and thoroughly sated as we snuggle in the afterglow.

"I'm glad you bought me," Chance eventually says, and I frown, my brain still scrambled from just how hard I came.

"Huh?"

He reaches out to tuck an errant lock of hair behind my ear, smiling. "At the auction. I'm glad you bought me." He snorts and looks up at the ceiling. "I was so anxious about doing that stupid thing for Charlie. I thought about pulling out a couple of times."

"Well then, I'm glad that you didn't," I tell him, wondering if any of this —of our relationship— would have been possible if I hadn't impulsively gone to the fundraiser, and even more impulsively bid on him when I saw him.

Chance just smiles softly and kisses my sweaty forehead. Echoing my words from earlier, when we'd snuggled on the couch, all he says is "Me too, baby. Me too."

And now that really is all that needs to be said.

Epilogue – Chance

With the symbolic sword of Damocles no longer hanging over our heads, I'm happier in life and love than I can ever recall being. I really do seem to have it all now: great friends, a boy I adore (whose bonus pup side I could never live without now that I have it) and, most surprisingly, my mother's unwavering support and affection.

In the weeks following my visit to my parents' house, Mom and I spoke at least every three days, until it got to the point where Kade demanded I just invite her over for dinner one night. The emotional look on his face when she wrapped him in a huge hug, tearfully telling him that she'd missed him almost as much as she'd missed me, is now forever imprinted in my brain.

We don't talk about my father, not even with Mom. It's like we've unanimously decided that he doesn't bear thinking about. He's in the past, everything worked out, and life is perfect.

We hang out with our friends a lot more, too. Together and

separately. So, it doesn't surprise me when Kade organizes to host a get-together at my house for the first time. It's been roughly six months since I (well, okay, since my Mom) sorted shit out with my Dad, and Kade and I have started talking about leasing out his apartment so he can officially move in. We're both aware that he spends more time here than there nowadays, but neither of us has been in a rush.

I like that about our relationship: we're easy going together, with zero expectations than to just love and support each other. Still, I do get a little revved up when I think of him calling my house 'home'.

"Where's the puppy?" Ash demands as he and Charlie barrel into the backyard where we're all set up. Winter is on its way out slowly, but there's more entertaining space out here than inside, so I've borrowed Ted's patio heaters and we're all rugged up in our jackets and thick jeans. Even the Littles are wearing warmer Little clothes.

"Little lamb," Charlie sighs and shakes his head fondly, "we've been over this…"

"I just wanna play," Ash pouts from underneath his mountain of curls and bats wide, wet eyes at his daddy. I have to smother a snort at how easily that melts Charlie.

"Sorry, Ash," I decide to swoop in and rescue Charlie from having to be the bearer of bad news, "Kade's not in pup space right now. But Josh and Matt are coloring if you want to join in?" I gesture to the second table we've set up specifically for Little play. On it there is a wide array of crayons, markers and stamps, and a bunch of coloring sheets and blank artist's notebooks. As promised, Josh and Matt are sitting shoulder-to-shoulder at the table, their heads bowed together as they draw and color. Josh's tongue is peeking out from the side of his mouth while he concentrates, and it's really quite adorable.

Mollified, Ash bounces over to his brother-in-law and their friend, and Charlie and I watch as the three of them whisper excitedly among themselves.

"Should I be concerned that they're conspiring together?" I ask Charlie, and he laughs.

"The worst they're gonna do is draw penises," he shrugs, then smirks. "I had the last masterpiece displayed on the fridge for a month. Until Mom came over and gave me a lecture on propriety." He rolls his eyes. "Like anyone invited into my house is gonna care, right?"

"Except her," I offer.

"Except her," he concedes ruefully.

We chat a bit longer about how his family's doing, how The Center is going, and light gossip about some of his staff as the rest of the group arrive in stages. Katie and Cherie are in the kitchen with Kade, and Ted and Zephyr are quite happy to sit at the 'adult' table to pick up a conversation with London and Emmett, where Spencer and Tony join us soon after.

It's not until the food has all been brought out and we're all about to dive in that I realize the vibe is weird. *Energized*. It's not a bad feeling, but it's like everyone's anxious for something to happen.

This is also the moment that Kade clears his throat and stands up from his seat down the table, sandwiched between Josh and Tony. "So, uh, thank you all for coming today," he says smoothly, and I'm thoroughly weirded out by how formal it feels. Like the beginning of a speech. But we're just hosting a casual dinner with our friends, so why the hell would he be making a speech?

I watch as my boyfriend pushes his chair back and starts

slowly walking towards me. "Everyone knows our whole story by now," he says, wearing a smile that I can't quite interpret. He looks nervous, but excited. A little wry, but also fond. "And nobody was surprised when I told them I wanted to take you off the market for good."

Wait...what?

I inhale sharply as Kade stops beside my seat and then drops to one knee.

Seriously...*what?*

I gape at him, then glance up at our friends around the table, then back down at Kade. My mouth won't work. Words won't formulate.

"I know we haven't even been dating for a year yet," Kade tells me, reaching for my hand. His elegant, pale fingers wrap around my chunky, stout ones. "But, Chance, I've known you for practically my whole life. I've been in love with you for more than half of it." He gives my hand a squeeze and then produces a ring box without ever letting me go. With his free hand, he pops it open and extends it towards me. I see the platinum band, smooth and flawless, but I can't focus on it. Instead, my eyes are drawn back to his. "Will you marry me, Chance? Be my Daddy forever?"

There's a collective hush over the gathering, and my mind is somehow frozen and simultaneously whirring at a thousand miles a minute. Of course my feisty, go-getter of a boyfriend is asking me to marry him, even though I'm the daddy and he's the boy-slash-pup. This is such a Kade move, taking the lead and putting the ball firmly in my court, and I can't help but fall even deeper in love with him for it.

"Of course, baby," I tell him, plucking the ring box from his hand and placing it on the table in front of me. "*Yes.*" Then

I'm grabbing him and pulling him up and into my lap, kissing him to the soundtrack of cheers and wolf-whistles from our friends.

Even though Charlie proposed to Ash pretty much just like this only a handful of years ago, it's perfect for Kade and me. We were reunited because of Charlie's Little Community Center, and I know that my friends' —*our* friends'— support and counsel through those early days helped to cement the foundations of our relationship. So it makes sense to include them in this moment, for them to cheer us on towards the new chapter of our lives.

I can only hope that my friends feel even half as happy in their relationships as I do right now. They deserve every bit of happiness, too.

And, as Kade slides the engagement ring onto my finger, I can't wait for us to make it official. To be Daddy and Boy-slash-Pup forever. To be husbands forever.

When I was eighteen, I never allowed myself to dream that it might be possible. Hell, not even a year ago, I sat across from Charlie and confessed much the same thing. Back then, I didn't feel like I fit in. I wasn't a Hot Daddy like the others, and I didn't see a happily ever after on the cards for myself.

But now I have Kade who makes me feel like maybe I really am a Hot Daddy, and I can see my happily ever after spread out in front of me. It's happening. It's really happening, and now the future looks bright.

The End.

Thank you so much for reading *Chance's Choice.* I genuinely hope you enjoyed it, because (as always) it was a lot of fun to write. This was my first time writing pet play/puppy play, and I hope I did it justice.

Anyway, I'd love it if you could leave a review on your retailer of purchase or on Goodreads.

Reviews not only tell the algorithms that our books deserve attention, but honest feedback also encourages and inspires me to keep writing. Even a star rating helps, and I greatly appreciate you making time to do so.

Speaking of my writing: if you're still enjoying the antics of the *Littles & Lace* crew, keep turning the pages for a sneak peek of Book 6, the final book of the series, titled *Josh's Jackpot.*

And, if you'd like a free ebook copy of *Charlie's Contentment* (a 10,000 word zero-angst, low-plot, high-fluff novella which functions as an extended epilogue for *Asher's Answer,* but can also be read as a super sweet stand-alone) subscribe to my newsletter here:

https://annasparrows.com/newsletter-subscription/

For updates, release dates, competitions and more, follow me on Facebook. The link is in the 'About The Author' page after the sneak peek.

Sneak Peek – Josh's Jackpot

Prologue – Roughly 6 Years Ago – Josh

I am an absolute wreck right now.

I am standing under fluorescent hospital lights and wondering whether my big brother is going to pull through from surgery after being shot on the job. He's a cop just like me. I followed him into the force. Everything Charlie ever did, I wanted to do, too.

I've always idolized him.

When I first heard the reports of an officer down from my precinct, I'd been concerned, but I'd never imagined that it would be Charlie. He was on an easy day shift, for fuck's sake. He wasn't even working the 'rough' parts of town.

I was wrong.

Our Captain let me leave work early, knowing I'd be too worried to be of any use anyway. And, instead of driving straight here, I went directly to Charlie's best friend's offices, where I knew I'd find both him (Ted) and Charlie's boyfriend, Ash.

I like Ash, don't get me wrong. I'm the one that introduced him to Charlie, albeit without the foresight that they might actually hook up. But he's a Little, and Charlie's his Daddy, and I was wholly unprepared for his irrational reaction when I broke the news about the shooting.

So sue me for snapping at him, okay? Ted made it very clear that *my* reaction was unjustified. Never mind that my big brother is currently on a table getting bullets pulled out of him, or that *I* don't have a Daddy to cuddle and reassure me right now, either. And having Ted scold me while he was simultaneously comforting Ash was a little hard to swallow given the circumstances.

Not that any of the guys know that I want a Daddy.

Oh, don't get me wrong: they know I'm a Little. But I've always maintained that I'm just a scene Little. They think that I'm just down for some kinky fun with a bratty twist, and that it's easy for me to step away from the headspace and live 'normally' outside of that.

'Normally'.

Ugh.

I don't like that word. What is 'normal' anyway?

Whatever it is, it's not me.

I'm just as kinky as the rest of my social group, but I've been pigeonholed and, to be honest, it's easier for me if they think I'm not a lifestyle Little. Could you imagine what might happen if they knew? Not to mention what they might say about me being a cop and all the stress the job brings, and the control I need to have over my Little side in order to make it work. All those protective Daddy types would become unbearable, especially if I ever found a Daddy of my own. They'd probably chase the guy away, or tell him how unbearably bratty I am, or *both.*

I can't have that. Especially when I haven't actually found anyone I've sparked with.

But I'm still young. There's time.

Charlie might not have time.

Fuck. So much for being able to distract myself.

The clock on the wall of this waiting room is ticking the seconds away, but to me it sounds like it's in slow motion.

Tick…tick…tick…tick.

Further into the room, Mom and my big sister, Maisy, are doting on Ash, with Ted hovering worriedly as well. My little brother, Axel, is sitting in one of the uncomfortable plastic chairs, looking stoic next to Dad. I feel like an outsider in this group right now, even though they're my family.

Thankfully, I don't have too much time to think about that before a knock on the waiting room door has my head swiveling in that direction.

A series of complicated feelings wash over me as I take in Max Dalton, Charlie's partner. He's maybe an inch or two shorter than me, and, even though he's muscular, he's nowhere as buff, either. I'm not sure exactly how much older than Charlie he is, but I know he's getting close to forty, even though his blonde hair and bright blue eyes make him seem much younger than that. But today he looks tired and stressed. His uniform is unkempt and stained, and I don't want to concentrate too hard about where those stains came from.

Without thinking, I make my way over to the doorway and embrace him, knowing that if it hadn't been for his quick thinking during the shooting, Charlie might have bled out before he could even make it into surgery.

"I'm so sorry, Josh," he murmurs into my ear. I shiver, but I don't know whether it's at the situation, or the proximity of his lips to my skin. I hope it's the former. Right now is a very shitty time to think about my crush on the man. Especially when he's clearly rattled. "I didn't see it coming. Neither of us did. It happened so fast."

"Nobody blames you, Max," I tell him, keeping my voice equally low. "If anything, they said that you compressed the wound and called it in in record time – fast enough to keep him alive so the bus could get there."

Max squeezes me, then thumps my back: a gesture that I return. "He's gonna be okay," he says, but I don't know if he's trying to reassure me or convince himself. Either way, of all the people in this room, he's the one I relate to most right now.

Obviously, I can't know what it's like to watch your partner get shot -*twice*- in front of you, but I know what the job itself is like. I know how much we care about our partners and our whole unit. Max's guilt is palpable, as is his worry. I'm right there with him.

Remembering our audience, I pull away from the hug and lead Max over to my family and Ted. I've barely introduced him before Ash's knees buckle and he drops to the ground, looking pale and horrified at Max's uniform.

Ash stammers out an explanation about the blood -*Charlie's blood*- and it's all I can do to not feel woozy as well.

"Shit," Max says, as if he's finally realizing that he's still wearing his uniform. He's immediately apologetic. "I didn't think. The paramedics let me go, I had to give my statement, and then I came straight here." As if he can sense how close I am to my own panic attack, he looks at me, his gaze piercing and fortifying all at once. "Any update?"

Unfortunately, all that does is make me antsy. That's better than close to hyperventilating or bursting into tears, I suppose. I shake my head. "Not yet. I only just got here."

Nodding, he chooses a seat near the door and lowers himself into it, waiting in tense silence while my mom peppers Ash with ridiculous questions partly to get to know him, and partly to distract herself (and him) from the situation at hand.

It's a relief when a doctor finally walks through the door in clean scrubs and tells us that Charlie made it through surgery and is awake, though heavily medicated. They're only going to let two people in to see him tonight and, knowing it's not likely to be me anyway, I voice my thoughts that Ash should be one of them. Charlie's gonna be asking for him, I just know it.

Dad agrees because he's a nice guy and, before I can blink, Mom and Ash are following the doctor out of the room, leaving the rest of us standing around awkwardly.

With the adrenaline rush over, I feel bone tired and shaky.

"Come on," Max says, giving me a gentle nudge towards the door. I find the weight and warmth of his hand on the back of my shoulder a comfort. Grounding. "Let's get you home. Did you drive here?"

I shake my head. My partner, Sam, dropped me at Ted's office building, and then Ted drove himself, Ash, and me here. I know I'll need to check in with Sam at some point, but right now I don't have the energy, and she's not expecting me back at work until Charlie's officially out of the woods anyway.

"You still living with your folks?" Max's question gets me to refocus and I sigh.

"Unfortunately."

I'm almost twenty-five but, to save money while I attended the academy, I remained living at home. It's not like I spent all of my time there: my last relationship was kind of serious, so I'd spent most nights at Declan's place. Until he dumped me almost a year ago, anyway. Since then, I've had the odd one-night stand, but I haven't gone out of my way to find a new relationship or a place of my own. I've been stagnant.

"Unfortunately?" Max questions, steering me down the rabbit warren of hospital hallways which all look the same to me, not that I'm really paying any attention to where we're going. I trust that Max knows the way out of here.

It's not that I don't love my family, because I do. But they're kind of a lot to deal with. Mom is a drama queen, Dad's an enabler, Axel is...well, he's a high school kid coming up on closing out his Senior year. Maisy lives with her husband but is usually having some sort of feud with Mom, and Charlie's probably the only one I can put up with for extended periods of time. Right now, with Charlie just out of life saving surgery, I just want a quiet space without all the drama.

I must be closer to breaking point than I thought because those words tumble out of my mouth without a filter, and I end on a confession that I would *never* make if I was in my right mind. "I need to be Little for a while."

Max's footsteps beside me falter for only a second as the blush creeps over my cheeks, but then he's walking just a little bit faster, the press of his hand between my shoulder blades just a tiny bit firmer, and I have no idea what he's thinking. I'm too embarrassed and exhausted to ask.

It's only as we finally approach his car in the multi-story car park attached to the hospital that he speaks. "Would you be comfortable at my place? I don't have any stuffies or anything, but we can make a stop on the way." I'm surprised by the question and the confidence with which he asks it. He meets

239

my gaze head on, his expression open and non-judgmental. When I don't answer, he says, "I'll be honest, Josh. I'm a Dom, not a Daddy. But I'm here for you. Whatever you need."

I'm surprised by his confession. I have never seen him at The Grove, but I know it's not the only BDSM club in town. The Grove is the best, though. It is high end, with exclusive memberships, NDAs, and intense vetting procedures. A part of me wants to ask why he's not a member there instead of wherever it is he goes instead, but I know that's just my squirrel brain focusing on the wrong details because I'm stressed and on the verge of unintentionally regressing.

"Does Charlie know?" I find myself asking instead of answering his question, still standing beside his car, my hand hovering over the door handle. He drives a dark blue sedan of some kind. I wasn't really paying that much attention to the make or model as we approached. It's definitely a good thing that I'm not at work if I'm not picking up those kinds of details right now.

He arches a light blonde eyebrow as he rounds the car and stands on the driver's side. "Does Charlie know what?"

"That you're a Dom."

He sighs and looks away. That's not a great sign. Then again, Sam doesn't know my secrets, either, though I wouldn't be surprised if she suspected them. She's a pretty switched-on cop.

"He knows I'm familiar with various BDSM lifestyles," Max eventually tells me, then he bends to open his door. I do the same on my side and we both slide into our seats.

"So that's a no, then?"

I watch him nod. "But he knows that I know about him and Ash. About their kink." He winces. "I told him earlier

240

today. Before we got the call out…" he trails off and shakes his head, then pops the key into the ignition but doesn't turn it. "I should have done a lot of things differently today."

I frown, realizing that he's as close to breaking point as I am, and I make my decision without any further thought, rationalizing that he mightn't be a Daddy, but a Dom's needs are to take care of their Subs. It's close enough for me. "If the offer's still on the table, I'd like to stay at your place tonight."

* * *

An hour and a half later, Max opens the door to his apartment and nudges me inside. We swung by my parents' place so I could grab my overnight bag with clean clothes and some comfort items, and then by his local Chinese restaurant for some takeout. It's still only early evening, but it feels like I've been awake forever. The need to just let go and be Little and let someone else take care of me is growing stronger with every passing minute.

Unfortunately, that usually makes me whiny and bratty: not the kind of attitude I want to have around a Dom. And not just any Dom, but my brother's hot older work partner who I have been crushing on since the day we were introduced.

"I'm just going to get changed," Max tells me, dropping his keys in a bowl on a little stand just inside the entryway of his apartment. He waves a hand around the space as he places the plastic bag of our takeout on the table. "Make yourself at home."

I nod, clutching my duffel bag closer to my chest as I step into the main living area. It's a small apartment, clearly only designed for one person or a very close couple. It's basically just a studio, though the bedroom and bathroom are separate to the rest of the living/dining/kitchen open-plan space.

Max has a big screen TV mounted on the wall, with a soft looking three-seater couch upholstered in a light cream color. There's a worn timber coffee table in between both items. Behind the couch is a little square dining table, also timber and scuffed, with two matching chairs. That leads into the U-shaped kitchen, with its windows looking out over the scrawl of suburbia with the city proper in the distance.

It's all neat and tidy, beige, and plain. A basic bachelor pad if ever I saw one. There's no evidence here that Max is a Dom, so anything of that nature must be in the bedroom.

I sit on the couch and nibble my lip when I realize that it's not a fold out or a futon. I'm 6'1", so I could sleep on it as it is, but it'll be a tight fit, especially with how broad I am. Still, I'd rather this than home right now.

"Josh?" his voice startles me, and I swivel around to where he's leaning against the doorframe that I assume leads to his bedroom. He's changed into loose gray sweats and a tight white t-shirt. He mightn't be as broad as me, but the man is toned and fit, and I try not to visibly salivate. His expression softens and he points towards the table. "Dinner?"

"Oh. Right. Yeah." I get up and walk over to the table while he grabs cutlery and a couple of cans of soda from the fridge.

As we dig into our boxes of noodles, I can't help but wish that I didn't have to do this for myself; that he would step in as the Daddy I need right now and feed me forkfuls like the overgrown toddler I want to be in the moment. I don't say anything, though. I just play with my food sullenly.

"Hey," I look up to see concern etched across his handsome

face. He gestures down to my box of barely touched food. "Not hungry?"

I am. I'm starving. But how do I explain that I'm so exhausted and stressed that I'm regressing beyond my ability to control it? That I want to eat, but I don't have the motivation or coordination to feed myself.

I just shrug.

That gets a reaction.

"*Joshua*," he says firmly, and fuck it if my dick doesn't take interest at the same time as my brain lights up like a Christmas tree, because Dom voice sounds a *lot* like Daddy voice. "Use words, please. I am not a mind reader."

With my cheeks burning, I blurt, "Can you feed me?"

Max's eyes widen, first in surprise and then with understanding. "*Oh*. Oh, yeah. Of course."

He pushes his own meal aside and then brings his chair around from opposite me to the space to my left, reaching for my box of noodles and fork. There's a gentle smile playing around the edges of his lips as he swirls the fork in the delicious umami mix then brings it to my mouth. "Open up," the instruction is quiet, but firm, and I comply without any of the brattiness that I'm otherwise known for.

For Max, I want to be good. At least for tonight. I want to be praised, and cuddled, and cared for.

We repeat the process over and over, and it's not long before the comforting fog of being little sets in properly. Later, I'll think back on how irresponsible it was to do this without negotiating first. To not discuss safe words or limits. Even though we're not doing this for sexual reasons (no matter how badly I wish he'd see me that way), leaping in without having that talk was a stupid idea. But right now, I don't think about such things. I just think about how Da-*Max* is being so kind and caring, and about how much I trust him to take care of me.

And take care of me he does. He finishes feeding me, then gets a washcloth to wipe my face clean. Then he ushers me into the bathroom and helps free me from my constrictive uniform while I whine and squirm and complain that "I gotta go real bad". We both breath a sigh of relief when I make it in time. While I'm taking care of business, he throws my uniform in his hamper, and afterwards, he makes sure I wash my hands and brush my teeth, then takes me back into the living room to grab my duffel bag.

Da-*Max* takes one look at the couch, then shakes his head, taking me by the hand and leading me into the bedroom where he gets me to lie on the bed as he pulls out the outfit he'd watched me pack earlier.

He also pulls out my diaper. If I were big, I'd question his limits. Ask him his traffic light color. Almost anything to make sure that he's really okay with this. But I'm not. I'm Little, and he's doing *exactly* what I need right now, so I let him pull my underwear down and awkwardly diaper me. I suck my thumb while he does, watching him from underneath my lashes, daydreaming that he could be my Daddy every day. Those thoughts don't go away. In fact, they get worse as he helps me into my pajamas -the *Paw Patrol* ones that feature Chase the police pup- and then hands me my matching Chase stuffy.

"Into bed, Josh," he says, gesturing towards the headboard. "I'll go sleep on the couch."

"No!" I cry out angrily. "No! Want Max here." 'Here' comes out as a whine, the 'r' sounding more like a 'w'. I'm a lost cause now.

Max hesitates.

I bring out the big guns, widening my eyes, not needing to force the tears that well up at the thought of being left alone in this strange room after the day I've had. *"Pwease* Da-*Maxie?"*

"Okay, shh, it's okay," Max agrees when the tears actually do fall. He drops onto the mattress and reaches for me, pulling me against his side for a cuddle. I clutch my stuffy under my arm, sucking on my thumb as I press my face against his warm, solid chest.

He rubs my back and continues to murmur sweet, soothing words until sleep finally claims me.

I wake suddenly in the morning after a nightmare. My heart is pounding, my diaper is wet, and the bed is cold and empty beside me. But I'm big again and I smother the desire to seek Max out, slipping into the bathroom next door and taking care of my needs myself.

My biggest mistake comes later when we're back at the hospital, having just seen Charlie. Max and I leave the room after Charlie and I both try to assure him that he's not at fault, and we walk silently back down the hallways towards the multi-level car park. Halfway there, I stop and grab his arm, tugging him into an empty room.

I don't like the resigned expression on his face, but I have to say my piece. "I just wanted to thank you for last night. For taking care of me like you did. It meant a lot."

Those blue eyes of his gentle again. "Don't mention it, Josh." Even though the words are kind, there's warning in them. I don't like that. Neither grown up nor little Josh likes being told no.

I don't know why I push it. Not really. But I lose all sense of reason, stepping into Max's personal space, even as he backs up against the wall.

"Josh…"

I ignore the more obvious warning there, too, pressing my lips to his.

I keep it chaste, but it's still sweet and affectionate. I probably give far too much away about my hidden feelings. But he kisses me back, if only for a moment, and it is *everything*.

Until it's not.

Hands as large as my own find my shoulders and gently push me back. "We can't do this, Josh," he tells me, and I swear I can feel my heart squeezing so hard it might stop. Last night was so good, so perfect, and my crush turned into something stronger. He was my Daddy, if only for a moment, and it's destroying me to know that the same man from last night is rejecting me now. "Not now, not ever. I'm sorry."

Then he walks away, and I'm right back to standing under the fluorescent lights of a hospital feeling absolutely wrecked.

About the Author

I've been writing* for as long as I can remember. I started with silly short stories as a kid, moved on to fanfiction in my teens (and still write it now), and am also a published MF romance author under a second pen name.

I have been an avid reader of MM romance my whole life. (Ask me about my beginnings with *Buffy* fanfic, haha.) I wrote a sweet and kinky MM romance novel in 2022 and the reader response changed my life. From there, I knew I had found my niche.

And thus Anna Sparrows was born.

*All of my writing is 100% my own. No part of it is generated by Artificial Intelligence (AI) software of any kind. Yes, that means that it's sometimes flawed, but I'm okay with that.

You can connect with me on:

🌐 https://annasparrows.com

📘 https://www.facebook.com/AnnaSparrowsAuthor

📷 https://www.instagram.com/annasparrows

Subscribe to my newsletter:

✉ https://annasparrows.com/newsletter-subscription

Also by Anna Sparrows

I write ridiculously sweet & steamy MM romance with guaranteed HEAs…and sometimes with a side of kink.

Littles & Lace Series
The Littles & Lace series is an MM Age Play series, following a group of like-minded friends in the BDSM community. You'll find mild ABDL, light Pet Play, Femme Play and more here.

Book 1: Asher's Answer

Book 2: Matteo's Mettle

Book 3: Ted's Temerity

Book 4: Spencer's Satisfaction

Book 5: Chance's Choice

Book 6: Josh's Jackpot

Dads & Adages Series
Visit Australia's sunny Gold Coast where an assortment of single dads find love and even learn a few life lessons along the way.

Book 1: Where There's A Will

Book 2: You Don't Know Jack

Book 3: A Match Made In Evan (release TBA)

Shifters Sanctuary Series
In a world where alphas are thought to be extinct, a number of 'human' men are about to have their worlds rocked.

Book 1: His Alpha Unlocked

Book 2: His Prodigal Alpha (release TBA)

www.ingramcontent.com/pod-product-compliance
Lightning Source LLC
Chambersburg PA
CBHW070553120726
47909CB00007B/2328